Desperately Seeking

EVELYN COSGRAVE

PENGUIN
IRELAND

PENGUIN IRELAND

Published by the Penguin Group
Penguin Ireland, 25 St Stephen's Green, Dublin 2, Ireland
(a division of Penguin Books Ltd)
Penguin Books Ltd, 80 Strand, London WC2R ORL, England
Penguin Group (USA) Inc., 375 Hudson Street, New York, New York 10014, USA
Penguin Group (Australia), 250 Camberwell Road, Camberwell, Victoria 3124, Australia
(a division of Pearson Australia Group Pty Ltd)
Penguin Group (Canada), 90 Eglinton Avenue East, Suite 700, Toronto, Ontario, Canada M4P 2Y3
(a division of Pearson Penguin Canada Inc.)
Penguin Books India Pvt Ltd, 11 Community Centre, Panchsheel Park, New Delhi – 110 017, India
Penguin Group (NZ), 67 Apollo Drive, Rosedale, North Shore 0632, New Zealand
(a division of Pearson New Zealand Ltd)
Penguin Books (South Africa) (Pty) Ltd, 24 Sturdee Avenue, Rosebank, Johannesburg 2196, South Africa

Penguin Books Ltd, Registered Offices: 80 Strand, London WC2R ORL, England

www.penguin.com

First published by Penguin Ireland 2008
1

Copyright © Evelyn Cosgrave, 2008

Set in 13.5/16 pt Postscript Monotype Garamond
Typeset by Rowland Phototypesetting Ltd, Bury St Edmunds, Suffolk
Printed in Great Britain by Clays Ltd, St Ives plc

A CIP catalogue record for this book is available from the British Library

ISBN 978-1-844-88145-1

www.greenpenguin.co.uk

Mixed Sources
Product group from well-managed
forests and other controlled sources
www.fsc.org Cert no. SA-COC-1592
© 1996 Forest Stewardship Council

Penguin Books is committed to a sustainable future
for our business, our readers and our planet.
The book in your hands is made from paper
certified by the Forest Stewardship Council.

For Mum and Dad

I

As soon as I heard myself say I would marry him, I knew I had hit rock bottom. I had seen it coming, I could have prepared an answer that declined his proposal absolutely but sweetly, yet still left him in no doubt of his worth as a person or in his ability to love again. I could have done it. I could do anything with this guy. But I had been lazy. I had become accustomed to him and I had forgotten what this was supposed to be. And now here I was telling him that I loved him too and of course I would marry him.

It was a lovely proposal. He didn't buy me a ring because he didn't trust himself to pick one without me. But he did take both of my hands in his and he looked at me so intently I had to turn away.

'I love you,' he said. 'You are the most amazing person I have ever known. Just put me out of my misery and marry me.' His gaze was still fast upon me when he added, 'I promise to make you happy.'

When I looked up again I was so overcome there was nothing I could do. The moment seemed to demand it. Nothing but a resounding yes would satisfy the universe. Otherwise something catastrophic might happen elsewhere in the world, to a butterfly, maybe, in South America.

'Yes,' I said. 'Yes, I'll marry you.'

Then I said that I really had to go to the loo, which was the first true thing I had said to him all evening. I had been about to go when he appeared so unexpectedly at my door. He was supposed to be away for the entire weekend, at some work thing, and I had been looking forward to an all-me weekend of pyjamas and pottering about. Had he been ten minutes later I would probably have been in my pyjamas. And he probably wouldn't have noticed. I can never work out whether that is something I hate about him, or love.

So I left my new fiancé in my neat beige living room and went off to think about what I had done. I stared at my surprisingly untroubled face in the mirror. What could I do? He was supposed to be my get-over guy, my feel-good fella, who was definitely not my type but would help me feel good about myself again while I got over one of the world's biggest bastards. Nobody had been meant to fall in love, especially not the get-over guy. Surely he knew I was a mess and not responsible for any of my actions. The only person meant to get hurt here was me, so what could I do?

However, as I continued to look at myself in the harsh light of the bathroom mirror, I was suddenly overcome by a need to get out. Even though an intimate evening in with your new fiancé is probably customary, I needed the intimacy of a big crowd. So I hauled out my machinery and began a little touch-up, which quickly became a full-on party-time make-over. Surely a girl deserves a party.

The only problem was who to conjure up for this party. My parents were an absolute no-no. If I had to deal with my mother tonight someone would end up in Casualty. My sisters? All of them? The noise would be deafening and then there was the Casualty issue. It would just have to be friends, any friends. All my friends.

'Keith, honey, I want to go out and celebrate!'

He had already poured champagne into the fabulous Waterford crystal flutes he had given me for Christmas.

'Oh . . . Kate, sweetie, I thought we'd celebrate at home,' he said, gazing at me sheepishly. It was his signature look – full of love and tenderness, but weak. 'This is a wonderful moment, for both of us.'

The look remained.

'Oh, Keith, I feel so excited! I just have to go out and tell people – I have to party!'

'OK, honey, we'll go out.'

I can be very mean when I want to be.

It was at somebody else's engagement party that I met Keith. Or birthday, or house-warming, I wasn't paying much attention. I think one of my sisters dragged me out, Lucy probably, but we were definitely locked deep in the heart of Limerick's newest and hottest new and hot pub – O'Flaherty's. I was still deep in the blues at this point, and getting pretty drunk, but I do remember noting that all the men there were lying, cheating, ugly bastards. Lucy told me later that I pinned some poor guy up against the bar and insisted he account for the sins of his sex. Apparently it's all down to genes.

I'm not usually this aggressive when I go out and I've never believed in giving men a hard time – it's much more fun to flirt with them and I'm normally a happy drunk – but these were not normal times. I do have a vague recollection of Keith from the party. He seemed to materialize somewhere near the end of the night, all neat shirt and affability. He was exactly what I didn't want – someone nice who wasn't drunk and foolishly thought I wasn't either.

'Hi!' he said.

'Pardon?'

'I said hi! Hello!'

'Oh. Hello.'

'This place is a bit insane, isn't it?'

'Is it? I kind of like it.'

'I prefer a quieter place myself.'

'No, I like it here, it's good and buzzy, you know? You feel like you're alive in a place like this. Where would you prefer to be? Somewhere like O'Grady's where everybody falls asleep watching the fire?'

'I like O'Grady's. But I see your point.'

'So why are you here?'

'Got dragged in.'

'Me too.'

'I'm Keith, by the way,' he said, proffering his hand.

'Annabelle,' I said immediately.

'Annabelle what?'

'Annabelle . . . Jones.'

I think we stalled there, and before he thought of anything else to say I was dragged off to look at someone's tattoo.

I went home and woke up with the hangover I deserved. He went home and looked up my number. (Which wasn't there, of course, because I never give out my real name to strange men in crowded pubs. And even if I did I've always been self-important enough to go ex-directory.) It seemed he had a hunt on his hands. Absolutely irresistible!

It was fruitless, however. Having surfaced for a brief moment, I returned to the depths of the city. Except, of course, that I bumped into him in the same pub the very next week. I think it was even the same table. That's Limerick for you.

I was more civil this time. Something at the back of my mind suggested I might owe him an apology. There wasn't any need to say much. For a quiet guy he was doing an awful lot of talking. A lot of gesturing, smiling, beseeching; he was being a bit girly, really. But it did give me a chance to sit back and take him in, size him up. Just to pass the time, really, because he was absolutely not my type.

He was one of those guys, and it only happens with men, that the instant you look at them you know exactly what they were like as a child. I could see him in primary school in grey trousers and maroon knitted jumper. His hair would be fairer and fuller but the expression of his eyes would be exactly the same. A queer mix of confidence – because he was intelligent and knew he was loved – but also an expectation of hurt, of not quite knowing what to do with the world. It's an image I can never fully separate from the thirty-two-year-old adult who likes to take himself just a little bit seriously.

'So what is it you said you did?' I asked, phasing back in for a while.

'I work in the chemical industry. At the moment I'm with a company in Shannon that blah blah blah blah blah blah . . .'

He didn't move his mouth very much as he spoke: his lips seemed to revolve gently around his teeth, which were even and pearly.

'And what is it you do?'

I was tempted to lie, I'm always tempted to lie, but I didn't.

'I'm a solicitor.'

'A solicitor?'

'A solicitor.'

'That's impressive.'

'No, it isn't. It's just a job. The firm I work for mainly deals with the small stuff. It's quite boring, really.'

'Well, I'm impressed. I must take your number in case I ever end up in trouble.'

I wished he wasn't so impressed and I assured him hastily that I would be useless to him were he to ring me from Henry

Street Garda Station in the small hours of the morning. He still seemed impressed.

The rest of that night went on with more people joining the table, people he knew, people I sort of knew, people it turned out we both knew. There were too many conversations happening at the same time. And none was about anything. It was just dawning on me that maybe I was getting too old for the super-pub scene. Already I was willing to make a fuss to get a seat and now I was finding fault with the kind of mindless chatter I used to find enchanting. God, I was becoming boring! But right then my only alternative to the super-pub was my empty apartment. At least here it looked as if I was having a super time.

Some time later that night, after I had slipped out for a sneaky cigarette, I was joined by Keith. I remember groaning, feeling sure I was in for a tedious rehash of the horrors-of-smoking routine but he said nothing. He leaned in and touched his lips against mine. He kissed my smoky mouth and he left.

I was surprised. I was even impressed. As a move, as a way to make an exit, to leave an impression, it was fabulous.

Suddenly I was interested.

Ages passed before I left the doorway of O'Flaherty's pub. I was, as they say, transfixed. Some light rain was falling, one of those late-evening autumn mists that remind you winter is coming and it might not be so bad. I had my bag with me and there was nobody left inside I wanted to say goodbye to, so I stubbed out my cigarette, which had burned away to nothing in my hand, and began to walk.

It had been a long time since I replayed an incident like that over and over in my head. I think it was the innocence of it that was so seductive. Nobody had paid that kind of attention to my lips, and only my lips, since adolescence, or childhood. I felt like I was in my own movie and I was the heroine. I walked around for ages, not ready yet to go home. I think I was afraid the feeling would disappear if I returned to the scene of my former life, my life before the kiss. The darkness and the mist were the perfect backdrop to my little fantasy.

For, of course, I knew it was a fantasy. Real people didn't behave like that and my experience of grand gestures has always been that they come at a price. But where's the harm in allowing it to run for a while? If you have a cold you take Lemsip, if you have a broken heart why not a daydream? I could wear it like a bandage until the wound went away. That was all I wanted. Where was the harm?

Yet, the following day I was surprised again. I was sitting at my desk plodding through a dossier, actually smiling to myself as I thought of Keith's notion that I was Ally McBeal or something, when I got a call. From Keith.

'Hi, Annabelle?'

'Ahm . . . aah . . .' For a moment my brain wouldn't work.

'Or is it Kate?'

'Ahm . . . yeah, this is Kate . . .'

'Are you busy?'

'Not really.' (I should have been.)

'Are you free for lunch?'

'Maybe.'

'Would you like to go to the Furze Bush?'

'Maybe.' Then, 'Wait a minute. Aren't you out in Shannon?'

'Nope!' I definitely heard an exclamation mark. 'I have the day off!'

'I didn't think chemical-engineer type people could do that.'

'It's rare, but it can happen.'

'Well, in that case I suppose I'll just have to meet you for lunch. I love the Furze Bush.'

'Will I meet you there at one?'

'OK.'

'OK, then.'

'Oh . . . and, ah . . . sorry about the Annabelle thing. How did you find out my real name?'

'The barman told me.'

'The barman?'

'No, actually, it was one of your friends.'

I felt quite foolish, but not foolish enough to run away. 'Anyway, sorry.'

'That's OK. I could have been anybody. See you at one, then.'

'See you.'

So I met him for lunch in the Furze Bush and then a drink in Mooney's. A few days later we had dinner at the Wild Tiger and then we were seeing each other all the time. We were going out. My Lemsip habit had become addictive. Nothing had changed. I still knew he was wildly not my type. I still found half of what he said profoundly boring and the other half delightfully ridiculous. But he did have a couple of things going for him. Mainly that he thought I was amazing. You have to like that in a guy. He said all sorts of daft things just when you weren't expecting them. He might be in the middle of explaining the minutiae of some documentary he'd seen on the Discovery Channel and then he'd say something like: 'You know, your eyes really do sparkle.'

'That's my sparkly eye-shadow.'

'You know what I mean.'

'I absolutely don't. You'll have to explain it to me.'

'You glow.'

'Well, now, that's just my Day Glo bronzing powder.'

'I'm serious.'

'You can't be.'

'I am. You light up a room.'

I had to laugh out loud at this. 'Keith, you're hilarious!'

Then he'd give up and go back to the documentary, and while my sparkly eyes gave the impression that I was listening, I would be thinking how nice it was that someone would think you could light up a room, no matter how ridiculous it sounded.

Another thing he had going for him was that not only was he a wonderful kisser (and not just the gentle lip-brushing kind, either) he was a bloody good lover too. You would never have thought it. He never seemed all that sexual in the normal course of things. Then again, I suppose you never know. That's the mystery of it.

I can't remember exactly when it was that we first slept together but it was several weeks after our first lunch at the Furze Bush. He liked to take things slowly. The main thing driving my desire to sleep with him was curiosity. I couldn't remember a time when things had been this, well . . . formal. I almost expected him to request an audience with my father where he would outline what he was going to do to me and where and when and was it OK? It was more of that early feeling I'd had with him that I was in a charming romantic comedy. I even began dressing in cute little outfits and taking more care with my makeup. Not to impress him, more that the role seemed to require it.

I had, of course, been thinking about it ever since that first kiss. After the lunch I knew it was inevitable so I indulged myself in bedroom fantasies. And some living-room fantasies, some kitchen fantasies, even one or two open-air fantasies, but those would have to wait for summer.

With someone new I always prefer to be on home ground. I think it might be a very, very vague remnant of my Catholic upbringing. Somehow, doing it at his place before there's even the remotest possibility that we might get married makes me a whore. And doing it at my place doesn't.

So, when I started to feel that he might be starting to feel he couldn't wait much longer, I suggested we spend a quiet evening in at my flat. (When, at the age of twenty-five, with no money and a travelling debt, my father suggested I invest in property I had no idea how grateful I would eventually become.) I did a quick tidy, made sure my bedroom was willowy and fragrant and that the lights were low enough in the living room to hide what I couldn't. I opened a robust red from the Côtes de Castillon and left it to breathe between two tall Waterfords. (I mainly prefer excellent wine drunk out of excellent glasses. But I have been known to drink any old rubbish out of any old rubbish.)

As for myself, I put on a Wonderbra, French knickers and Chanel No. 5. Over that I draped a silk wrap-around dress that clung suggestively to all my best bits.

We had very different taste in music so I went for a neutral moods compilation. It was the kind of stuff that usually made me sick, but lately my tolerance for schmaltz had been growing. He arrived a little early, something that bugged me to distraction normally but, as I said, I was mellowing.

He, also, looked nice. Essentially, Keith isn't a handsome man. He still has too much of the boy in him but he's too old to be boyish. His features, while perfectly fine and regular, are just a little too soft. His colouring is nondescript but leans towards a mousy brown. You wouldn't pick him out of a crowd but you couldn't justify throwing him out of bed either. He has a nice face. A face that gets nicer with knowing.

He came in and took off his coat. The shirt was new. Possibly the jeans also. Usually he would hang his coat carefully over a chair but tonight he simply threw it against the back of the sofa from where it promptly fell to the floor. He didn't pick it up.

'You look nice,' he said.

'Thanks, so do you.'

I thought I detected a little shortness of breath in his voice so I poured the wine straight away and suggested he sit down. He drank the wine too quickly and spilled a drop on his shirt. He didn't seem to notice. Then he kissed me. It was a long, lingering kiss, a kiss you could live in for ever. 'You know I love you,' he said.

Suddenly I got it. With all the talk about glowing and lighting up rooms, this was what he had meant. He was in love with me. This kind, sweet, intelligent, unmarried man was in love with me.

'I love you too,' I said.

Right at that moment I did. I'm certain of it.

He kissed me again and rubbed the back of his hand gently across my cheek. 'I've never known anyone like you.'

'I'm not so special.'

'You are. You're the most –'

'Honestly I'm not. Kiss me again.'

He obliged but broke off quickly and stood up.

'What's the matter?'

'Nothing . . . I . . . do you . . .'

'Keith . . .' I said, sidling up beside him. 'Is there something you want to say?'

'Well . . . I was just wondering if . . . seeing as we . . . if maybe . . . you were thinking . . .'

'If I was thinking what?'

'If maybe . . . you were ready . . .'

'You know, Keith, you're going to have to learn to talk properly, I have no idea what you're trying to say . . .'

It was too much for him. He grabbed me by the waist and kissed me furiously, the kind of kiss that extends beyond you and takes your clothes off and leads you into the bedroom. And after his first sigh at the sight of the Wonderbra and French knickers, he sighed again, and then again as he opened first one hook and then another, and as he slipped the silky underwear from my hips, over my buttocks and down my legs he began to groan, and he continued to groan as I undid the buckle on his belt and dug my hands deep inside his trousers. There was hardly time to take the rest of his clothes off before he was inside me. It felt good to have him there; it erased certain memories I wanted rid of. He kept kissing me and groaning, and I kept kissing him back and sighing, and I even started a little gentle screaming and by the time he came I was on the verge of an orgasm myself without even having to try very hard. For the last thrust I climbed on top of him and was delivered of sweet ecstasy. All in all it was a pretty good shag.

I lay there afterwards thinking that this wasn't a bad place to be a couple of months after the worst break-up of my life. So, I wasn't completely sure what I was doing but when was I? So, he seemed to like me more than I liked him. I was more than happy to try that for a while. A nice guy, and great sex, where was the problem?

'You *cannot* be serious!' said Lucy, when she arrived at my engagement party.

'No *fucking* way!' said one of my other sisters, Marion.

'I am not being your bridesmaid!' said my colleague

Denise. (I had no intention of asking her to be a bridesmaid.)

'You must be so happy!' said Angela, this total pain in the ass I work with. (Texted her by mistake.)

'Well, it's time for you. How old are you now? Thirty? Nearly thirty? It's time for you!' said my plain-speaking friend Colette.

'No, seriously,' Lucy again, 'you can't marry him. I mean he's nice and all, I know you like him. Hell, I like him, but you can't marry him. It's wrong, sweetie, you know it's wrong. He's not the right man for you. You're not the right woman for him. Marriage is a serious business, you know. All joking aside, Kate, you can't.'

'I know you're not going to go through with it,' Marion this time, 'you haven't thought about it properly. Mum won't know what to think. And Dad's only going to get upset. He's very easily upset these days. It's too sudden. I don't know why you're doing this. How long have you known him, for God's sake? You don't even believe in marriage. What's the point? Why are you doing this?'

'I think it's brilliant!' Denise. 'It's about time one of us got married. You are going to be so happy. Oh, I know he's a bit quiet and everything, a little bit nerdy, but he's a really nice guy. I'd have him any day. Well, obviously, I wouldn't, but you know what I mean. And, actually, he's not all that bad-looking. He kind of grows on you, you know. I don't really like his hair colour, and it *is* receding, just a bit, but that doesn't matter in a man any more. You know?'

Angela: 'Of course, it's very unusual to get engaged without a ring. When my sister got engaged they'd had the ring for ages. Six whole months! They got it when they were working in Dubai. Diamonds are much cheaper over there so they were able to get a much bigger one than they could have afforded if they'd got it here. I mean, her fiancé has a very good job – he's a manager in Intel – but diamonds are so expensive now and you never really know what you're paying for. It's platinum. Gold is out now. It's all platinum. I suppose you're getting platinum?'

'I mean, why not? Everybody gets married eventually. Or wants to, eventually. What's the big deal? Marry him. You'll be happy, or you won't. Either way, it's not the end of the world. He's perfectly fine. Better than most. It'll do you good. Just don't get carried away. That's where people go wrong. They start expecting too much. It's not *Sex and the City*. It's much more like your mother says it is. But it's still better than a lot of things.' That was Colette.

O'Flaherty's was buzzing. Or maybe it was me. Something was making a ferocious noise inside my head. Maybe that was the Jack Daniel's. Or maybe it was the Coke. Coca-Cola. Friday night is always a buzzy night in town. It's a night for the working people. Students go out on a Thursday, the leisured on a Saturday. It's something to do with all that steam being let off mixed with perfume and deodorant and the air of expectation. Even girls who haven't gone home after work have tarted up their office gear. Buttons have been opened, skirts hoisted up, bellies revealed. And the men – they're loud and sweaty and deeply attractive. I looked around and thought I'd happily snog the head off several of them. But every time I looked around Keith was there, smiling idiotically and laying his hands all over me. He was like a half-witted octopus.

I kept saying to myself, over and over and over, that this was my engagement party but it was like that dozy cow said: it's so strange to get engaged without a ring. I began to wonder what kind of a ring I might like. Diamonds are clearly the best but they're so boring. Oh, what a lovely solitaire! Oh, what a lovely diamond cluster! I like the coloured stones but they're so old-fashioned. I think I'll have a ruby studded with sapphires and encrusted with emeralds. That would be very nice. I'll have it specially made by a designer in Bangladesh. Yes, that's what I'll have.

And that wasn't all. If I really was going to get married there would be a whole wedding to plan. Hotels, bridesmaid dresses, cakes, cars, honeymoons. Yes, we'd have to have a honeymoon. I was in need of a holiday. A little continental sun would relax me no end. I wondered if we could get away with a little pre-honeymoon holiday, an engagement break? After all, weddings are supposed to be incredibly stressful. We'd need to build ourselves up.

I was looking for Keith to put this to him when Lucy nabbed me. Her sweet face was wrinkled with concern. 'Look,' she said, 'it's not that I'm not happy for you, or that I don't want you to be happy and I definitely don't want to spoil the happiest night of your life so far, but you really have me worried. And Marion too. You know how we never like to agree on anything but she's as bothered as I am. You don't love him, Kate.' She fixed me with her deep opal eyes and pleaded with me to come to my senses.

Unfortunately, despite my love for Lucy and my general high regard for her opinions, I wasn't budging. The drunker I got and the more people gave me advice, the more I was warming to the idea of marrying Keith. Being engaged and getting married were very exciting. It was nice to be the centre of attention for a while. It was about time my family looked at me for a change. I might be the youngest of the brood, the runt of the litter, but my time had come. I was taking control and I was getting married. To Keith. Keith was my choice. And that was that.

So I took my favourite sister in my arms (the only one

who hadn't yet taken the plunge) and told her not to worry. Whatever it looked like, this was right for me.

And there was Keith in front of us, more than a little drunk himself, his face shiny with sweat and delight. He put his arms round the two of us and squeezed tightly. 'I'm such a lucky man,' he was saying, somewhat indistinctly. 'Not only do I get this fabulous girl, I get all her fabulous sisters as well!'

Lucy extricated herself, with further congratulatory mumblings to Keith, while I remained locked in his embrace. 'I'm so happy, Kate,' he whispered into my ear.

'Oh, me too, Keith, me too.'

'I cannot wait until you're my wife!'

'Slow down there a while. We have to get used to being engaged first.'

'I'm used to it already,' he said, nuzzling my neck, 'I feel like I've been engaged to you for ever.'

'Well,' I said twisting myself round to face him, 'I'm not. I want to enjoy this time. I want to do it properly.'

'OK, my love. Whatever you want. You shall have whatever you want.'

'Come on,' I said to him, 'let's find some of your friends. They're a happy bunch. They think it's really cool that you're getting married.'

And so we joined Paul and Jack and Aiden, an accountant, a tax inspector and a chemical engineer, who treated me as if I was some kind of exotic plant and their friend as if he was James Bond. We had more to drink before eventually stumbling home to bed. We slept very soundly, very contentedly. The sleep of the newly engaged.

2

It always annoys me when people start talking about families and the positions of the children. They get it totally wrong as far as my family is concerned. The oldest is supposed to be sensible and proper and the middle child traumatized, while the youngest is the pet, loved and spoiled by everyone. Well, our oldest, Jean, has been known to behave less than sensibly on occasion, and our middle two, Lucy and Anna, are delightfully sane, and nobody, not sane, mad, traumatized or otherwise, has ever spoiled me.

Then people start talking about the gaps and say that makes the real difference. When she was pregnant with Jean my mother read a book that suggested the perfect gap between your babies was two years, so that was what she strove for. Having six babies, I'm amazed she strove for anything, but my mother is a very strong woman. However, the two-year thing didn't quite work out. I've lost track of how old the rest of my sisters are, but between me and number five there is considerably less than a year. So, you see, Ruth was supposed to be the youngest and she was the one doted upon and spoiled. I arrived completely unasked-for (apparently Mum and Dad had decided they had enough and began to practise the rhythm method) and, to be frank, I kind of got forgotten about.

Of course I don't mean that I wasn't fed or changed, or brought to the doctor when I was sick, my parents aren't criminals. I think they were just parented-out by the time I came along. And it didn't help that Ruth was a difficult child. She had all the diseases – colic, asthma, food allergies (lactose and yeast), measles, mumps, rubella. She carries their legacy with her still and she's as strong as an ox. I have always been remarkably healthy myself, but for years I tried desperately to break something, anything: leg, arm, collarbone, wrist. My entire sports career was based around breaking something, but that was just as unsuccessful as my sports career.

However, being somewhat neglected as a child has probably left me a little needy. I'm the last one to navel-gaze, I believe you should just get on with things, but if I were to psychoanalyse myself for five minutes I'm sure my issues with men come down to a lack of attention in the play-pen.

Such thoughts were with me as I strolled across the new bridge towards the North Circular Road on the Sunday morning following my engagement party. Keith felt it was important we arrive before noon. Otherwise we might appear sloppy. I kept having to pull him back to stop him striding away from me. He thinks my family's marvellous. He thinks there's something innately good about a large family, especially one that's all girls. He's from a gaggle of two boys. (That's one good thing – in marrying Keith I can't inherit any more sisters.) The thought also struck me that maybe he liked my family more than he liked me, but I dismissed that one fairly quickly. Keith liked me. A lot.

It wasn't just his eagerness to go forward that kept me pulling Keith back but also a dread of my stomach going too far forward. You'd think that after years of abusing my liver like this it would have got more efficient at dealing with the toxins, yet nowadays every hangover seems worse than the last. Well, I'm nearly not in my twenties any more. Every time I stopped and leaned over the railings to take in the docks and the estuary beyond I thought, I should really be taking stock of my life, but then my stomach heaved and I realized I had more pressing matters at hand. Keith was a sweetie, rubbing my neck and holding my hair back in case I was about to hurl. I suppose that's one definition of love.

Eventually we made it. It's only a twenty-minute walk from my flat on Hartstonge Street to the North Circular but we got there in about forty. We could have driven but Keith felt the need for a ceremonial walk and I thought the air might do me good. It didn't. By the time we arrived at Sycamore Lodge I was in need of my bed and a stomach pump.

Our family home is a sizeable early-twentieth-century residence on Limerick's exclusive North Circular Road. It is detached, lies on three-quarters of an acre, bordered on three sides by old stone and on the fourth by even older oak. It is the house I was born into and have grown up in and will, presumably, be the house I get married from. My father bought it in 1963 with money he made from his first property deal. He always says it's the best investment he ever made.

Dad was in the garden raking up twigs that had blown off the trees. He's no gardener but likes the way gardening makes him feel. A long time ago his family was dispossessed. I think our huge garden makes up for it a bit. He looked up and smiled at us, and in that moment I wished I had different news, something that would make him proud of me.

'Hey, Dad!'

'Hey, kids. Your mother's inside.'

'Oh, good. I thought she might still be at Mass.'

'We're going to the ten o'clock, these days. Your mother got very fed up of a choir that couldn't sing. How are you, Keith?'

'Very well, thanks, Mr Delahunty. Lovely morning, isn't it?'

'Not bad for April, now.'

'Are you coming in, Dad?'

'I'll be in in a minute. There's a bit of work to be done first.'

Whatever my dad does, whether it's closing a business deal or lining up a golf shot, he likes to classify it as 'a bit of work'.

'Well, don't be long. We've got some news.'

Even with that tantalizing rejoinder, I knew we'd be waiting a good twenty minutes for him.

My mother was in the kitchen, her favourite room. She was wearing last year's good tweed skirt and long-sleeved silk blouse. She would have changed immediately out of this year's good tweed skirt and long-sleeved silk blouse on coming in from Mass. She has always maintained a hierarchical wardrobe. Every year, new garments, very like the old ones, are acquired, and the existing garments relegated accordingly. This year's are Sunday (or other) Good, last year's are Sunday Home, the year before that's are Everyday Meet and Greet, before that Everyday Home and so it goes. Eventually they become dusters or go to a charity shop. Whatever the occasion, Mrs David Delahunty is always dressed for it.

She was also wearing an apron, a very nice designer job Dad had bought her in Meadows and Byrne. Sunday lunch was well under way. This week it was roast spring lamb with rosemary stuffing, creamed potatoes, steamed broccoli in lemon butter, followed by *Good Housekeeping*'s apple crumble. Late in life, Mum discovered that being a good cook was socially acceptable.

She turned round from the cooker and beamed at us. 'Kids! What a lovely surprise! I was only saying to Daddy this morning that we hadn't seen you two in ages. Of course, you have loads to occupy you but I was hoping you'd drop in. I don't know why I bother with a roast any more. I hardly see any of you. Even Jean is staying away. I don't know what's going on with that girl lately – she's as moody as she was as a teenager, and I don't know when I last saw Lucy but there's nothing new there. You'll have to give me all the news. And how are you, Keith? You're very quiet.' Mum was in great form. It's when she goes quiet that I get worried.

'I'm great, Mrs Delahunty, really great.'

'Well, that's good. I get so worried about ye young people. There's always a drama somewhere. And how are your parents? Is your father recovered from that cold? If you ask me it's the flu injection that causes the colds. They can tell me anything they like, I know what's happening. He's recovered so?'

'He has, yes. He's in great form again.'

'That's good. Kate, you're looking a little peaky. But there's a surprise. I told you to take those vitamins. You need something to build you up when you won't eat properly. Isn't it true, Keith? I keep telling her but she never listens. Now, where's my balloon whisk?'

At this point I had to sit down even though my mother believes you should only sit down to eat. Soon we would be getting the idleness-of-youth speech. I keep trying to tell my mother that none of us is all that youthful any more but she never listens. I asked her if there was any coffee and she told me it was too late in the day for coffee, dinner would be served soon. So I sat on the edge of a kitchen chair and tried not to fall off the edge of the universe.

Keith, however, was full of good humour. 'You have a fabulous view from your kitchen window,' he said directly to my mother.

27

'You're right, Keith. It helps to alleviate some of the drudgery of cooking.'

'Smells gorgeous.'

'Oh, thank you. It's nice to be appreciated.'

'You must give me the recipe.'

'It's as simple as anything. I'll write it down for you before you go.'

I'd find Keith's appreciation of my mother and her kitchen truly sickening if he wasn't truly genuine. What a great son-in-law he'll make.

Suddenly there was a commotion at the kitchen door and Dad appeared with Lucy and Marion in tow. Then I had a flashback to the night before. I was holding forth in the luxury loos of O'Flaherty's nightclub, impressing upon the two girls my need to assert myself and bring my life to the next phase. Marion tried to impress upon me that the 'next phase' didn't have to be marriage – for one who rushed into marriage herself she takes it very seriously now. They must have been a little worried about me still, or maybe they were just curious.

Anyway, here everybody was, so, grabbing Keith's arm for support, I hoisted myself up, took a deep breath and said, 'Hey! We're getting married!'

At first I thought the silence might kill me. My father was the first to move. 'Well, that's great news altogether. Congratulations!'

He gave me a soft squeeze, a bedtime squeeze, and he shook Keith's hand heartily.

Then my mother awoke from her stupor. 'Yes,' she said, 'oh yes, yes, this is wonderful. My little baby getting married. Oh, yes, yes, yes.'

She hugged and kissed us both and, though I'm not absolutely sure, I think she shed a tear. All in all, given that this was the fifth time one of their daughters announced an engagement, they were suitably moved and delighted.

So, we sat down to the marvellous lamb and a very fine Châteauneuf-du-Pape. Dad had wanted to open a bottle of champagne but Mum persuaded him to leave it until dessert. The lamb would get nothing from the champagne and the champagne would be spoiled by the lamb. She was right, of course. As I looked round the table at everybody I was almost happy. Keith was beaming like an idiot, Mum was wearing her patented smile of satisfaction, but I'm not sure if that was for us or because the lamb was a success, and Dad was grinning into his wine, thinking I don't know what. Lucy was getting drunk and Marion was just glad that everything was going smoothly.

Suddenly Dad decided it was time for the champagne. One of his great pleasures in life is his wine cellar. It was the first improvement he made to the house. The second was a wall-to-wall bookcase in the living room to house his books on the subject. When all the other parents were attending meetings on how to keep your children from drink, Dad would be holding tutorials on the wine regions in France. Occasionally he held informal tastings, mainly when Mum was out of the house. He inculcated in each of us a healthy respect for wine and other forms of alcohol. The disrespect came later.

We moved out to the conservatory, already drenched in the afternoon sun. Draping myself across one of the loungers I felt sure I was going to fall asleep. It seemed that so much had been accomplished and even more set in motion that I needed to sleep off the effects of the exertion. I felt I needed to sleep for a very long time. But with my mother in the room there was no chance of that.

'You know that Virginia's Bridalwear is closing down?

I was talking to Eleanor Fitzmorris at the concert hall the other night and she told me there were some irregularities with the accounts. It's all since the son took over. I mean, I don't know what kind of a job that is for a man. No wonder he wasn't any good at it. And I said to Eleanor was he gay and she said, no, he definitely wasn't, he just wanted to give the business a go. Out of respect for his mother. Well, she'll be turning in her grave now.'

Lucy topped up her glass but said nothing.

'You know, Mum,' Marion said, 'that's just gossip. Eleanor Fitzmorris is a nosy bint who likes nothing better than to slag off her neighbours. You should know better than to listen to what she says.'

'Don't you tell me who I shouldn't listen to, lady. She's a good friend of mine and I know for a fact that every word she says is true.'

'Oh, whatever!' Marion also topped up her glass.

'I've heard that Top Man is the best place for men's dress hire.'

This was Keith. I'd forgotten he was still there.

'Not any more, Keith, dear. The whole thing has been taken over by a franchise and the service is not the same. No, the only place to go now is McGinty's. It's shabby, but they know how to treat you.' She sighed as she said this, and shot the rest of us a dirty look. As usual, she was the only one willing to keep the conversation going.

I must have actually fallen asleep because the next thing I remember is Daddy putting all the furniture back in place and nudging my shoulder. 'I think you should go and see to your boy,' he said.

I wandered off into the house but nobody seemed to be anywhere. Still sleepy, I decided my old bedroom was as good a place as any to look for people. To give Mum her due, she's never been one to go turning your bedroom into a library or a gym just because you haven't lived there for a decade or so. She's kept our rooms ready for use. Maybe some part of her wishes we'd return, tails between the legs we should have kept together. Anyway, it's a comfort to know that even if I can't find clean underwear in my flat, there's always a freshly made bed waiting for me at Mum and Dad's.

I've always loved my room, even when I had to share it with Ruth. Luckily she was the kind of child who had to be always in the middle of everything so I was often able to spend whole afternoons alone there. Of course, there was the odd occasion when I chose to share my room with somebody else. Somebody like Bobby O'Gorman who lived across the road. I might feel ashamed now of the things we did together (oh, just doctors and nurses when we were about fifteen, but still fairly innocent), if it weren't for the fact that I was deeply in love with him. He had jet black hair and inky blue eyes and the roundest, softest, sweetest smile I've ever seen on a boy. He was also extremely reticent but curiosity carried him just far enough to satisfy mine, for a while.

I was about to enter a very comfortable reverie when there was a knock at my door. It wouldn't be Mum, she was well past the cursory I'm-pretending-to-respect-your-privacy-but-we-both-know-I'm-coming-in-anyway knock, and Dad would never bother you if you were in your bedroom. If it was Keith he could join me for a little sleep. However, it was Marion and Lucy who barged in before I could finish my thought.

'Hey, honey.'

'Hey, Luce.'

25

'You doing OK?' asked Marion, as she sat beside me on the bed.

'I'm fine, sweetie. I'm a little drunk but, hey, what's new?'

'Are you sure you're OK?' said Lucy.

'Look, there really wasn't any need for the two of you to come over today. Mum and Dad are absolutely fine. We're absolutely fine. I know I probably went on a bit last night but everything's fine. Honestly!'

The two girls said nothing for a minute, then Marion took my hand. 'Look,' she said, 'there's another reason we came over today.'

'Oh!'

'Yeah. We heard a bit of news yesterday we thought we should tell you. Well, Lucy heard it first and then I was able to confirm it.'

'Oh?'

'Yeah, aahhm . . .'

'Daniel O'Hanlon's wife is pregnant,' Lucy blurted out.

'Oh.'

'We're sorry. But you're better hearing it from us. It'll be all over the place soon. Apparently, they're thrilled. It's sickening, I know.'

'I'm really sorry, sweetheart. You could do without this.'

I was genuinely unable to speak.

'Will we leave you alone for a while?'

'No,' I said. 'Stay. I think I might be sick.'

3

You always believe there will be one person in your life who will make the difference. The person who makes sense of everything – you, the world, your family, love. The person for whom you would do anything because anything you do for them is something you do for yourself. The person with whom you fall wholly in love. For me, that person was Daniel O'Hanlon.

We met through work. I used to say that finally I understood why God had made me a lawyer. He's with one of the other big firms in town – in fact, he's a partner and his firm is the biggest. Apart from being strikingly good-looking, he's one of the most admired men in his profession. Everybody knows who he is; everybody wants to know him. For a green young apprentice who had only just managed to pass her Blackhall Place exams (third attempt) and was contemplating a change of career, he was a symbol of the unattainable. In every sense of the word for, of course, he was married.

When he first started paying me attention I was merely flattered. It wasn't unusual for men, particularly older men, to find me attractive. I'm a natural flirt and I've always found older men to be so much better at the game than those my own age. Perhaps it has something to do with older men not feeling threatened by a younger woman. And most married men who flirt do so playfully – at least, that's what I'd always believed. So I didn't think there was any harm in his phoning me up after the Law Society dinner at which we had been introduced. I didn't think it was unusual that he asked me to join him and a few of his colleagues for a drink after work. Or that all of his colleagues disappeared after two quick drinks. I only thought how fabulous it was that Daniel O'Hanlon had so much to say to me and found my chatter so fascinating. That first evening we sat in the snug of the Merry Widow until near closing. We didn't even drink much, we just talked and talked and talked. I can't remember anything about our conversation; I was star-struck and he was – well, I still haven't worked it out. Why does anybody start an affair? Sure, loads of people stumble into it, but he seemed to set out to do it. And why did he target me? Was it so obvious that I was easily impressed, slightly lost and of dubious moral character?

He walked me home that night. I do remember feeling that the streets had never seemed so alive with possibility. This was my city and anything could happen. All future events were mine to lay claim to. The sodium lamps seemed to be lighting the way into something that, for the moment, there was no good reason to turn away from. He brought me to my building and said he'd really enjoyed our talk. He hoped we might do it again. I said I hoped so too and kissed him briefly on the lips.

Over the next couple of weeks I kept bumping into him. He'd be in our building meeting one of the partners. He'd be having lunch at the same place I was. Or there he'd be, on the street, just a few feet away. And each time I saw him my body would contract, my mind would paralyse; I would be rendered a fool. Yet he never seemed to notice me. I thought it a little odd that someone who had appeared so besotted could now behave as if I was a nobody. But I didn't think it was odd enough to pin him as a jackass and move on. Perhaps if I'd been better at my job I would have been too busy to obsess about a jumped-up lawyer who thought he was God's gift.

I hadn't had a boyfriend in a while. Philip was still sort of on the scene but we both knew it wasn't going anywhere. We had fallen heavily in lust with each other while working on a portfolio together. But when we had had time to get to know each other we realized, as you do in these situations, that we had nothing in common. He was quite boring with little interest in anything other than his job, and sport. He was immature, a bit mean and far, far too fond of himself. It was while I was realizing all this that it dawned on me I'd been doing this sort of thing for too long. After I'd got over the notion that I might marry every man who excited my interest I gave up on the idea of serious relationships altogether. After all, a girl has the right just to want to have fun. But for a while now it hadn't been fun. I was bored and a little tired. However, a hot and heavy affair with a married man was not what I needed.

We met again by accident one night at a party. It was somebody's fortieth. I hadn't been planning to go but Colette persuaded me. She and I have been friends for years, as far back as schooldays when we were in the same class, had the same hairstyle, liked the same boys and told each other everything. But we went to different universities and followed different careers. We liked different boys, and by our mid-twenties we had little in common. She got married and had kids and I didn't. Then we ended up back in Limerick and there seemed to be enough between us for a rekindling. I admire Colette: she's so together and sure of herself. On that particular evening she fancied a night out and wanted me along for company. I owed her one. The person turning forty was some friend of her husband's but she reckoned she needed the night out more than he did.

We arrived together but soon drifted into disparate groups. Colette and I always work a party well. We give each other breathing space but we'll still be there for the other if needed. I was having a very good time. I had fallen upon a group of young men who were delighted to find even one attractive woman under thirty. I flirted with them and we decided collectively that it was better to shoot yourself than to turn forty in your own living room with a bunch of even older old farts. The house was a big, sprawling affair in the suburbs so we were able to drift off into some side room that might have been an office, or a gift-wrapping room. We had requisitioned a bottle of vodka and were about to begin an elaborate drinking game when Daniel O'Hanlon appeared at the door.

He seemed drunk. 'Can I join you?' he asked. 'Or is there an age limit?' he added a little sourly.

I said nothing.

I didn't need to. One of my junior companions hopped up and launched a near obscene licking-up session: 'Oh, hi, Mr O'Hanlon! We were just taking a break from all the craziness next door. Great party! Do you know the hosts? Smashing house. Do you live around here?'

He went on and on, but nobody was listening, least of all Daniel, and his mates were about to make off with the vodka. Daniel came further into the room and sort of shoved the sycophant out with the others. Then he closed the door. 'I've missed you.'

'Oh?'

'Yeah.'

'Well, you were doing a pretty good job of ignoring me.'

'I wasn't ignoring you, I was resisting you.'

'Resisting me! Give me a break, Mr O'Hanlon.'

'You are gorgeous, you know.'

'Yes, I know. Thanks!'

Suddenly his look changed and he seemed less drunk than disoriented. There was something vulnerable about him, something that suggested he needed help.

'Look, Kate, I know I've messed you around since that night in the Merry Widow but I've been thinking about you constantly. I didn't tell you this before, but I'm married.'

'I know you are.'

'Oh!'

He took a step back and leaned against the edge of a table. He was about to say something, but changed his mind. He covered his face with his hands and let out what could only be described as a cross between a sigh and a howl. I felt as if I'd been watching him for eternity. Then he glanced at me and said he was sorry. He looked sorry. He looked like the sorriest, saddest man I'd ever seen. So I went closer to him, close enough to smell the fresh sweat on his body. Our heads touched first, temple to temple, then our cheeks, then our lips. It was one of those kisses that is born somewhere deep inside you and grows as it moves to the surface, then bursts out of you. Then there is aftershock after aftershock as your whole body trembles. It's what an orgasm used to feel like before you knew what an orgasm was.

As we kissed I was convinced that I loved this man and that I wanted to be with him, no matter what. His touch seemed to be the touch my body was crying out for. If there were danger signals I couldn't hear them for all the noise in my head. When we finally let go of each other I knew there was only one thing I wanted to happen next. I told him I was leaving the party. I asked him if he wanted to leave with me. He said nothing, but bundled me out of the back door. A few minutes later he reappeared carrying our coats and fumbling for his keys. Suddenly I remembered Colette.

31

I couldn't leave without telling her. I told Daniel I'd only be a minute and rushed back inside.

It took me ages to find her, but eventually I saw her sitting at the top of the stairs, smoking a cigarette.

'Look, Colette, I'm going, OK? Will you be all right to get a taxi home?'

I was hoping this would be enough and I could slip away without further explanation, but Colette knows me too well. 'Wait a minute!' She scudded down the stairs. 'You're going home with somebody?'

I hadn't told her, or anyone, about my first evening with Daniel. 'No. Yes. I'll tell you tomorrow.'

'You're going home with someone you shouldn't be going home with?'

'Look, I'll tell you tomorrow.'

I didn't want to be impatient with her but I didn't want her to persuade me out of anything either.

'It's important. It's big.'

'OK, then. I'm sure you have no idea what you're doing. I'll talk to you tomorrow.'

I touched her arm and walked out of the back door.

Daniel was waiting in the car. I asked him if he was all right to drive. I don't know if I was worried about him losing his licence or about him killing the two of us. He leaned over, took my hands in his and said he was fine. Then he kissed my cheek so softly and asked if I was all right about this. I still had no full idea what 'this' was but I knew I wanted it.

All the way back to my flat we said nothing. He parked on the street and held my hand in the lift. As soon as I closed the door behind us we fell upon each other, kissing wildly, even biting. We were naked in seconds. The way we made love that first time was furious, as if neither of us had ever done it before and might never do it again. It was profoundly physical, yet I felt as though I couldn't separate my mind from what was going on. I felt as though something terrible would happen if he were ever to leave my body. And he, also, seemed to find less pleasure in that first time than a necessary relief. Our lovemaking would become more relaxed, but that night we were both exorcizing something.

Of course he couldn't stay the night. We both slept and when we woke it was almost three o'clock. He had to get up and leave. As he walked out of the door, with one last hurried but passionate kiss, I should have felt something like guilt or remorse. But I didn't. I had either had a one-night stand with a married man or was about to begin a long-term affair with one, and everything in me hoped it was the latter. I had never felt passion like that before and I desperately wanted more. All I could think of was him, his touch, his smell, his body. All I wanted was to have him again.

The following day was Sunday so I slept in. I stayed in the bed we had made love in, replaying our night over and over. If my memory was to be wiped of everything but that, it would have been enough.

Some time late in the afternoon, after I had finally dragged myself out of bed and taken a shower, my door buzzed. It was Daniel. I let him up.

'I want you to know,' he said, 'that last night was amazing. I love you. I want to keep seeing you.'

I guess I had my answer.

Since we had been engaged for more than thirty-six hours and I still had no ring, Keith decided we were taking Monday afternoon off to go shopping. I was less than useless at work that day so my boss had no problem letting me go. In fact, everybody at work was still bemused by my announcement. Most people in the office didn't take me for the marrying kind, especially those who were privy to my recent romantic history. But everybody wished me well; some of them meant it, others looked forward to another crisis. You know the sort – those who lead monumentally boring lives but take unnatural delight in the messes other people make.

I skipped down the beautifully restored staircase of our carefully preserved Georgian building and lunged into the pink light of a warm April afternoon. I felt positively buoyant.

We had arranged to meet for a coffee first in Lily's Café. It had become a regular spot for the two of us. It was central, offered good coffee, great cakes, friendly service and was always open. It was one of my favourite places. It occurred to me one day when I was sitting there waiting for Keith (I was early for once) that this was something I hadn't done in a long time. I hadn't dated. I hadn't simply gone out with somebody to the cinema or to restaurants or to the pub. And I liked it. There was something pure about meeting your boyfriend at a café, then going to the cinema. Or getting dressed up for dinner in a special place, then going home to fall asleep watching a video. When you have an affair with a married man in a small city, you spend a lot of time behind closed doors.

Keith was waiting for me, and he had ordered me a cappuccino. It was all falling into place. Here was the man who would look after me for the rest of my life. He would open doors, order drinks, remind me when the bills were due, fix the washing-machine, cut the grass, talk to my parents, program the remote control, and buy me jewellery. I could live with this. As he sat by the window, illuminated by the afternoon sun and the pale pink shirt he had changed into on leaving work, he was the very picture of connubial bliss.

As soon as he saw me approaching the table he stood up and kissed me somewhat formally on the cheek. 'Hey, honey,' he said, holding out a chair for me.

'Hey,' I said, with what I intended to be warm emphasis.

'I don't know if you've thought about what you'd like,' he began immediately, 'but I was looking in McDermott's window and they have some lovely stones.'

'No,' I said, surprised, 'I haven't thought about it. I'm sure all the rings are lovely.'

'Oh, sure, they might look nice but you have to know what you're getting. An engagement ring isn't just any piece of jewellery.'

'Oh!'

'Well, not only will you have it for ever but you'll wear it for ever and probably hand it down to your children and grandchildren.'

'Yeah . . . I suppose so . . .' I'd never thought of it like that.

'I want it to be the right one for you.'

'I'm sure I'll like them all.'

'I don't want you to rush it now, I want you to be sure.'

'It's fine, Keith. Let's go and pick a ring.' I wished he wouldn't make such a big deal of it.

'Right, we'll go so,' he said, pushing away the last of his coffee. 'We want to give ourselves plenty of time.'

'Sure. Fine.'

By the time we made it to McDermott's and entered their richly carpeted emporium, the euphoria I had been feeling at the start of the afternoon had almost dissipated.

Unlike many of my peers, I had never had a particular interest in engagement rings. I had never pored over the fingers of my engaged friends or sisters, I had never cruised the windows of jewellery shops, I had never held my left hand in the air and fantasized about diamonds.

Neither had I ever asked the price.

I was astounded.

I had no idea that these tiny pieces of stone and metal could cost so much. Frankly, I felt a little nauseous. Was I really going to let Keith pay out several thousand euro of his money to buy me a ring, symbol of our love, hopeful indicator of our future together? As far as he was concerned, no ring was big enough or expensive enough, and he knew what he was talking about. He kept asking about carats and clarity and other things I'd never heard of. I tried on several: a solitaire so big it made my wrist hurt, a clump of three diamonds, a clump of five that dazzled so much I had to look away, then an emerald cluster that would have been useful in a street fight. They looked like interlopers on my hand. The jeweller detected something of my discomfort and assured Madam that many young ladies are unsure at first which ring suits them best. I found Sir's consideration even more suffocating and finally I turned to Keith and asked if we could leave.

I ran out of the shop and drank in the poisonous air in the street.

'What's wrong?'

'Nothing's wrong.'

'There's something. Tell me what it is.'

'There's nothing. Can we go home?'

'Tell me – tell me what it is.'

I couldn't articulate it. I couldn't say that, somehow, by putting a price tag on our relationship, it had disintegrated. I couldn't say I felt a fraud, that I, and not the ring, was the interloper. The ring belonged – it belonged to somebody who deserved it.

I told Keith I was feeling a bit woozy and asked him to take me home. So he did.

He brought me back to my apartment and put the kettle on. Surprisingly, a cup of tea was very welcome. I've always envied the way some people can find endless comfort and relief in a cup of tea. I suppose when you've gone looking further afield for your comfort, the humble mix of caffeine and tannin loses its power. Keith pottered about in the kitchenette, putting things away, wiping up, noting I was out of milk and fresh bread. It dawned on me that Keith wasn't going to be my husband: he was going to be my wife. They say everyone needs a good wife; if women had wives instead of husbands the world would be a very different place. He said he was going to run down to the shop to pick up a few things. Before he went he kissed my forehead.

I lay down on the couch and wished life was simpler.

I began to think about my mother's life and her reasons for getting married. Mum has never been one for sitting down with her girls and telling us how it was that she met Daddy and fell in love and got married and lived happily ever after, but from time to time she would intimate that she had no real choice in the matter (I don't mean she couldn't choose whom she married, rather that she couldn't choose not to get married) and that our problem was we had endless choice. Which course to study in college, whether or not to pursue post-graduate studies. To travel abroad or start work immediately? To fall in love with this man or that other man? To marry him or live with him? To have children now, later or never? To handle your life with reasonable reasonableness or to make mess after mess without ever thinking about what you were doing or learning from any of your mistakes? Oh, yes, so many choices.

But it was easier then. You married the nicest man you could find and had babies with him and cleaned the house and nobody expected you to have a career, much less be good at it. If you were lucky you had a nice house and good neighbours and – and . . . Oh, who am I kidding? Most of them were miserable because they didn't have what I have.

And then I thought about Daniel O'Hanlon's wife. They'd got married having just left college after going out together since the middle of First Year. Daniel said that neither of them had had a serious relationship before and both were virgins. He said it was inevitable they would get married. He said they got on really well together, they still did, but there weren't any sparks. He said there never had been. Naturally I believed everything he said.

She became pregnant almost immediately. It wasn't exactly planned, Daniel said, but they were both delighted. She didn't go back to work after the first child, a boy, and they had a second straight away. Another boy. Meanwhile, Daniel was kicking ass at Webster and Jones making tons of lucre for the missus and the sprogs. Somewhere along the line they had two more kids, a third boy and a girl. Four kids! And now she was pregnant again.

When Daniel went back to her he said it was for the family. I hadn't realized there was to be more family on the way. It's practically obscene to have five children in this day and age. Five young O'Hanlons running about the place!

He said he would have liked to have a baby with me . . .

There was no point even thinking about it.

I had already had my cry with Lucy and Marion and I wasn't going to start again.

And then there was Marion's marriage. She had been

going out with this guy from Dundalk for ever when he broke it off. He never explained why. He just said he didn't want to marry my lovely Marion. To be honest, the little I knew of him I didn't like. I think Marion was dying to get married because Jean was married. She's always looked up to Jean, though I cannot fathom why. She says I don't understand Jean because I was only a child when she did her growing up. Whatever!

Anyway, as soon as Marion was dumped she started going out with this old boyfriend from school, Nick. They'd never actually broken up, just drifted apart. Within a year they were getting married. Everybody said it was a rebound thing and that Marion was far too eager to walk up that aisle (my mother). But the funny thing is that of all my sisters' marriages, I think theirs is the happiest.

Suddenly I was roused by Keith charging back into the flat.

'I'm going to cook you a little something,' he said, laying a bag of provisions on the table. 'I think you might be hypoglycaemic – you never eat properly.'

I was tired of telling him that someone the size of me eating properly and someone the size of him eating properly were not the same thing. But he insisted on whipping out his shiitake mushrooms and sautéing them in the pan while mixing in creamy scrambled eggs seasoned with nutmeg. (He had walked an extra block to our new organic deli.) He served me the meal (including a glass of chilled chablis) on a tray so I wouldn't have to move from the couch. Then he took a small box from his inside pocket and placed it on the tray. 'It was my grandmother's. I know why you freaked in the jeweller's. I was being foolish. This ring is much more you. It's unique and amazing, like you are.'

The ring was beautiful – a delicate sparkling ruby cluster.

He placed it ceremoniously on my finger and I felt a surge of love for him.

'Oh, Keith . . .' I said.

And, even though it was probably far more valuable than some ring from a shop, I accepted his grandmother's ring, and kissed him.

4

I knew it would only be a short time before Mum told me about the engagement party she was planning. I knew that by the time she told me her guests would be invited and it would be on a night that definitely didn't suit me. I knew there was no point in arguing, but I did.

'We've already had a party, Mum.'

'That neither your father nor I was invited to!'

'It was informal, impromptu. We're informal people.'

'An engagement isn't informal. What would the family think if there was no proper marking of the event?'

'I really don't want a party, Mum. And neither does Keith.'

'Oh yes he does! I was only talking to him about it last weekend when you disappeared for half the afternoon. He thought it would be a nice surprise for you.'

'Oh, he's only thinking of you. He doesn't really want a party.'

'Kate, thanks to your habit of running away every time a member of the family pays a visit, Keith has hardly met a single one of your cousins, not to mind my sisters. I was on the phone to Mary last night and I got the distinct impression she doesn't believe Keith exists.'

'Oh, God, Mum, Keith exists! Who cares what Auntie Mary thinks?'

'I care and your father cares. And your sisters care. Jean was on to me as well, wondering when she was going to meet your mystery man.'

'Mum, Keith is no mystery.'

'I'll need you over here on Saturday at four o'clock. There's a lot to be done, and seeing as the party is for you, I'll need your help.'

'Saturday? This Saturday?'

'Of course this Saturday. We couldn't wait any longer.'

'But we're going to Dublin to see a play. It was a present from Keith's parents.'

'Well, you'll have to cancel.'

'But they'll be insulted.'

'They won't. They'll understand. They're sensible people.'

'How many have you invited?'

'Not many. Just the family. About seventy.'

'Seventy!'

'The house can easily take seventy. If we open up the doors between the sitting and dining rooms you wouldn't even see seventy.'

'So, all the aunts, then? And all the uncles? And most of the cousins?'

'And a few of our neighbours. Just some good friends of mine. You'll know everybody. I don't know why you're not delighted.'

'No, Mum, you misunderstand me. I *am* delighted. This is me being delighted.'

'Look, madam, I don't misunderstand you at all. Saturday at four. And wear something nice.'

Something nice, according to my mother, would have been a version of her own expensive blouses and skirts. She didn't like trousers on women, although now that her sisters were getting into them she was beginning to understand it didn't mean the end of civilization as she knew it. (Unlike Mum, some of the sisters were gaining a little weight and found the trousers very comfortable.) She didn't like anything

42

short, long, see-through or low-cut. She didn't like anything bright (garish), patterned (cheap), or flimsy (suggestive). Since my mother stopped buying clothes for me I have never worn anything she liked.

So, on Saturday afternoon, after spending the morning in bed, I opened my wardrobe and laid my party clothes on the bed. Until recently the pile hadn't been added to much. Since Keith and I started going out there had been more occasions for the glitzy stuff. Before that my wardrobe had remained low-key. Except for my lingerie drawer.

There were a couple of fancy Karen Millen dresses, but one I had worn to death and the other was so fancy that nobody would dry-clean it for me. There was a red formal Monsoon two-piece I'd bought for last year's Christmas party, but I didn't like it any more. Then there were some miscellaneous pieces – trousers, skirts and tops that I liked to mix and match but none was right for that afternoon. There was nothing for it – I'd have to go shopping.

Keith had tried to persuade me that the perfect way to begin our special day would be to meet in town for lunch, shop around for a thank-you gift for my mother for such a thoughtful gesture, then head out to the party together. I assured him that if I was to have any chance of surviving the evening I would have to be left alone until the last possible moment. Eventually he agreed.

I tried a few of the smaller boutiques first but they had only casual summer gear. I needed something that would make a statement, of some sort, to somebody. I needed something my mother would hate. Several shops on and still nothing. I thought about going for the ripped-jeans look with a belly top but I couldn't bring myself to do it. I was nearly thirty, after all, and besides, I have more taste than that. Brown Thomas was my last stop; it should probably have been the first but my BT credit card was maxed out and, well, there was never anything going cheap in Brown Thomas.

I love stepping off the escalator on to the first-storey fashion floor, especially when I haven't been there for a while. There's always so much choice, so many possibilities, so many roles you could play. Who would I be tonight? Sexy and sophisticated in Diane von Furstenburg? Sexy and girly in Whistles? Or sexy and sexy in a tight little number by Karen Millen?

It would have to be all three. I ran round picking them up, then raced to my secret changing cubicle at the back of the shop that nobody else seemed to know about. I tried the dress from Whistles first. It was gorgeous, but not on me. It made me look too much like a girl and not in a good way. The DVF was divine but didn't say 'party' (it might have been better suited to a party for two).

I was just taking it off and reaching for the Karen Millen when I became aware of people outside the cubicle, waiting for me to leave. Two women were talking in low tones but it was just possible to make out what they were saying. Only one was trying on, the other seemed to be offering moral support, which the one trying on appeared to need – she kept going on about her weight and nothing fitting her any more. Then the other said she didn't know what she'd look like after her fifth baby . . .

Suddenly the thing that had been niggling me about these women became clear. I knew I recognized one of the voices. I pulled off the last of the DVF dress and slumped to the floor. There I was, semi-naked and sweating, and there she was, the jolly pregnant wife of my former lover.

*

I had encountered her before, at another of those Law Society dinners. She hadn't been at the one where Daniel couldn't keep his eyes off me. This dinner was in aid of some charity and everybody was there. Daniel and I had been seeing each other for about six months, and I was deliriously happy. Everything about him was wonderful. It was sexy and exciting and provocative. I felt like I was the only adult in the world because only I could handle such a complicated relationship. Daniel loved me and I loved him, but he also loved his wife and kids and I had no problem with that. What he had with her was quotidian, pedestrian, and what he had with me was dynamic, passionate. I wasn't so rooted in middle-class orthodoxy that I couldn't handle sharing my man. I didn't want what they had – the family life, the tedium, the reliability. What I wanted was a man so besotted with me he would risk the happiness of his family, the regard of his friends and colleagues, for mere moments in my company. I didn't care who knew. We were in love; it was nobody else's business.

Daniel, however, cared. It was agreed between us that the only way for this to work was to make sure nobody knew. That suited me fine: it added to the excitement and my growing sense of superiority over the rest of the inhibited boyfriend-or-husband-having world. I had a secret, which made me special.

So, at that dinner, at which I was unencumbered by an escort, I carried with me an air of smug delight. I knew she would be there. I couldn't wait to meet her. What Daniel had told me about her made me confident she held nothing on me. I wasn't disappointed. She was attractive, certainly, but in a conventional way. She was about my height and build, maybe slightly shorter, slightly heavier. Her hair was expensively cut into a bob, which framed her face well, and carefully dyed to enhance her skin tone. For her age (she had to be in her early forties) her skin was bright and free of lines. But there was nothing remarkable in any of her features. Eyes that were nicely made up but not particularly expressive, a mouth that was a little too small and lips that didn't reveal anything. You would look at her and admire her, but you wouldn't look again.

I was deep in conversation with one of the senior partners when she and Daniel came up to us. They joined in the conversation and later, as an afterthought, Daniel performed the introductions. Of course, she knew everybody else so she put out her hand to shake mine. 'Very pleased to meet you,' she said. 'It's great to see women staying in the profession. I'm afraid I never practised myself.'

She gave her husband one of those highly intimate mock-frowns that tell the world they're of one mind about every-thing. Then, as the men continued the conversation, she marshalled me to one side to ask about conditions and present work practices, saying she could never get a straight answer from her husband. I played my part but I was eager to be away from her. I wasn't suddenly struck down with guilt but I certainly didn't want her as a confidante.

Naturally I went home alone that night but Daniel made a special effort to get over to me the following evening. He said he had been incredibly proud of me. He said I was the most stunning woman in the room and it was killing him that he couldn't run home with me there and then. He said he couldn't believe what we were doing but he wanted it never to end. He said he cared for me so much it hurt. We made love on the floor of my living room and hours later I had to prise him away from me and send him home.

There were other occasions. It was one of those instances in which as soon as you become aware of a person you see them everywhere. She was at an art-exhibition opening; she was three people ahead of me at the checkout in Dunnes; she was coming out of the beautician's as I was going in. Limerick isn't London, or even Dublin, but it's not that small. I have good friends I don't see as often. And every time I'd see her I'd feel less and less comfortable. It was one thing to parade in front of her in my best party frock buffeted by cheap company champagne, and quite another to come up against the wife of the man I was sleeping with in a multi-storey car park as she piled her kids and her shopping into the family car.

Now here I was, trapped in a space so small I couldn't even stretch my legs to relieve the tremors in my body. There was absolutely no way I was going to face her. Because now she knew who I was.

So, I decided to make myself even more ridiculous by remaining in a department-store changing cubicle for as long as it took the two women to go away. Nothing that they or anybody else thought could be worse than dragging my clothes back on and walking out in front of her, party dresses in tow. So I waited. I heard them wonder to each other if there was anybody in there; I felt them tug at the flimsy curtain that divided me from them; I could smell her perfume as she leaned in to try to see what the hell was going on. Still I didn't move.

I was hoping they'd find the whole thing too weird and go away without alerting a sales assistant. For a moment I contemplated putting a scarf over my head and making a run for it, but I couldn't get my limbs to respond. So I continued to wait. I was aware of how utterly ridiculous the situation was but there was nothing I could do. I wasn't equal to a meeting with this woman.

Suddenly I felt the curtains being tugged a little more roughly and then the other woman spoke, in a voice quite unlike the one I had heard when she was worrying about her weight: 'Look,' she said, 'we don't know what you think you're playing at but we're about to call a manager and Security.'

I was petrified. I didn't even have the wit to pull on my clothes. Was I really about to be discovered in all my shame?

'Oh, leave it, Trish,' I heard Daniel's wife say. 'It's not worth it. I need to sit down anyway.'

'No way! We have a right to use this changing room. I'm not leaving here until she comes out.'

She kept tugging at the curtain; it was only now I realized my knuckles were white with the effort of clinging to it.

'Just leave it. Obviously something's not right.'

'I'm not leaving it!'

'Fine!' And that was when Daniel's wife shoved her bulk past her friend and forced her way in. I didn't even feel the curtain leave my hands. Suddenly she was towering over me, heavily pregnant with her husband's baby, her expression moving rapidly from surprise to recognition to disdain and, finally, to disgust.

'Come on, Trish, let's go,' she said, turning round. 'I told you something wasn't quite right. There's a foul stench in here.'

Then the friend was in the cubicle, looking down on me with a sneer that told me she, too, knew everything.

'Oh, my God,' she said. 'Is this . . . is this . . . *her*?'

'That's right. This is the little bitch who screwed my husband.'

I was still unable to speak. There was a tightness in my throat that felt like stones rubbing off each other and my mouth was so dry my cheeks seemed pasted together.

The lights seemed to be flickering, and even though I was practically undressed, I was about to pass out with the heat. A pain I had only just become aware of was shooting through my head and out between my eyes. If one of those women had taken a gun to me, it would have been a relief.

'Let's go,' she said. 'I don't need this. Scum like her shouldn't be allowed in here.'

And then she was gone. Mrs O'Hanlon walked off the fashion floor of Brown Thomas with her head held high; she had forgiven her husband and taken him back for the sake of their children. She had nothing to reproach herself for. As for me, I was everything she said I was.

I don't know how long it took me to gather my wits and pull on my clothes, but by the time I left the cubicle, the shop was nearly closing. As soon as I was out in the air again I rang Lucy.

'What's wrong?' she said immediately.

'Can I come over?'

'Of course. *What's wrong?*'

I couldn't say the words.

'What's wrong, Kate?' she said again. 'Has something happened?'

'I just met her,' I said. 'I just met his wife.'

'Where are you? I'm coming to get you.'

'I'm just outside BT's,' I wailed.

'Well, stay there. I'll be up to you in a minute.'

'I'll walk down towards you . . . Oh, Lucy, it was awful . . .'

'Don't worry, honey. I'll be with you in a minute.'

Lucy must have sprinted all the way because I had barely turned off O'Connell Street when she was beside me. She put her arms round me and even though I was in the middle of Limerick's central business district I blubbered uncontrollably into her shoulder.

'It's OK, sweetie,' she said. 'It's OK. Come on, we'll go home and have a big old drink and you'll be fine in no time.'

Lucy shared a flat with one of her old art-college friends down by the quays. They used to have a fabulous view of the river but then someone went and built a hotel in front of them. What can you do? I like their flat. It still has a partial view of the river (exactly how much river do you need when you have a life?) and everything about it suggests relaxation. It's always clean, but never too tidy. There's always wine in the fridge and something interesting to read on the floor. Their couch is very comfortable and doubles as a bed. And Lucy's always glad to see me. The minute we got in the door she went to the fridge and mixed me a long, cool gin and tonic with very little tonic.

'Oh, Lucy, the Bombay Sapphire – you're too good!'

'Oh, well, I save it for the very best occasions – and the worst. Now,' she said, sitting me down beside her on the couch, 'tell me exactly what happened.'

I told her, and the bizarre thing was that as I described my predicament that afternoon, the whole thing felt a bit ludicrous.

Of course Lucy's reaction helped: 'Don't mind what that cow says. She's the bitch, she's the one who's scum, talking to you like that. Her husband isn't her property and her husband did the dirty on you. All you did was love the gobshite!'

'But, Lucy, you should have seen the look on her face . . . and the friend! Oh, my God, there was poison in that look!'

'She has no right to make you feel that way. Sometimes people end up loving the wrong people. It can't be helped. It wasn't your fault.'

'Well, I suppose I did commit adultery . . .'

'No, you didn't, he did! And you're supposed to be the lawyer!'

We laughed.

'But really, Luce,' I said, feeling a bit better now, 'you don't have to excuse what I did entirely. I was in the wrong with Daniel.'

Suddenly Lucy got up and swung about the room. 'Relationships are complex,' she said, as if she was searching for the right words. 'It isn't always a simple case of not loving someone because they're married or because they're . . . Well, it's not simple anyway.'

'You do a pretty good job of keeping it simple,' I reminded her. 'You like a guy, you go out with him, you get tired of him, you dump him. I've never known you to have a relationship crisis.'

'Well . . . that's because . . .' She stalled mid-sentence. She was scratching her head and running her tongue repeatedly over her lips. 'That's because I . . . well, I . . .' She was swallowing hard.

I was afraid all this talk was beginning to grate on her. 'That's because you're so sweet,' I jumped in, 'and I'm a bitch, like Mrs O'Hanlon says, but you know what? I don't care any more. It happened, it's in the past, and right now I have an engagement party to go to, and I still don't have anything to wear.'

'You're right,' said Lucy, smiling broadly at me, 'and I have a wardrobe full of fabulous things for you to borrow.'

It didn't take us long to fashion an outfit that I would love, my mother would hate, and Keith wouldn't understand. We found an embroidered pair of jeans with strategic rips and put a wildly patterned silk wrap dress on top that would slyly reveal the killer bra I was going to wear underneath. At home I had boots that would set off the jeans and a necklace that would direct attention to the bra. Yet as I stood in front of Lucy's mirror, the jeans hanging off one arm, the top draped across my chest, I couldn't quite hide from the train wreck of the afternoon. I so badly wanted to forget about that whole time and wished it was as easy as putting on a new outfit.

That was one of the great things about being with Keith: he always made me feel good about myself. He was like a great big fur coat that insulated me from my own unpleasant thoughts. I texted him and told him I was looking forward to seeing him at the party. 'I love you . . .' I wrote, and clicked send. And then I clicked send again and then again and again until I must have sent the message twenty times.

He texted back 'ditto'.

5

By the time we reached the North Circular Road my mother was in a right state. Everything was done but she was still in a state. Why was I so late? Where had I been? Had I no regard for her feelings? Why wasn't Keith with me? I hadn't done anything stupid, had I? And what on earth was I wearing? I wasn't in the mood to take it so I breezed past her into the kitchen and poured Lucy and myself a glass of wine. Then we took up positions in the conservatory and let my mother rant on her own. My sisters were arriving, causing a bottleneck in the hall and a distraction for Mum.

We're always a noisy bunch whenever the gang of us gets together. There's Jean at the top, then comes Marion. There's me at the bottom, with Ruth just above me. That leaves Anna and Lucy in the middle. Anna is the only one not still in the environs of Limerick. She lives in New Zealand with her husband, Tommy, and their two kids. We hardly ever see each other; we don't talk much except for Christmas and birthdays. We get along just fine.

Even though Jean has never been my favourite sister, her wedding stands out – probably because it was the first and I was so young. She was twenty-one when she met Mike, and I was eleven. They got married three years later when I was fourteen, too old to be a flower-girl and too inconsequential to be a bridesmaid.

Their courtship alleviated some of the tedium of my childhood. At eleven I was already bored with school and most of my friends. Life for a child was different then. Now, the average four-year-old has more engagements in a week than both of its parents. No childhood is complete, it seems, without ballet and drama and chess and violin and harpsichord and God knows what else. When I was four I played with my dolls. I took their clothes off and put them on again and brought them for walks. Or I played with my friends. We played house, or hospital, or school, or Mass. We looked around us at the adults and thought, I can do that. It was all very low maintenance. We didn't have mobile phones or Gameboys. We had toy phones and boys who were sometimes game for a bit of girly fun. Television didn't open until five o'clock in the afternoon and then it was only for *Bosco* or *Wanderly Wagon*. I'm not saying it was any better and by the age of eleven I was well fed up with it. The only interesting thing on the horizon was secondary school, which of itself wasn't interesting but would involve crossing town every day, and who knew what exciting things might happen as I waited for my bus in the evenings? So when Mike came a-calling I was charmed by the diversion.

Jean was still living at home when she met him. She had come back to Limerick after trying and failing (rather spectacularly) at college in Galway and had started a secretarial course in Miss Mac's. It was always meant to be a stop-gap for her – Jean never saw herself as anybody's secretary. Yet when she got a job in a travel agent's and realized she could spend all her wages on herself, she talked less and less about 'reading' politics and modern history at Trinity.

She met Mike through a girl at work. He had just moved to Limerick and was sharing a flat with this girl's brother. They all met up one evening and that was the start of it. There had been other boys before him – a Paul, who took her out to dinner but never offered to pay; a Frank, who took her to a ball but went home with somebody else; a John, who thought she was easier than she actually was. Initially, nobody took any notice of Mike, we probably thought he'd go the way of the others, but after a while it was obvious that he was a keeper. My mother says he's the steadying influence Jean needs. I always wondered what she was that he needed. But, then, there's no fathoming other people's relationships. (Or even your own!)

What I remember is how nice he was to me. I was the awkward, annoying, totally pain-in-the-ass sister of his girlfriend, but he never forgot to talk to me or buy me Mars bars and bottles of Coke. And it wasn't even as if he was impressing Jean by doing this. In fact, it annoyed the hell out of her that he had so much time for me. And, naturally, I thought he was the greatest thing since – well, he was the greatest thing ever. A person, an actual man, who cared, or at least gave the impression of caring, about what I thought. We would have long silly conversations about the teachers at my school – he even knew one of them. He lent me his records – he said there was no decent music in our house. Of course, it was Jean he was lending them to but she had no interest in Blue Oyster Cult or Deep Purple or Led Zeppelin.

Sometimes, Mum would make Jean take me out with them on their dates. Something would have come up and she'd need someone to keep an eye on me. Or she fancied the house to herself for a while. So I would tag along to the cinema and they'd bring me to the pub afterwards, though I was always sworn to say we'd gone for coffee. During those illicit afternoons in Souths or Nancy Blakes, I used to imagine marrying Mike myself in about ten years' time, and as they sipped their beers I'd fill in the details of our life together. But after a while I'd be forced to admit that a lot might change in ten years and that, really, they did seem to like each other a lot. So, given that I probably had more exciting things coming, I surrendered him to my sister.

Lucy's my favourite. One of my aunts once said that Lucy was pretty on the outside and pretty on the inside. It's a daft thing to say, but I've always thought it was true. Lucy has the kind of features that make her seem ageless. She's thirty-four, though she could easily pass for mid-twenties. Tonight she was particularly lovely in cropped combats with a chiffon and sequin halter-neck top and cute little sequinned fake Birkenstocks. Her dark blonde hair had been cut to make an alluring sweep along her cheekbones, and she had dabbed just the right amount of a shimmery electric blue on her eyes and a light pink gloss on her lips.

Her attitude and outlook are very mid-twenties too. She's still somewhat directionless, even though she has a good job that she likes, as a graphic designer, and has been in it for several years with no sign of moving. But it's the way she treats each day that's characteristic of someone not quite settled. It always seems with Lucy that it's mere accident she ends up going to work every day and coming home to the same flat on Steamboat Quay every evening. She has never yet announced that she's off to South America, but you always feel she might. In a way it's more surprising that she's still here.

She never has a boyfriend for longer than a couple of months and she has certainly never let a man break her heart. All of the boyfriends are great, too – good-looking, intelligent, funny and absolutely crazy about her. But she has never fallen for any of them. She says she's yet to find something she hasn't already found somewhere else. Except for the part about broken hearts, I've always felt our attitudes to men are similar; she stays cool, while I rush in like a bad black-and-white heroine, but we end up not having found quite what we're looking for.

There was a man on the scene at the moment, an out-of-work sculptor called Luke, whom Lucy quite liked, but it was obviously going nowhere. He'd been hanging around her flat a lot lately, but I think that was mainly because he'd just been evicted from his own.

Ruth and I avoid each other as much as possible. I'm sure a psychoanalyst would say I'm jealous of her because she got all the attention when we were younger and she's still my mother's favourite. But I don't think that's it. I just don't like her. She's needy and small-minded. She has no vision beyond her own life and absolutely no interest in mine. She lives out of my mother's pocket. I don't think she's capable of making the smallest decision without consulting her. Of course, she doesn't think much of me, either. She says I'm a selfish know-it-all who never thinks of anybody but herself. She may be right. She's married to Phil, whom I have no real opinion on, but if he was the only person left in a room for me to talk to, I would leave the room.

If Lucy's my favourite sister, then Marion's my second favourite. She's not as soft as Lucy but I think it's her clear-headedness I admire. She calls a spade a spade, and sometimes no other name will do for a spade. She has always looked a little older than she is – or maybe 'settled' is the word, but now, in her late thirties, she has grown into herself and appears very youthful. Her skin has always been fabulous and she's taken very good care of it. Her strong features are arresting, whether she wears makeup or not. She has never obsessed about her appearance: she's either quietly confident about it, or she doesn't give a damn. She's not an effusive person but in her quiet way she's happy, and it's always nice to be around happy people.

It was Jean who was arriving now, thankfully diverting Mum. Mike had brought some fancy wine he'd got over the Internet so there was a huge commotion while Dad hauled out his books and established its pedigree. Mum thought it was so thoughtful. Mike is the favourite son-in-law.

Further commotion – Ruth playing the martyr with some drama about how she'd tried every single shop in town for the low-salt crackers Mum claims to like but couldn't find them so she'd brought three alternatives instead – allowed Mike to drift away from Party Central and into the conservatory to find Lucy and me pouring a glass of Pouilly Fumé for him.

'C'mere, Mike,' hollered Lucy. 'It's safe! There's only ourselves and a very nice bottle of wine.'

'Hey,' he said, pulling up a chair beside us but remaining standing behind it, 'congratulations. Congratulations, Kate! This is great news!'

He stood for a moment longer behind the chair, then walked rather clumsily round it to plant a kiss on my cheek.

'Thanks!' I said, pleased to have his approval. I felt he had witnessed every fiasco of my life and I wanted him to see I could get it right for once. 'I know it's a bit quick, but what the hell, I'm not getting any younger. And I want to have a great big wedding while Mum and Dad can still afford it.'

'Oh, it's all on the parents, is it? I thought modern couples paid for their own.'

'God, no! Why should ye ould ones have had it easy and we young things have to suffer because times have changed a bit? Daddy always said he'd pay for our weddings, isn't that right, Luce?'

'Listen, leave me out of this. If I ever do get married, I certainly won't be having a wedding.'

'Oh, come on, a wedding is great gas. You'll never have a better party.'

'I'm out of here,' said Lucy, unfurling herself from the chair. 'Nice seeing you, Mike. And don't listen to any more garbage from her. The wine's already gone to her head.'

'So,' I said to him, motioning for him to take Lucy's seat beside me, 'what do you think? I'm getting married! Did you ever think you'd see the day?'

'Ahm, it's great.'

'You know,' I said, refilling my glass – he hadn't touched his, 'there was a time when I'd convinced myself I was going to marry you.'

'Oh?'

'Yeah.' I giggled. 'I did. When you were going out with Jean and Mum used to make ye take me on your dates when she'd nowhere else to offload me. Do you remember?'

'I do.'

'And I wasn't even that young, but I do remember thinking that when I got older I'd just marry you. It seemed the sensible thing to do.'

'And . . . what were you going to do about Jean?'

'Oh, I didn't think that far ahead. I probably presumed you'd have got tired of her by then.'

'Really?'

'Oh, don't look so serious, Mike. I got over you when I fell in love with George Michael. Though it didn't work out with him either . . .'

Mike didn't seem to find my joke as funny as I did. 'So where's Keith? It's usual to invite the fiancé to the engagement party.'

'Oh, he'll be along in a while. I told him things would be starting a little later than originally planned. I'm only thinking of his heart – he has no idea how much stress my mother can generate at one of these things.'

'Anyway, Kate,' he said edging a little closer, 'I really hope you'll be very happy. You deserve it.'

'Thanks, Mike, I really appreciate that.'

It was odd, but as he took my hand and gave it a squeeze, I did wonder that he wasn't a little happier.

Just then, as if on cue, Keith materialized in front of us. He just stood there for a second as if he didn't quite know what to do. Mike got up immediately, pushing his chair back with undue force, and put out his hand. 'Congratulations, Keith,' he said quickly, almost automatically. 'Well done. I hope ye'll be very happy.'

'Thanks, Mike,' he said giving Mike's hand a perfunctory shake. 'I'm sure we will be.'

Suddenly Jean crashed through the door with a tray of canapés, howling about how I never lost it and it was so typical of me to be sitting on my ass while everybody else did the work. Didn't I know that everybody was in the sitting room waiting for us? Didn't I realize this party was for me? To shut her up I grabbed Keith and descended upon the crowd waiting anxiously in the sitting room where there followed an obscene amount of hugging and kissing and wailing, all of it conducted about two octaves above what was healthy for the human ear to deal with.

Keith rose manfully to the occasion, saying the right things, hugging heartily, kissing tenderly, even blushing slightly. I got dragged into the centre of it while everybody admired the fabulous vintage ring and congratulated Keith on his great taste in jewellery as well as women, and for a moment I revelled in the attention, even though I was still unsettled by the events of the afternoon. Thankfully, my father interrupted the orgy of well-wishing – he had urgent need of Keith in the cellar – so I went off to find Lucy again.

However, it wasn't long before every room in the house had filled with my extended family, and Lucy and I had no option but to join the throng. Lucy was accosted by some long-lost neighbour in the hallway and I situated myself centre stage in the sitting room. It was packed with people I didn't care about, but that couldn't take from the feeling of warmth I always get in that room. It hasn't changed much since we were kids, but unlike most seventies living rooms it was never done out in shades of orange and brown polyester. My mother's taste in clothes translates well to a high-ceilinged turn-of-the-century drawing room. The walls are white where they aren't bearing some interesting, if largely unnoteworthy, artwork. These pieces are Dad's choice. The furniture is a mixture of mahogany, maple and oak, all of it antique. The periods are mixed but the theme is not: each piece – the sofa, the leather armchairs, the *chaise longue*, the maple sideboard, the bookcase, the end tables – is functional and beautiful.

I spied one of my aunts sitting gingerly on the edge of Dad's favourite chair and was turning away when she caught my eye. 'Kate, petal, sweetheart, congratulations! We've been dying to see you. Your father's run away with your lovely man. We hardly got a chance to say hello but he looked very nice, very handsome. Are you delighted, my dear?'

This was Mary, the aunt who apparently hadn't believed in Keith's existence. It would have been too wonderful if I could have kept her away from Keith all night.

'Hello, Auntie, yes, we're delighted.'

'And your mother tells me there's no date set and nothing booked. You can't hang around, these days – everything's booked years in advance. I was only telling your mother how your cousin Gina couldn't get a Saturday in the Castletory

Park for three years! Of course, the Castletory Park is a premier hotel – you might get something if you went further afield. So, when are ye thinking of?'

'We don't really know, to be honest. There's been so much going on we haven't had time to think about it. Sure you know yourself.'

'Absolutely!'

Then it was the turn of another aunt to swing round and berate me for being so sly and keeping everything so tight. But at least Auntie Brenda was making herself useful by carrying round a tray of drinks, so I helped myself and wandered into the dining room. There were as many people there, but it didn't seem as crowded as everybody was forced to give way to the large mahogany table in the centre of the room. It radiated a profound sense of calm. Jean was sitting by herself at one of the large sash windows.

'Hi, Jeanie! You enjoying yourself?'

'Oh, hi, hon! Listen, sorry for screaming at you earlier. I really am delighted for you, if a little surprised. It's a bit rushed, isn't it?' Jean knew who my last boyfriend had been.

'Oh, not really. It just seemed right, you know? I suppose it is a bit rushed but we're not getting any younger here.'

Jean smiled and gave me a squeeze. She's not a bad old sort sometimes.

'And how are you?'

'Oh, fine. Busy. Nothing new.'

She paused and seemed to be about to say something else, but changed her mind. She looked quite pretty tonight. She had allowed her hair to grow longer, which suited her. Also, she had stopped dyeing it herself and invested in a good colourist. She was even wearing makeup, which she seldom did. I decided to tell her. 'You look really nice tonight.'

'Hey, thank you. I *did* make a bit of an effort, given the occasion.' She smiled again, reminding me of a photo Mum has in the sitting room. She had just made her confirmation and believed herself to be filled with the Holy Spirit.

We were interrupted by yet another aunt; this time it was Auntie Joan, trying to get the five sisters out in the hall for a photograph. 'Come on, come on,' she was going on, 'we're nearly there now. It's all down to you, Lucy.' I tried telling her that we were missing Anna and suggesting that we'd better wait until all six of us were together, but nothing would put her off. She already had Ruth posing at the foot of the stairs; Marion was leaning against the jamb of the sitting-room door, refusing to move; Jean and I remained highly sceptical behind Auntie Joan, and Lucy was nowhere to be found. My mother was flapping around, not sure whether she objected more to the fact that her sister was taking over or to the fact that nobody would co-operate with her. I suggested going off to find Lucy but Auntie Joan was letting nobody go. 'She'll make her way back to the drinks soon enough,' somebody said.

Meanwhile Dad returned with a camcorder. He'd borrowed it from one of the neighbours and thought it would solve the problem of elusive and uncooperative daughters. We posed reluctantly and he captured us all, then handed the camera to Auntie Joan and told her to go and find Lucy. He said he had an idea she was out in the back garden somewhere. 'Your mother would love a little word,' he said to me.

'What?'

'About the party and how well it's going. How much you appreciate her and all that.'

'Oh, yes, Dad, sorry.'

'She's talking to your auntie Margaret in the dining room.'

I eventually found my mother sitting alone at the kitchen table, sipping a glass of Harvey's Bristol Cream.

'Hello, love,' she said. 'Don't tell your father I'm drinking this. He thinks it's awful rubbish.'

I knew it was her favourite. Her parents used to drink it by the bucketful when they could afford it.

'Of course I won't. You OK, Mum?'

'Oh, I'm a little tired. It's a lot of work, after all.'

'I know, and I really appreciate it. It's been a great party. Everybody's having a brilliant time.'

'They are, aren't they?'

'All your sisters are very impressed. And the house looks great.'

'Yes, we were right not to go meddling with the sitting room. It's perfect the way it is.'

'Why don't we join them there now? Everyone's looking for you, and Daddy's about to cut the cake.'

'All right, dear. You know, that dress or blouse or whatever it is you've on you is really quite nice.'

'Thanks, Mum. It's Lucy's.'

I don't think we've been that close in years.

After the cake-cutting, the speech-making (Keith acquitted himself very well) and the photograph Auntie Joan insisted on, everybody disappeared again. Even Keith. I had just located Mike sitting on his own by the window in the dining room and was making my way through the crowd to join him, when I heard Lucy's laughter coming from the study.

'Here you all are!' I said, almost accusingly, on finding Jean, Marion and Lucy in a huddle on the floor round a bottle of champagne. 'It's my party, you know.'

'That's why we didn't want to be stealing your thunder,'

said Lucy. 'Oh, come on so,' she added, 'I'll pour you a glass. Where's Keith?'

'I don't know. Everybody's acting weird tonight.'

'No, honey,' said Marion. 'It's just you.'

'We were saying,' said Jean, 'that this is quite a good party. You have to hand it to Mum. She knows how to put on a spread.'

'Yeah,' added Marion, 'but do you remember how she used to be, when we were kids, before the cookery classes? A dinner for every day?'

'Oh, God, yes!' shrieked Jean. 'A dinner for every day! Let me get this right now. Monday was bacon and cabbage, because it could be bought the week before and wouldn't go off.'

'Yes,' said Marion, 'and even though she hated it and never ate any of it, she cooked it every week because Dad loved it.'

'I remember,' said Lucy. 'She thought it was common and only for poor country people. It killed her to have to cook it. The smell of it stayed in the kitchen for ages. That's why she cooked it on Monday – to get it out of the way for the week.'

'It killed her more that Dad liked it so much,' continued Marion. 'He didn't insist on much, but bacon and cabbage was sacred with him.'

'Do they have it any more?' I asked, not remembering the days of the set menu.

'Sometimes,' answered Marion, 'I can still smell it there the odd time, but Dad's watching his cholesterol now and he's less insistent than he used to be. To be honest, I think Mum's grown to like it and cooks it for herself.'

'So,' went on Lucy, 'what was Tuesday?'

'Right,' said Jean, getting back into her stride. 'Tuesday was steak, to make up for the poverty of the day before.'

'Yes,' said Marion, 'and she always went to town on a Tuesday.'

'Always, and stocked up at the butcher. But she wouldn't buy meat for too many days for fear of it going off.'

'Oh, yes! People were always getting food poisoning in those days. And Mum didn't believe in freezing meat. She said it ruined the texture.'

'Now, Wednesday was always chicken, roast or fried, and Thursday was lamb-chop night.'

'I remember the lamb chops,' said Lucy. 'They were lovely if she baked them but horrible if she grilled them. I don't know why she ever grilled them.'

'She grilled them,' said Marion, 'when she didn't have time to bake them. She was often out and about on a Thursday afternoon, visiting her friends or one of her sisters. Remember? She often got Doreen O'Doherty in from next door to mind us.'

'Ah, I remember – Dopey Doreen.'

'She wasn't Dopey,' said Marion, mock-crossly. 'She was just a little too innocent for this world.'

'Whatever you say. I remember that she used to get really upset at *Wanderly Wagon*. I don't know if it was the lost princess or Sneaky Snake, but something about *Wanderly Wagon* had her in tears every evening.'

'Poor Mrs O'Doherty,' said Jean, then fell over herself laughing.

'Wait now,' Lucy broke in, between the tears of laughter, 'you haven't finished the week.'

Jean was trying desperately to pull herself together. I felt the tiniest bit peeved that I didn't remember the good old days according to bad housekeeping. By the time I was on solids three times a day, Mum was producing things like quiche and spaghetti Bolognese and *coq au vin*. She was a regular Delia Smith.

'Oh, let me think,' Jean continued, 'that leaves Friday – fish, of course, whatever was freshest in Saddlier's, but usually whiting. And never chips. We didn't know what a chip was. We thought chips were some delicacy you could only get once a year in Kilkee.'

'I'd forgotten about the chip embargo. Another nasty, fat-ridden item that only poor people ate.'

'That leaves Saturday, which was either a mixed grill or shepherd's pie, depending on her mood, I think, and then on Sunday – what we'd been waiting for the whole week – the big, leathery, indigestible Sunday roast.'

'Oh, God, no,' burst in Marion. 'That was in the days when lamb was something you only got in spring, and the rest of the year you had mutton. Mutton! You couldn't chew it and it tasted of sheep – literally!'

'Oh, yes, the overcooked meat – because rare meat was something else Mum didn't believe in at the time – piled up on your plate so you had no hope of finishing it. Oh, wow, happy times.'

The three girls were exhausted and delighted with their reminiscing. While Lucy and I share a lot of memories, I sometimes wish I remembered things the others share. Ruth and I were around at the same time, experiencing the same things, but I spent a lot of my time avoiding her, pretending she didn't exist. I remember I had a friend in primary school who was an only child and I thought it must be the most glorious thing in the world. Whenever Ruth and I do reminisce we end up contradicting each other. It's like we grew up in different houses.

'So, were Mum and Dad really that different when ye

were young?' I asked, curious for more tales of these people I didn't fully recognize.

'Well,' answered Marion, 'Mum was definitely a little more strung out then. I don't think the whole business of house-keeping and bringing up children came naturally to her. She'd probably have been better off working, but that wasn't an option. It wouldn't have occurred to her to get a job. And she would have been brilliant at so many things. It's a pity, in a way, she didn't work for Dad. She would have loved it and it would have made a big difference to him. One of his biggest worries, always, was getting people he could trust.'

'Really? I thought she liked swanning around in her expensive outfits, visiting her friends and organizing the school garden fête.'

'And what a fête it was! Its success was largely down to Mum, you know. When she finally retired from the parents' association they stopped running it.'

'Would Dad really have wanted her working with him?' asked Jean, dubious of Marion's take on things.

'I think so. He has huge respect for her, even though he doesn't always give that impression.'

'Do you remember their rows?' asked Lucy, full of interest again.

'Oh, you could hardly call them rows. They consisted of Mum banging round the house, huffing and puffing about not being appreciated and Dad just holing himself up in the study, refusing to talk.'

'Oh, yes! Then he'd go out for a walk or something and come back with flowers.'

'And she'd bang about for another while until Dad told her about the dinner reservations he'd made for that evening.'

'Then she'd huff and puff some more about her hair being in a state until he told her to go off and get it done.'

'And they'd go out that evening and everything would be hunky-dory again until the next big coolness.'

'I don't think they ever talked about whatever had caused the problem. It was just understood between them that it was Dad's fault and he'd eventually apologize.'

'You know, they could do with a holiday, the pair of them,' Marion said, her tone suddenly quite serious. 'They haven't been away properly in ages.'

'Yeah,' said Jean. 'That trip to Donegal was the last, and it was only for four days. What's stopping them? Sure Dad's practically retired now.'

'I don't know,' Marion went on. 'I think that might be part of the problem. 1 don't think he wants to retire and lose control.'

'It's a pity none of us wants to take over.'

'But is that the case?' Marion asked. 'He never encouraged any of us, did he?'

'Well, no, but nobody showed any interest either,' said Jean. 'I mean, you work in the company and you're not that bothered.'

'Well . . . no . . . but . . .'

'Why? Would you be interested?'

'I don't know.'

'No – really? Is it something you might like? If it is, you should tell Dad. Maybe that's what he's waiting for.'

'Maybe . . . I don't know . . . Anyway . . .'

Just then Keith appeared at the door, looking very dejected.

'Oh, hiya, love, I was looking for you everywhere.'

'We're just reliving old times here,' said Lucy. 'Come and join us.'

'Well, I was kinda hoping that –'

'It's OK, Keith,' I said, getting up from the huddle on the floor. 'I've had enough of this anyway. Let's find a nice quiet corner and snog.'

I led him away from my sisters' laughter, and while no one was looking, we ducked upstairs.

'We really shouldn't do this, you know,' he said, as I guided him into my old room. 'Everybody's downstairs . . . your mother . . .'

'Oh, they won't mind. They have their own rooms.'

'No, seriously, Kate . . . I want to talk to you.'

I climbed on to the bed and eyed him seductively. 'Are you quite sure you don't want to take me here, on this former virgin's bed?' I teased.

'Mmm,' he said, 'maybe not *quite* sure. But I want to talk to you first.' He squashed in on the bed beside me. 'I don't know about you,' he continued, 'but I feel sometimes that this whole engagement thing is getting away on us. It's like it's everybody else's business but ours. You know what I mean?'

'Yes. Yes. Yes, I do.' In fact I had been contributing to that feeling.

'Well, I feel we need to take control ourselves – take charge, you know.'

I sat up. Was he about to announce that we were eloping? Were we about to tie the sheets together and make our escape through my bedroom window? Were those airline tickets sticking out of his shirt pocket? (Wait a minute, there was nothing sticking out of his shirt pocket. Was I seeing things?)

'. . . so, do you think it's a good idea?'

'Sorry, what did you say?'

'A holiday. Just get away on our own and not have families

or anybody asking questions or organizing parties. Just the two of us. What do you think?'

'Keith, it's a brilliant idea. A holiday's just what I need. What we need. That's brilliant. When are we going? And where? Maybe we should never come back.'

'Hold on there – we'll have to sort out work. I've nothing booked yet, just made enquiries. But you do think it's a good idea? Nothing too extravagant, given all the expenses we'll have soon.'

I was about to ask what expenses, but then I realized. 'No, Keith. This is your most perfect idea yet.' And then I persuaded him into something that that little bed had been looking forward to all of its life.

6

A holiday was just the ticket. I'm no sun-worshipper and neither is Keith, but when some crowd on the Internet can fly you to a sun-drenched village on the Spanish coast for the price of your car insurance, you'd be a fool not to whip out your bikini and factor forty-seven. And when your boyfriend insists on paying for the whole thing (well, as he said himself, he didn't have to fork out for the ring) you're already at the beautician's being sprayed from head to toe the sun-kissed bronze you'd never have the courage to allow the sun to kiss you.

We had an early start on the Saturday morning but everything, including the flight, was on schedule. Keith had supervised my packing the previous evening because he didn't trust me to be ready on time. His own bag, a medium-sized case he had borrowed from his mother, was already in the boot of the car, complete with combination lock and multiple labels. Before we left the flat he laid all our essential documents on the table: two passports, flight confirmation and hotel details, credit cards, euros (which he secreted in five different places about our persons), important phone numbers and his mobile phone, which now had 'roaming'. My own passport had taken some time to find, but I eventually located it in a drawer behind last year's Christmas cards.

Keith was the master of order and calm. On the way out to the airport he made lists of the things we could do when we got there. He had done a bit of research on the resort and apparently there was no end to the activities we could get involved in. I kind of switched off as he went on; all I wanted was a week of sun and nothingness. In the end it hadn't been difficult getting the time off: my boss simply reminded me that I had already used up a considerable portion of my annual leave, and were I to need any more extensive periods of time off this year, it might prove difficult. He was skirting round the issue of the wedding, of course, but I had never said it was going to be this year. Nobody had set a date. Keith, on the other hand (who is really good at his job and whose boss hates to let him go), had had to practically beg for the time. (I think he had to leave one of his kidneys in storage.) But he was determined. He was in need of this holiday even more than I was. His love affair with my family had plateaued and he was in need of time away to refresh. It was just as well – I was a little tired of him never seeing things as they really were.

When we pulled into the long-term car park we were well ahead of Keith's schedule. He had worked out that by arriving an hour before our check-in time we would avoid the queues and have plenty of time for a leisurely breakfast and shopping in Duty Free. Even though the value isn't as good as it used to be I can't help picking up a few essentials from Dior and Chanel, so I was happy to go along with it. But as we were placing our luggage on a trolley, Keith began to hurry me along insisting that queues were forming even though he couldn't possibly see through the brown glass. As we approached the entrance he was banging his coat pockets to check he still had our essential documents.

'You have them,' I insisted. 'You've already checked twice.'

But he kept stopping to pull them out and go through

them one by one. I was getting a little impatient, but he was fine again once we were in the (four-deep) queue at the check-in desk.

Our breakfast wasn't as leisurely as I had anticipated. We had been looking forward to a full Irish but as soon as we sat down to eat, Keith lost his appetite. Then he was hopping up and down to the toilets. At this rate I'd never get any shopping done. The third time he got up to go, I actually shouted at him: 'Oh, for God's sake,' I snapped, 'what is the matter with you?'

I don't think I had ever spoken a cross word to him before.

'Nothing! Nothing's wrong,' he said, and ran.

When he came back I told him I was going on into Duty Free and he could follow me when he was done going to the toilet. And that was when he broke down. 'Oh, God, no, no! Don't leave me here!' he whimpered. 'I'll never make it if you leave me.'

'What?' I said, aghast.

'Oh, Kate,' he said, sitting back down at the table (he seemed to need the support), 'I never told you ... Well, I was hoping I wouldn't have to ...'

'Never told me what?' I asked, unable to keep the note of impatience out of my voice.

'Well,' he said, covering his face with his hands, 'ahm ... I, ah ... I don't fly very well ...'

'Oh!'

The idea of someone not flying well had never occurred to me. From a very early age I had been on and off planes regularly. Flying didn't cost me a thought. Of course I had *heard* of people being afraid of flying, but I had always assumed them to be slightly hysterical women looking for attention. It had never crossed my mind that a man, a steady, sensible, grounded man like Keith, might have a problem becoming airborne.

I sat down beside him and emitted a large, unhelpful sigh. 'How bad is it?' I asked, wondering if we were going to get away at all.

'Well, I don't know,' he said. 'It's been ages since I flew.'

'And what happened then?'

'I can't remember.'

'Come on,' I said, bundling him up, 'let's go to the bar and have a drink.'

'It's a quarter past eleven,' he protested feebly.

'Well, it's drinking time somewhere,' I said (I didn't have any other ideas). 'Anyway, we're on holiday. People do daft things when they're on holiday. A drink will do us both good. You should have said something – Ruth always has a stash of Valium for emergencies . . . or I might have been able to scare up a joint.'

The bar was surprisingly busy for a quarter past eleven on a Saturday morning, and the clientele weren't all foreigners either. I ordered us two vodkas and orange, and made his a double. He drank his quicker than I'd ever seen him down a drink, so I ordered another. He was smiling feebly at me, begging me to forgive him.

'It's OK,' I reassured him. 'You'll be fine in a minute.'

'But I'm ruining your holiday . . .'

'No, you're not. It's our holiday and nothing's ruined.'

Of course, all I could think about was missing my run round Duty Free, at best, or never getting off the ground, at worst. Poor Keith had probably worked himself up into an awful frenzy about this holiday. Part of the reason he was so keen to get away was that he thought he'd have a better chance of pinning me down to talk dates and times and which side of the city we wanted to live on: he'd been trying to broach these subjects for weeks and I kept evading or jokingly dismissing him. On holiday, with little to do all day except lie about and pick a restaurant for the evening, he must have thought he'd have a better chance of getting me to agree to something.

It had been more difficult lately: there's only so long you can dance round a topic that needs an airing. Even more than setting a date, Keith was anxious about a house. I tried reminding him that we both had houses and suggested we couldn't possibly want the hassle of buying another. But he saw this conjugal buying of the family home as an important symbolic move. He was more than ready to sell his own house in Clareview, bought purely because it was a sensible thing to do with his money and on the right side of town for work. He saw my flat as a good investment and a steady source of extra income if we decided to let it. He also saw it (though he would never admit it) as a steady source of income to replace mine when, inevitably, I gave up work to start a family. It wasn't that I objected utterly to his unconscious forward planning or that one small part of me wouldn't go along with it all (who was I kidding, anyway, that I had a career?), but that the whole thing was far too real, far too practical to consider when I was only barely used to the idea, to the theory, of marrying him.

He had been coming home every day recently with brochures from estate agents, many of them big glossy portfolios detailing the forty-five fabulous bedrooms you could have for barely half a million if only you were willing to move out to the sticks. Which I wasn't. Even Keith had to admit, since he'd been practically living in my flat, that being in the middle of everything had its advantages, but he had in his head something he must have seen in a picture book as a child. He wanted it all – big rooms, lush garden, wooden shed, privet hedges, picket fences, the lot. I thought men weren't supposed to care about things like that.

His moving in had taken place accidentally. Neither of us suggested it; he didn't want to be presumptuous and I know how he likes an ordered living environment so I thought he'd probably prefer to live at his own place. Yet, gradually, after a couple of late weekend nights, he hadn't gone home. And when he did go home he came back with clean clothes, toiletries, some books and CDs. I thought at first I'd find the place claustrophobic with him around all the time but he was very quiet and, apart from the way he kept tidying up after me and the way he kept cooking really nice meals, I hardly knew he was there. And in bed he was so warm and reassuring. In a way it was as if we were already married, had been for years. He was still passionate, and very easily aroused, but mostly he was like that comfort bear you had as a child. The one you didn't pay a lot of attention to during the day, because he was old and sad-looking, but wouldn't go to bed without. Maybe the reason I was so reluctant to talk houses with Keith was that I was happy with our present living arrangements. Or maybe I enjoyed teasing him.

After his second double vodka and orange Keith seemed a little better. 'I'm really sorry, you know. I thought I had this fear-of-flying thing licked. I thought that if I was just organized enough I could force myself into it. I guess I was wrong.'

'It's OK,' I said softly. 'It doesn't matter. You can't control the things you're afraid of. It doesn't matter if we don't go to Spain. We could drive up to Galway and spend the week there. I've already got a tan.'

'Oh, but that's just it. With you I'm not afraid of anything. I feel like I can conquer the world. That's why I'm disappointed that I'm having trouble conquering Duty Free.'

We both laughed, and for the first time I really didn't care if we ended up in Los Almiras or Oranmore.

'Do you want to give it a try? We can take it one step at a time and we can turn back if you don't want to go any further.'

'Oh, Kate, you are wonderful. What on earth are you doing with me?'

'Well, I love you, you eejit.' I said the words without thinking, and as soon as they were out of my mouth I realized they might be true.

So I took his hand and we glided past Security, right through the waiting area (bypassing all the potions and perfumes) and on to our gate. By this time the plane was nearly boarded so we walked straight on. All the time Keith kept a tight grip on my hand, and when we finally sat into our seats, he took that hand and kissed it. 'I love you,' he said.

'I love you too.'

It was strange to think that Keith might occasionally need something from me, and rather than it being a total pain in the ass, it was actually rather endearing. He fell asleep before we took off and when he woke up, somewhere over northern Spain, he was surprisingly like his old self.

Our first day in Los Almiras was heavenly. When we'd arrived at the resort the previous evening (after a, thankfully, uneventful flight) we had barely enough energy to unpack a toothbrush before falling into bed. We slept surprisingly well, given the hectic day, and when we woke it was like we had entered a parallel universe or something. I had the notion, even though I knew how ridiculous it was, that we were on our honeymoon. I looked across at Keith and thought, Yeah, I could do this for a while. Then we rolled together, had the best sex since either of us could remember and fell into a deep post-coital sleep that washed away any lingering fatigue from the journey. I think Keith was anxious to recover a sense of manliness, because he was particularly dominant that morning. Usually, sex with Keith was very safe – satisfying, predictable and low maintenance while still hugely enjoyable, but that morning he was flipping me about, throwing my legs over his shoulders, even engaging in a little dirty talk. I was enjoying the diversion: it made me feel like I was doing something naughty, and with Keith, that was some achievement.

When we climbed out of bed and into the shower it was nearly one o'clock, and by the time I'd decided what to wear and Keith had worked out that we had no English-speaking TV channels it was a quarter past two. Clearly siesta time. We decided to take it in the shaded bar area at the far side of the pool. From there we could sip our watery cocktails and view, at a safe distance, the swimming masses. I love to swim but only when I have the pool virtually to myself.

As it was still only May, the weather was pleasant but not so hot we couldn't take a walk round the village without feeling too sweaty and simply not up for it. That's the great problem with sun holidays: the sun, and the attendant heat. It's great to fantasize in the middle of an Irish winter about clear blue skies and the hot sun on your back as you prepare to dive into an azure sea but I've never found the reality lives up to my fantasies. There are always too many people, too many of them non-exotics who probably live round the corner from you at home; the blues are never quite as intense and the heat is always so intense you wish there was a knob somewhere so you could turn it down. The lack of control is part of the problem – in winter, if you're cold you put on more clothes and turn the heat up. But in summer, once you've taken off everything common decency allows, there's nothing more you can do. You either sit in the shade or go indoors but that defeats the purpose of being in the sun. As I said, I'm not a sun person.

We returned to the bar and had several more cocktails, each one a little more watery than the last. We toasted each other on how clever we were to get away and what a fabulous place we had chosen. I knew Keith had the same ridiculous notion in his head that this might be our honeymoon but to say it out loud would have burst our bubble. We were served odd-looking canapés that were deep-fried and tasted fishy but had the desired effect of making us think about dinner. During our stroll round the resort we had come across several bistros that looked like they could be the setting for romantic dining but we decided to stay in our hotel for this first night. The restaurant was on a balcony on the first floor and looked out over the bay, which at this time was emptying of bathers and sun-worshippers and taking on the aspect of a tropical-island hideaway. We got a table where the view was at its finest and settled into a meal of grilled fish (caught locally that day), a salad tossed lightly in a piquant dressing and a wine so white and cold and sharp it might have been pure mountain spring water (with a delightful kick, of course).

All through the meal Keith was gazing at me as if I might actually be the woman of his dreams, and it was so intoxicating I began to indulge the notion that he was right. We talked only about each other, as if the world was spinning on an axis entirely of our making. I thought how even one day of sun had given his skin a radiance it didn't usually have, how even the contours of his face seemed more sharply defined. I wondered if I was actually falling in love with him, really in love, in love beyond all reasonable control.

Perhaps the way I felt and the things I'd said in the airport hadn't been brought on by early-morning drinking on an empty stomach. And if I'd never been in love before I'm sure I would have believed this to be the real thing. What more could a girl want? If this wasn't love what on earth could love be? But I had been here before. And even though none of it might have been as real as it was in my head at the time, the feelings I'd had for that man were beyond anything I had believed possible for one person to feel about another. It might all have gone horribly wrong but when it was right it was the best bloody thing in the universe.

We finished our meal with a good espresso, and as we were about to leave the terrace we discovered a set of stone steps leading down to the beach.

'Come on,' he said, delight in his eyes. 'Let's go down to the beach for a walk.'

I looked ahead to the perfect moonlit sand and the perfect shore and I knew it was the perfect setting for a romantic stroll for the perfect couple. This was the stuff movie moments were made of, but suddenly I didn't want to be in anyone's movie, not even one that was entirely made up. 'I'm not so sure, Keith, I feel a bit sleepy after that meal.'

'Oh, come on – I'm not asking you to go jogging, just a short walk.'

'Honestly, I'm still a bit tired after the flight and every-thing. Maybe tomorrow.'

But he knew as well as I did that tomorrow the moment would have passed. Indeed, if he had to try so hard to get me to do something that seemed so natural to him, it was already past.

'All right, then, whatever,' he said, letting go of my hand. 'It's no big deal.'

'The beach will still be there tomorrow.'

'It's fine. It's not a problem.'

Without saying any more we headed back to our room where I undressed and climbed under the crisp white sheets. Keith took up the remote control and was still flicking between one incomprehensible station and another when I drifted off to sleep.

Somehow we never did get round to that moonlit stroll.

Daniel and I had spent a short holiday in Paris. That was also in May. He had a meeting in London and arranged to join me in Paris the following day. He figured he could safely get two more nights away. So I flew out from Shannon on my own, got a train from Charles de Gaulle to the city and a taxi from there to a little three-star hotel in Pigalle. Daniel knew the area. It was close to everything, he said, including the red-light district but, typical of Paris, even the red-light district is less seedy and more socio-historical. I arrived there early on a Friday evening, knowing I had at least two more hours to wait before Daniel might arrive. He had phoned earlier that day before I left Limerick to say he was thinking about us every moment and couldn't wait to leave London and everything else to be with me. I couldn't believe we were finally going to spend the night together. Two whole nights together. He had been feeling guilty recently, knowing he was spending a lot of time away from his family. Late nights with me meant he didn't see his kids before they went to bed. His wife understood that he often needed to work late, she was used to it, but not seeing his kids was different. So, we had slowed things down, only meeting at lunchtimes or briefly before he went home in the evenings. And that had become unsatisfactory very quickly so he promised he'd work something so we could get away together. And he had.

I would have been happy to meet him in London but he said he had always imagined bringing me to Paris. I didn't argue. I might not have thought it then but I'm sure part of the reason he didn't want to meet in London was that it was still too close to home. He has many connections there and knows the streets almost as well as he knows Limerick's. Even though London's big you never know who you might bump into. (The irony was that, despite all Daniel's precautions, his wife was going to find out anyway, thanks to some helpful office gossip.) But at the time none of that occurred to me.

I checked into the room using my own name. It was booked in Daniel's and as I signed I couldn't help smiling at what I was doing. If this had been a movie made in the fifties I would have pretended to be his wife. I would even have had to wear a wedding ring. But it wasn't a movie, it wasn't even Ireland: it was twenty-first-century Paris and the times had moved on. Still, something about that deserted foyer and the blank stare of the concierge made me wish for something other than a covert liaison with my married lover. But for now it was all I had.

By the time Daniel arrived (he was more than an hour later than the latest he'd said he could be), I was sleepy and a little drunk, having helped myself to the contents of the mini-bar. I would have gone downstairs in the hope of some company but apparently three stars in Paris doesn't buy you a bar. So Daniel arrived weary from his day to find me weepy and petulant. That was the start of it.

He stood in the doorway, bags in hand, squinting, trying to adjust to the dim light in the room. I don't think he was quite sure for a moment that I was there. For a moment I wasn't sure that I recognized him. He seemed older that his forty-two years — even in the light of the one lamp in the room I could detect lines in his face I hadn't noticed before. His body, usually so virile, seemed thinner and somewhat shrunken. Yet even as I was mentally taking note of this, part of me was sure I was imagining it. Here was my dashing man, come to soothe my ache for him and assure me that all was right with the world. But as soon as he spoke there was a weariness in his voice I didn't recognize. Was it the room? Or was it us?

'You're here. I've been waiting for ever.'

'I know. I'm sorry. I had to get a later flight. The meeting ran late. The traffic was unbelievable. I'm sorry.'

'You look tired.'

'I am.'

'I love you.'

Then he walked across to where I was lying on the bed. He bent low and kissed me. 'I love you too.'

I wanted to climb inside that kiss and hide away for ever. 'What will we do? Will we go out and get dinner? I saw a gorgeous place on the corner.'

'Oh, Kate, I'm exhausted, absolutely wrecked. All I'm fit for is sleep. We'll do Paris tomorrow. We'll see everything. I promise you.'

'Oh. OK.'

If there was complete devastation written across my face, it was unintentional.

'Ah, Kate, don't do this. I've been up since six. I haven't stopped all day. Just let me sleep. I'll make it up to you tomorrow, I promise.'

'OK. I'm tired too.'

Tired of waiting.

I went to the bathroom to wash my teeth, and when I returned he was already in bed, practically asleep. He grunted something, which I took to be a request to get in beside him but I ignored it. Fatigued as I was, I wasn't ready for sleep yet. I leaned over him, kissed his forehead and told him I was going out for a walk. He mumbled something else and I left the room. As I passed the concierge he barely acknowledged me. It wasn't the same guy as before but he wore the same expression.

The night was cooler than I had expected and I had forgotten to bring a jacket. Maybe a jolt of cold air was what I needed. I knew I was being a touch unreasonable but I thought it was perfectly understandable. Sure, he'd had a long day, I could see he was exhausted, but he must know how important this night was for me. For us. I had spent the entire day without talking to anybody who wasn't in some way paid to talk or listen to members of the public. I had spent my day waiting for him. And now here he was, asleep before he could even ask how I was. My flight hadn't been so great. I had been delayed for an hour and a half. One of my bags had been mislaid. I didn't have enough clothes for the next couple of days. I was hungry. I'd been waiting to have dinner with him. I had drunk too much, just when I'd decided to cut back. I'd been lonely all day. I was still lonely.

I decided to turn back towards the hotel. I was finding it hard to think while having to keep in mind how far I'd wandered. There was no one to turn to if I got lost. Another couple was waiting for the lift as I approached. They acknowledged me, then returned to their contemplation of each other. They got out on the floor before mine.

I opened the bedroom door as quietly as possible. Daniel was snoring loudly. I undressed and got in beside him. Eventually, I was asleep too.

*

85

But tomorrow was a new day. Daniel woke first and before I had even adjusted to where I was he was edging my pyjama bottoms over my knees and himself as close as my sleepy state allowed. Realizing suddenly that we were finally here, that we had actually spent the night together, I forgot any misgivings I'd had and plunged on to him. It was wonderful – I loved him and we were on our own for two full days. It would be as if there was only the two of us, no wife, no kids, no work, just us. It would be perfect.

And that morning was. After our lovemaking (Daniel's energies were well restored), we decided to have breakfast in one of the many authentic restaurants on the surrounding streets. The hotel dining room seemed too provincial, too much for tourists. We had the whole city to explore. The very place I had wanted to have dinner the previous evening was open. We sat outside, even though it was almost too cold, and indulged in strong aromatic coffee and hot buttery croissants. It tasted like heaven. This breakfast tasted like every breakfast I ever wanted to have again. Daniel was in great form: either he was intent on making it up to me for the night before, or he was truly as happy as I was.

'I couldn't stop thinking about you all day,' he said, placing a morsel of croissant in my mouth. 'I was imagining you naked in the middle of those old bores. I nearly had to leave the room.'

'Get away! I'm sure you didn't think about me once. I know what you're like when you're working.'

'Honestly! I had this mental picture of you sitting cross-legged in the middle of them all. But then I had to stop because they were having heart-attacks.'

'That was considerate of you. Listen, Daniel,' I added, 'I'm sorry I was so snippy – it was just that I was so . . .'

He put his fingers over my lips. 'It was my fault. I should

have been there sooner. I'm sorry I was so tired when I arrived.'

'Well . . . we're both here now.'

'And I'm going to show you the very best time Paris has to offer.'

'Oh!' I suddenly remembered. 'I have no clothes. They lost one of my bags.'

'Well, we'll buy some new ones. Don't they make clothes here in Paris? Some guy called Chanel?'

'Well . . . woman, originally, but yes, Chanel is here and Dior and Chloé . . . Are you really going to kit me out from Chanel? They are a little expensive.'

'You're worth every penny.'

We let our buttery fingers entwine and it seemed like nothing could ever separate us.

In the end, of course, I didn't let him embellish his credit card with ladies' couture; I found the equivalent of the high street and bought a few nice things with my own. However, I did let him buy me an antique brooch from a quaint little jeweller we found in the Latin Quarter.

After popping back to the hotel to get our coats, we set off along the Paris streets with the general aim of finding the Eiffel Tower. (There are some touristy things you simply have to do.) Daniel said the view from the top was breath-taking. (I had been to Paris once before but only passing through *en route* from Germany. I had been broke and not in the mood for sightseeing.) After a while we found our-selves at the Opéra where we boarded one of those open-top bus tours. Its kitschiness was delightful and after a whistle-stop tour of other sights we were deposited right outside the tower. Whatever about the view from the top, the view from below is pretty amazing. How could somebody not adore this elegant construct of nuts and bolts? We decided to climb the eighty or so flights of metal stairs, stopping briefly on the *première étage* to buy a disposable camera. We pressed on to the *deuxième étage*, every twinge in our calf muscles a register of our determination. I was quite pleased to find out we had to take a lift to the third floor. I was enjoying being a pioneer but enough was enough.

The lift was large and square, glass-walled and glass-roofed. The minute I stepped inside I felt fear. The concentration I'd needed to climb the stairs had kept me from being truly aware of how high up we were. Suddenly I saw I was about to travel to nine hundred feet pressed tight against the wall of a glass box. Everybody around me looked no more animated than if they were getting the lift to Homewares in a department store. Daniel, too, was perfectly calm.

He was trying to get a picture from each side. He kept disappearing behind the increasing numbers of people crowding into the lift and when, for what seemed like a very long time, I couldn't catch sight of him, I panicked. I screamed that I couldn't breathe and flailed at the people on all sides of me, yelling at them to let me out. I tried to break through the crowd, desperate to find Daniel or the exit. Faces kept emerging to stare at me as if I was truly insane, yet nobody helped me.

My heart was palpitating and sweat streaked down my back. Eventually the lift operator, who was about to close the doors, grabbed my arm and guided me out on to the terrace. The next thing I remember is Daniel prising my fingers from the metal railings and holding me close to him. 'It's OK, it's OK,' he kept repeating, 'you're fine. You're out of the lift now. It's OK.'

'I'm not OK, I'm not OK, I'm such an eejit,' I wailed at him.

'You're not an eejit. That was a very small overcrowded lift.'

'But nobody else minded it. You didn't.'

'Kate, love, it doesn't matter, it was just a small panic-attack. I'm sure they see worse here every day. Everything's all right now.'

He squeezed me tightly and I began to believe him.

'Do you want to walk down slowly, or will we get a cup of coffee first?'

'No, no, I think I'm ready to go down. It was just the lift . . . so high and so crowded. I couldn't breathe in there.'

'It was a foolish idea to go all the way to the top, anyway. God knows we're high enough here.'

'But I wanted to see the top.'

'Another time . . .'

We started our descent, and while the climb down those steps didn't bother me, something was still niggling at me, something other than claustrophobia or the mortification of making a public spectacle of myself. I didn't know what it was or how deeply it was buried but something had made me panic in that lift, something other than a mild fear of heights and a distaste for crowds

'Come on,' I said to him, when we got to the bottom, 'let's go and get drunk.'

The rest of our holiday in Los Almiras was passed in typical style. We did the trip to the one landmark in the region that had any pretensions towards archaeological importance; we visited the neighbouring beach, which wasn't half as nice as our own; we met the other Irish couple, who could have been our *doppelgängers* except that they actually were on their honeymoon; we had several walks on the beach and while none of them was moonlit, they were delightful; we made love every day and had orgasms like they were going out of fashion. By our last evening I was truly regretting that we had to leave. I'd thought Keith might drive me a little crazy – but what do you know? He hadn't.

We were having dinner with that other Irish couple, Don and Lorna, on the terrace restaurant. It was their last evening also; they had been on our flight out from Shannon and would be on our flight home. They were maybe a little older than us and had only been going out together a year before they got married. Both of them had been in long-term relationships before in which they had nearly made it up the aisle.

'I just woke up one morning,' said Lorna, 'and realized that Steve didn't love me. I suppose I'd sort of known it for ages but when you've been with someone nearly for ever you don't analyse every little feeling you have about them. You just presume.'

'Yeah,' said Don. 'It was similar for me. Áine and I had been going together since school. It was a running joke with both our families and all our friends that we still weren't married. But by the time we'd both finished with college and had done a bit of travelling and were saving for the deposit on a house, we kind of realized that we'd done with each other. It was almost like we'd lived a whole life together and were ready to move on. It was a shame, but it was true. It hit our families the worst.'

'My break-up was pretty messy, though,' continued Lorna. 'I knew Steve didn't love me and I knew there was no point in us getting married but a big part of me wanted to get on with it and be married and deal with the rest later. Steve was furious when I confronted him. We'd already spent an awful lot of money on the wedding and everybody had been invited. It was the money and the humiliation that bothered him most. Eventually he admitted that he was just going along with it to keep me happy. He said that, no, he didn't think realistically he would have been faithful.'

'And then we met,' said Don. 'Speed-dating, would you believe?'

'I didn't want to go,' said Lorna, 'but a group of my friends dragged me along. As soon as I saw Don I knew he was the one.'

'I felt the same way,' said Don. 'You just know when it's right.'

'Oh, you do,' I said emphatically, because it was what their two pairs of expectant eyes were demanding, but it made me wonder if I had ever had that feeling deep in my gut that it was right with Keith. Anyway, what does 'right' mean? Nobody can know for sure that they're going to live happily ever after. There mightn't even be any such thing.

I had enjoyed their company over the few days, but I was glad they lived in Fermanagh. Nobody expected you to keep in contact if you lived in Fermanagh.

I had made only one cursory phone call home all week. The obligatory no-we-didn't-die-horrific-deaths-in-the-worst-air-crash-of-the-millennium-even-though-it-didn't-make-the-evening-news phone call. My mother was suitably nonplussed about our adventures and merely told me not to forget to bring back something for my aunts. 'I don't want a thing, you know me, but your aunts would really appreciate the thought.'

I had already filled a bag with the appropriate kind of tat. I would pick up some White Linen for my mother at the airport.

So when we got back to the hotel on that last evening and there was a message for me saying simply, 'Ring Lucy,' I was more than surprised. Oh, God, had something awful happened? Was I being punished for daring to have a good time – or for having led a dissolute life up to now? Ring Lucy. There was nothing for it but to do it.

'Hey, Luce, what's up?'

'Come home quick. Mum's in a state. Jean has left Mike.'

7

I came back to a madhouse. We landed in Shannon at seven
o'clock and less than an hour later I was in the thick of it at
Sycamore Lodge. Before we could even think about Jean or
Mike we had to deal with Mum. Despite the efforts of Lucy,
Marion, Ruth, Dad, her GP and the local pharmacist, she
was still hanging from the chandeliers (almost literally).
When I arrived through the door she was leaning over the
landing banister, threatening to drive herself to Dublin.

'Don't be silly, love,' Dad was saying from the hall below.
'Nobody's going to Dublin. We don't even know where
Jean is.'

'Don't call me silly. I'm not the silly one here. I'm not
the one throwing up my marriage on a whim. And I've been
tempted. Believe me, I've been tempted. I've had far more
to put up with than that girl has.'

'Yes, love, we know. Now, will you come down here and
we'll have a cup of tea?'

'I don't want any tea.'

'Look,' he continued, pushing me in front of him, 'look
who's home.'

'Kate, is it? I'm sure you had a hand in this, Kate.'

I wasn't ready to be attacked the minute I got in the door.
'Honestly, Mum, I don't know a thing about it.'

'Hrrmph!'

Marion came out to greet me and responded to my look
of desperation with one of her own. 'We've been at this all
afternoon,' she said.

I decided it was ridiculous to be shouting at Mum up the stairs so I began to go up to her.

'Don't come near me!' she flashed. 'I don't want anyone near me.'

'OK, OK, Mum,' I said, turning on my heels, wondering if anybody had tried leaving her on her own for a while. 'We'll be in here if you need us.' I grabbed Dad by the shoulders and led him forcibly into the sitting room. 'She'll be fine, Dad. I really don't think she's going to throw herself over the banister.'

Keith followed us in but remained standing by the door. He didn't know what to do with himself.

'I wanted her to take a Valium,' piped up Ruth, 'but she refused. Valium's good for her – it's always been good for her.'

'Oh, take one yourself,' snapped Lucy.

'I'm only trying to help!'

'Maybe she'll have one later,' said Marion, 'but right now Kate's right. We should leave her alone for a while. We still need to get out of her what Jean actually said.'

'So Jean was here last night,' I established, 'and said she was leaving Mike?'

'Well,' said Lucy, 'it seems she said something about going to Dublin on a course, some two-week thing for her job. And then when Mum asked if Mike was going to join her at the weekend she said, no, he wasn't and that actually she was leaving him. And that was it. According to Mum, she just waltzed out of the house, having dropped her bombshell.'

'I don't believe it. She wouldn't do that. Where is she now? Has anyone spoken to her?'

'I've been ringing her mobile,' said Marion, 'but it's switched off. I've tried her work and they won't say where she's staying.'

'She must have told them not to,' said Ruth.

'What about Mike?'

'Mobile and house phones are ringing out. And he wasn't at work today.'

'But why would Jean leave Mike like that? They weren't unhappy, were they?'

'Who knows?' said Marion. 'But I don't think so. I mean, she never said anything to me anyway.'

'Or to me,' said Ruth.

'Mike did say something at your engagement party,' said Lucy.

'Oh, yeah?'

'Yeah. I suppose I wasn't taking that much notice – I mean, when has Jean ever been exactly happy?'

'Well, what was he saying?'

'Oh, just that she was working very hard and she wasn't around much in the evenings. She always had somewhere else to be. He wasn't saying anything in particular, but he seemed a bit concerned about her.'

'Concerned she'd tire herself out? Or concerned she was going to leave him?'

'Oh, I don't think he had any notion she was going to leave him. He just seemed a bit . . . bothered, you know?'

'Yeah,' said Marion. 'He was a bit quiet that night.'

'Was he?' I asked, trying to remember.

'You probably didn't notice, but he was a bit off form.'

'So what do we do now?'

'I'll go and check on Mum,' said Ruth, getting up.

'Hold on a minute,' said Lucy. 'Don't go fussing her.'

'I'm not fussing her. I'm just concerned about my mother.'

'Look,' said Marion, 'we're all concerned about her. Let's give her a few more minutes.'

Ruth sat back down with a thump and crossed her legs with vigorous intention.

'What do you think, Dad?' I asked him, suddenly aware that he had been silent all this time.

'I think,' he said slowly, 'that whatever's going on, they'll sort it out eventually.'

Just then Mum appeared in the doorway, pale and drawn but otherwise quite well. 'I'll have that cup of tea now,' she said.

'I'll make it,' said Ruth. 'You put your feet up. I'll get you a little sandwich too – your blood sugar's probably gone very low.'

'Just the tea will be fine.' Mum came fully into the room and sat on the edge of the couch. 'I can't believe she's done this.'

'What exactly did she say?' asked Marion, gently.

'What did she say? She said she was leaving her husband! Leaving Mike! Mike! She was lucky to get him and now here she is leaving him. She won't get another husband, not at her age.'

'Did she say why, Mum?'

'She did not!'

'Like, do you think it was a sudden thing, as if they'd had a row, or do you think it was something she'd planned?'

Mum considered this. 'You know, I think it was planned. Yes – yes! She said she'd thought about it for a long time. Yes, that's what she said.'

Marion and I looked at each other.

'Had she ever mentioned being unhappy, Mum?' I asked.

'Oh, Jean's always complaining about something. Of course, if she had children she'd know what it was like to have something to complain about. And she certainly wouldn't go walking out on her husband if she had children.'

Jean's refusal to start a family had always been a sore point with Mum.

'Children don't automatically fix things,' said Lucy.

Suddenly I was reminded of Keith's presence by the particularly annoying sound of him repeatedly clearing his throat. 'Honestly, Keith,' I said, transferring my frustration to my fiancé, lurking uselessly by the door, 'you should go home. You're exhausted and there's no need for you to be here.'

'But how will you get back?'

'I'm perfectly capable of getting myself home. You could do with going to bed.'

'Poor Mike,' Mum continued. 'He would have loved a son.'

'OK, OK,' said Marion. 'We're getting off the point here. So, we can't contact Jean. At worst we'll hear from her in two weeks when she comes back from Dublin. Mike isn't answering his phone but he has to be at home some time so we could go out to Kilconnel and try to talk to him.'

'That's a good idea.'

'I'm afraid you'll have to count me out, though,' said Marion. 'Nick isn't back till tonight and I can't leave the kids with his mother any longer.'

'No problem,' said Lucy. 'Kate and I will go out. OK, Kate?'

'Fine.'

'I'll drive you,' said Dad.

'I'll drive you,' said Keith, already fingering his car keys.

'No!' I said firmly, then added, more softly, 'No, you go home, Keith. You're wrecked, and if we do find Mike he might be a bit embarrassed in front of another man.'

'But how will you get out there?'

'Ruth will drive us, right, Roo?' Lucy said, as Ruth returned, carrying a tray laden with tea-things.

'What will I do?'

'Drive Kate and me out to Kilconnel to find Mike.'

'Oh . . . ahm . . . of course, but . . . Well, you know him much better than I do . . . He mightn't like . . .'

'We don't want your counselling services, just a lift in your car.'

'Well, OK, then.'

And so it was decided. Keith headed back to the flat while we piled into Ruth's brand-new people-carrier. We left Mum picking her way through crustless sandwiches and dainty fingers of fruit cake while Dad took up the newspaper and drank his tea in silence.

When we got to the house it was clear that nobody was home so we took a vote and decided to wait a while in case he came back. I couldn't decide which was more ridiculous – camping outside Mike and Jean's house, or taking a vote to decide to do it. We put on the radio and listened to the sea area forecast while Ruth treated us to a lecture on the trials of marital breakdown. Ruth and her husband Phil have done a few stints on a pre-marriage course and feel themselves to be experts. (The local priest was desperate and they were the only married couple who regularly attended Mass but Ruth likes to tell everyone they were chosen because of the beauty of their marriage. Whatever makes her happy.) However, after about forty-five minutes we could take no more so we pulled round and headed back to Limerick. Still no Mike.

Ruth dropped us off on O'Connell Street. (We decided one of us was enough to report back to Mum, and Ruth was still itching to give her that Valium.) I figured Keith would be asleep by now – he wasn't answering his mobile – so I persuaded Lucy into a nightcap at the White House.

Suddenly a long, cold pint of Guinness seemed a very good idea.

'You know,' said Lucy, bringing two gorgeous pints to our table, 'I didn't want to say it in front of Mum and Ruth, but Mike did sort of give the impression that something was wrong the other night.'

'Oh? What else did he say?'

'Well, nothing very specific but when I asked him, half jokingly, if he thought she might be having an affair, he answered like he'd really thought about it. I mean, he said, no, he didn't think so, but obviously . . .'

'Wow!'

'I'd never have thought she was the type, but I wouldn't have thought she was the type to walk out either.'

'Did you ask about their . . . sex life?'

'Of course I didn't! What do you think I am?'

'Mum's right about one thing, though.'

'What's that?'

'Mike *has* always wanted children.'

'I thought they'd resolved that.'

'Resolved it in so far as Mike agreed to go along with what she wanted. What was it she said once? That they'd both agreed there was enough in just the two of them?'

'Oh, well, I don't know. The only thing I said to him was that maybe he should talk to you.'

'Me? Why me?'

'You two have always been close and maybe if Jean was . . . you know . . . if she did . . .'

'You mean if she was having an affair I'd be able to tell, given my history?'

'Not exactly.' Lucy was visibly cringing.

'It's OK. I know what you mean.'

'Anyway, he didn't want to bother you, it being your big night and all.'

I wish he had bothered me. In all the years I've known Mike I've always thought of him as an absolute rock – not only for Jean but for the whole family. I can't imagine life without him.

'Actually,' continued Lucy, 'that wasn't the only thing I was talking to Mike about the other night.'

'Oh?'

'Yeah, I was going to tell you that day before the party . . . but . . . well . . .'

'What is it, Lucy?'

'Well, you know the way I've never had a boyfriend for very long and how I've never really been in love?'

'Yeah?'

'And how I've never really had that kind of passion – you know, that uncontrollable sort of passion – like you had with Daniel?'

'Yeah?'

'Well, I think I might know why.'

'Oh?'

'Yeah. I think I might be a lesbian.'

'A what?'

'A lesbian. I believe you've heard of them. Into women rather than men.'

'Seriously, Lucy, you think you're gay?'

'Yeah, I do. Well, actually I don't think it. I know it. I'm gay. I am.'

'Wow. Well, congratulations!'

I hugged her. It had taken a minute to sink in but it made perfect sense. Lucy was gay. And she was delighted.

'Does anybody else know?'

'No, you're the first. Well, except Mike. I told him because he's so level-headed. If it sounded right when I said it to him I'd believe it more myself.'

'And what did he say?'

'He was delighted. He said I was the best-looking lesbian he'd ever met. And that womankind was lucky to have me.' She laughed.

'Wow,' I said again. 'How long have you known?'

'I'm not sure. Maybe I've known all my life. But I met this woman recently and I suppose she kind of helped me work it out.'

'Oh? And is she your girlfriend?' I asked, grinning.

'No. I don't have a girlfriend. Not yet anyway. She's a friend.'

'So what's your plan now? Are you . . . "out"?'

'I suppose so. Though I don't want to go advertising it. I'll tell the others – well, maybe not Ruth, not yet, and not Mum and Dad. I'll leave them alone until they've got over one bombshell.'

'But you're happy about it?'

'Oh, Kate, I'm so happy. I'm a bit scared too . . . that people will look at me differently. But it's not like I've changed or anything, I'm still the same person. It's just that I won't be having any more boyfriends.'

'I suppose that means you and Luke have split up?' I asked innocently.

'Poor Luke. He's a sweetheart. He won't even notice.'

I laughed, and as the laugh turned into a yawn I realized how tired I was. I had woken up in the travel-brochure harmony of Los Almiras some sixteen hours earlier and now I was in the midst of broken marriages, missing wives and lesbian sisters.

'Come on,' said Lucy, gathering up our things, 'let's get you home to your man. It's been a long day.'

'You really are a dark horse, Lucy. I'd no idea all this was going on.'

'I guess you never know what people are hiding,' said Lucy, with a smile, as we left the pub.

We strolled up O'Connell Street, enjoying the relative brightness and warmth of the evening, and rounded the corner into Hartstonge Street. It was just as we were about to part at the steps to my building that we saw him. He was sitting, crumpled, on the floor in the foyer. He saw us immediately and was on his feet in seconds. He was distinctly embarrassed to be caught like that. He looked as if he hadn't slept or eaten in days.

'OK, Kate,' he said. 'I think you know something about this. What's going on?'

His voice was forced. He was trying to be calm but it was costing him a huge effort.

I could only tell him I knew nothing. 'Mike,' I began, 'this is the first I've heard of it. I had no idea.'

'Oh, come on,' he said. 'You knew what was going on. Lucy said you knew something.' This was where Lucy jumped in to say, no, that wasn't what she'd said, she'd just thought I might have a clue as to what was up with Jean. His face was contorted now, an ugly expression I'd never seen before forming across his features.

'What is it with you girls?' he almost spat. 'Has none of you any respect for what it means to be married?'

I knew he probably didn't mean it but it hurt to hear him say that. He was looking directly at me as if he truly despised me. Suddenly I forgot that this was about Jean and nearly launched into an explanation of my past (and present) behaviour, but Mike wasn't hanging around to hear it or anything else.

'I'm wasting my time here.' He barged past us and tried

to get out of the door but missed the subtle lifting mechanism. He tugged at it, making a racket that would have woken the dead. I tried to assist him in raising the catch, but as soon as I was near enough, he shrugged me away. Tears of frustration were running down his cheeks; I would have given anything to help him. Eventually he got the door open and slammed it behind him without another word to us. Lucy and I turned to each other. Neither of us had ever seen Mike like that.

After everything had finished between Daniel and me, I resolved not to feel any guilt about it. I'd decided I'd been hurt as much as anybody and I tried to convince myself I'd done nothing wrong. That's the story I stick to mostly. At times like this I feel wretched and crave absolution. I've even thought about going to confession, but I don't know if there's enough of the Catholic left in me to believe in the forgiveness, even if I could muster the courage to confess to a priest. It would be such a quick fix, yet it isn't really the wrath of God I'm worried about. I suppose living with occasional wretchedness is the price I have to pay.

Lucy and I decided there wasn't much point in mentioning this incident at home so we made a quick phone call to say we'd seen Mike briefly and he was still quite upset. We didn't know what else to do. One thing was for sure: this break-up was for real and it didn't look like there would be a way to fix it.

I had expected Keith to be in bed but he was still up, laying out his clothes for the next day. 'I looked for something of yours to iron,' he said, 'but I couldn't find anything clean.'

'Oh, for God's sake,' I snapped, rather unfairly, 'who cares about clean clothes?' I knew he was only being helpful, but Keith and his concerns seemed rather mundane right now. I wondered if I walked out on him would he still be putting a crease in his trousers or would he be out wandering the streets like a madman?

'Come on,' I said to him, 'let's go to bed. I don't even know if I can face work in the morning.'

He put the iron away and followed me into the bedroom.

8

Sometimes I wake up in the morning and feel far too well dressed for the world. I feel like I'm not feeling anything. I get out of bed and have a shower without realizing I'm awake. I go into the kitchen and make a cup of coffee and I don't remember boiling the kettle. Then I get dressed. First, I pull on my underwear, which is usually fashionable, clean and matching although there are times when it's not. Then I put on my suit. That's where the real problem lies. I was never meant to wear a suit. There's something about a tailored suit that puts a strain on my mind. I can feel the fabric on every part of my body. 'Conform,' it's saying. 'Conform. Disappear into the background. Be indistinguishable from the crowd. Do not be yourself.'

Ever since I became self-aware I have been obsessed about my appearance. Somewhere between the ages of one and two, when I realized that the little girl in the mirror was me, I've been trying to alter her. It's been exhausting at times, but always fun. When I was a teenager I went through a Goth phase – mainly because of a boyfriend I had for about three weeks, and because I had the time. I used to get stared at constantly and, of course, that was part of the attraction, but now, when I get dressed up in my big fancy work suit and nobody looks, or if they do, it's only to nod acceptance, I realize that I was much more myself in the ridiculous black get-up than I ever could be in my stylish two-piece.

When I was at school I was one of those silly girls who

knew that, with a little sustained effort, I could do quite well in the Leaving Cert. There were loads of us. Our school was small, single sex and highly academic. It specialized in turning out very confident young women who would enter the professions but would probably leave them before too long to get married. Therefore it didn't matter what you chose to study at college as long as it sounded good. There was, of course, a small number of girls who had their heads screwed on much better than the rest of us, who thought about the future as something real that might affect the rest of their lives. They chose career paths they hoped would bring them satisfaction and fulfilment. As I said, I was not one of those girls.

All of us Delahuntys have good brains; we get them from both sides of the family. But while most of the older ones had no great desire, or were not expected, to dazzle with their jobs, by the time us later ones were leaving school, the whole country had become gripped by Leaving-Cert points mania. It was the newest status symbol, replacing the foreign holiday and the brand-new car. Whose son got medicine? Whose daughter just missed veterinary? Whose child got pharmacy with points to spare? If you had the ability, you were expected to perform.

My own parents, being sensible in the main (even my mother, when it comes to such things), tried to impress on me the importance of choosing a career I would be suited to, of picking a college course based on my likes and aptitudes. My father, in particular, encouraged careful thinking and prudent choices. He did not encourage my choice of law. 'I don't think it's for you, sweetheart,' he said.

But I was determined. Several others in my class were going for law, and my determination to beat them, if nothing else, kept me focused. In the end we all got it. I'm the only one still practising (yikes!), even though I was easily the least suited to it. At the time, my father was recommending I think about an arts degree, which would probably have suited me but it would have meant wasting my points so I dismissed it. He suggested the art college where Lucy had spent four happy years, but I knew that wasn't for me. I'm much too square. So I lined up the high-points contenders and picked them off one by one. Definitely not medicine. It seemed much too like hard work. I'm not keen on blood either (I flinch at the sight of a nail cut too low), and a white coat would do nothing for my figure. Ditto veterinary. Ditto dentistry. (Why would anyone want to be a dentist?) And pharmacy seemed too much like shop-keeping. And so, in the year I did my Leaving Cert, the only big hitter remaining was law. Hence, I chose law.

Now here I am at my desk, dressed in my Quin and Donnelly suit, wondering what I should have done differently.

It was while I was sitting there, idling with some correspondence, that I had a phone call from Jean.

'Hi there', she said, maybe meekly.

'Hi there,' I said, as flatly as I could.

'I hope you don't mind me phoning you at work.'

'I mind you phoning me at work as much as I mind you phoning me,' I said, rather pedantically.

She ignored the tone. 'I won't keep you long.'

'Why are you ringing me? Why aren't you ringing Mike?'

'I need to talk to you first.'

'Why? I've nothing to say to you.'

'Please, Kate. I will talk to Mike, but I want to talk to you first.'

'You're an absolute bitch, you know.'

'Yes. Yes, I know.'

'Well, good.'

Now that that was out of the way I could give way to my curiosity and talk to her.

'Look, I know it must have been weird for everybody but it was something I had to do. I thought you might understand.'

'Why does everybody think *I* would understand?'

'Well, you feel things strongly. You're not afraid to do what you need to.'

I wasn't sure what she was talking about. Did the fact that I was insane enough to have an affair with a married man qualify me as a couples counsellor?

'I'm not going to justify what you've done, Jean.'

'I know. That's not what I want. Look, will you meet me? Can I buy you a drink?'

I was in need of a drink. 'When?'

'Whenever you can get off work.'

'I can probably sneak away in an hour.' It was three o'clock.

'Great. I'll meet you in Malone's so, at four-ish.'

'OK, then. See you there.'

I wondered if I should contact Mike and tell him where she was. But I believed her when she said she would talk to him, and I kind of understood why she wanted to talk to me first. Whatever she had to say I would probably under-stand, a bit at least. When you're being dysfunctional it's always better to be with someone who has a history of dysfunctional behaviour.

I shuffled around the office conspicuously for half an hour or so, then announced I was going to the library to do some research. With any luck nobody would need me for the rest of the afternoon. Malone's was a short walk down town; it was one of Jean's favourite pubs. It used to be a favourite haunt of the two of them. She was waiting for me when I got there; she had two gin-and-tonics at a low table near the back. She got up as I approached, and held out her hand in a rather old-fashioned gentlemanly way. I took it, and automatically we had a deep, lasting hug. I was surprised by how much I needed to hug her. We had probably never hugged each other like that before, or certainly never meant it. She felt soft and pliant, not how I usually thought of her. There was distinct moisture in her eyes when we parted.

'Hey,' she said. 'Thanks for coming.'

Suddenly I knew that, no matter what she told me, I wouldn't judge her. Suddenly I felt like the older sister who would be happy to share her wisdom. 'So,' I said, 'tell me everything.'

She took a sip from her glass, inhaled deeply, and began. 'It wasn't easy. I've thought about nothing else for ages – for years, even. Mike is the best, you know that. He's one of the really good ones. I'm lucky I even know him, not to mind be married to him. And he's still the best. Nothing's changed. He's always done everything he can to make me happy, and God knows that hasn't been easy. I'm a very selfish person and Mike isn't. He's the opposite of selfish He's – '

'I know what Mike is,' I assured her.

'Well, then you know that, in a way, he's not right for me. He was right for me eighteen years ago when I was a mess and needed someone to love me no matter what. He's been right for me all these years but in a way he's been too good for me because now I feel . . . Please don't hate me when I say this but I'm trying to be as honest as possible . . . Now I feel, well . . . that I don't need him any more. Is that terrible?'

'No, it's not terrible.'

'I do realize that I wouldn't be the person I am if it weren't for Mike. You mightn't think it but I'm a fairly together person now . . . I'm confident, I'm enjoying work – I'm even reasonably happy with the way I look. I don't want to sound like some self-help testimony, but I'm a lot happier now than I used to be. I'm probably what most people manage to be by their mid-twenties. But now that I'm there, or here, or whatever . . . I kind of want to go it alone. I want to see what I can do by myself. Does that make sense?'

I also wanted to be as honest as possible. 'I suppose it does, sort of . . . but does your marriage have to end just so you can feel like you're doing it for yourself?'

'Yes, I think it does. Mike would always be a security. I would never feel independent if I were still with him.'

I was getting suspicious. How transparent was her honesty?

'Jean, is there someone else?' I asked her, straight out. 'Is that why you wanted to talk to me?'

'No, there isn't.' She was emphatic. She paused. 'But I want to have the option of there being somebody else in the future.'

'Oh.'

'You must remember, Kate, that I never did the running around you did. I had a couple of boyfriends, then Mike, then wedded bliss for fifteen years. Can you believe I've been married for fifteen years? I need to be free to explore. And . . .' she paused again '. . . I know it sounds terrible but I don't think I love Mike. I mean, I love him for who he is, and all he's been to me . . . but I'm not *in love* with him, not how you should be, even after fifteen years.'

She was quiet again and took another sip of her drink. I

could see that everything she'd said had been wrangled out of her, probably very slowly and very painfully.

'Hey,' she said, before I had a chance to speak, 'want to go outside for a sneaky cigarette?'

'Sure.'

I'd been having a lot fewer sneaky cigarettes lately (Keith being good for me that way) but I was always ready to jump off the wagon. And it had probably been about fifteen years since Jean and I had shared a smoke. During their courting days, when Mum used to dump me on the two of them, Jean would often let me have an illicit drag on her cigarette. Mike hated it and used to get cross with the two of us, especially Jean because she should have known better. And Jean should have shopped me to Mum, but I think she liked the company. There's twice the pleasure when there's two of you. She's been smoking on and off for years; like me, she started at school, in the laneway behind the gym, or underneath the laburnum tree in the nuns' garden. Until now she'd been totally off them for ages. I suppose this was part of her needing to break free and do the bad thing.

It was lovely outside. Ever since the smoking ban, pubs had been making a real effort to provide a makeshift beer garden. Malone's were lucky: they had a paved area to the side that used to hold their bins but they'd tidied it up and put out some cheap garden furniture and the obligatory gas heater and, to any boozy smoker, it could have been the Latin Quarter. Now that we were outside I could see Jean's face properly. She looked younger, almost like she'd looked when we'd last shared a cigarette. Was it because she was so much happier now or because I hadn't actually looked at her in a very long time? I was enjoying the moment – I couldn't but be happy that my slightly estranged sister and I were bonding over Silk Cut Blue – but I was still mad at

111

her. I still held in my mind the image of a deranged Mike crumpled on the foyer floor in my building. It was something I shouldn't have seen and she was responsible for it.

'Jean,' I decided to ask her, 'why the dramatic exit? Why did you tell Mike you were leaving him before you went away? Why didn't you wait until you came back? You really, really wrecked his head.'

'I know.'

She rubbed her face with her hands. 'I know that was probably the worst part of it but it was the only way.' She was pleading with me to understand. 'I knew that if I just went up to Dublin without saying anything I'd lose my bottle by the time I got back. I'd tried to say something before but I could never muster the courage. This way I could say it and leave and not have to deal with it until I had time to come to terms with it myself. I know it was lousy, but it was the only way. If I'd stayed to have it out with him I'd probably have ended up backing down because . . . well . . . it's pretty hard to say no to a really loving man who's been everything to you for nearly half your life. You know what I mean?'

'Yeah,' I had to admit. 'I think I probably do. But,' I added, 'it was still a horrible thing to do to Mike. He didn't deserve that.'

'I know.' Her voice quivered. She was crying.

I hugged her and held her tightly until her body stopped heaving. In a way I admired her. She had done a very difficult thing.

'I am going to talk to him.' She was blowing her nose. 'I want to see him and explain. But I couldn't have done that if I hadn't given myself the chance to get it straight in my head first. After saying it to him and to Mum there was definitely no going back.'

I had forgotten about Mum.

'Oh, God, Mum,' I blurted out. 'She had to be sedated. There was consternation!'

We burst out laughing. We're truly terrible daughters.

'Oh, no,' said Jean. 'She's not too bad, is she? I had a few qualms about that – I didn't want to be responsible for bringing on an early death. But I had to tell her. She's a tough old bird and she needed to be told the truth. I'm actually more worried about Dad. He really likes Mike, and he'll hate me for doing this to him.'

'He won't hate you. Dad isn't capable of that. You're his first born. He loves you. But, yes, he is disappointed. And a bit bewildered. It's not within his realms of understanding why someone would leave any marriage, let alone a marriage that involved Mike.'

'Oh, stop, you're making me feel bad.'

'Well, I'm sorry, Jeanie dear, but bad is how you've got to feel. At least some of the time.'

'I know, I know. But you do see why I had to do it?'

'Look,' I said to her, 'if you're sure you've done the right thing. *Are* you sure, after all you've said to me here, that you want to end your marriage, leave your life as you've known it for the past fifteen years – and for no good reason either, mind you, other than that you want to rediscover your wild youth?'

She paused, whether for effect or to think, I didn't know.

'Yes,' she said eventually. 'I'm sure. It's the right thing.'

'Well, OK, then.'

It was getting a bit chilly and our G-and-Ts needed freshening so we went back inside. Jean was visibly lighter in spirit, almost buoyant. I'd never thought a marriage break-up could be so pleasant. We found our table again and settled down with our drinks and a packet of crisps.

'You know,' she said, after a while, 'this isn't all bad for Mike. Once he gets over the shock, he'll be much better off.'

'How do you make that out?' I asked, intrigued and dubious.

'Well,' she was taking her time, choosing her words carefully, 'it's been a while since Mike was in love with me.'

'That's not true!'

'It is. I'm not saying there's anything bad in that. I'm not saying I'm fleeing a loveless marriage, but he isn't in love with me any more.'

'How do you know?'

'Oh, you just know. He'd never be obvious, but it's there. When we were married first, he used to tell me he loved me all the time. And he really meant it. It came so naturally to him, he'd say it any time, and I'd know it was true. And then, whatever, years go by, and suddenly I realize he doesn't say it any more, or at least not like he used to. And if I ever force it, he'll say it, but I know he doesn't mean it and I know he hates lying.'

'Are you sure that isn't what comes of being married for fifteen years?'

'I'm sure. But it's OK. In fact, it's much better. I'm not leaving him because he isn't in love with me. I'm leaving him because I'm not in love with him. When he has time to think about it, he'll see how this is a good thing for him.'

'Whatever you say, Jeanie.'

'No, it's true. Mike is . . . I'm not . . . Well, I'm not that adventurous . . . sex-wise, and . . . Mike would like to be, if you know what I mean.'

'Oh, yeah?'

'Well, I mean I do like sex, I just like it simple.'

'OK, then.' I couldn't suppress a smile. It was so odd to

hear Jean talk like this. She really was being as honest as she could be.

'Mike didn't have that many girlfriends before me, either. And he's still very good-looking. I mean, he's actually better-looking now than he was when I met him. And I've seen other women look at him. Young, attractive girls. He might like to find out where that leads him. You know what I mean?'

I did. Mike is one of those guys who grow into their looks as they get older. He was attractive in his twenties but now he's in his early forties there's something casually distinguished about him. He was never one to pay particular attention to his appearance, but as he's aged, he's taken care of himself. He's probably fitter now than he was in his twenties; his body has more muscle and is better toned. He has always worn his hair slightly long – the legacy of too many bad razor jobs in childhood, he claims – and a little scraggy. If he's not seeing clients he can go without shaving for days and it looks well on him; he makes other men appear to have made far too much effort. He usually dresses casually in jeans and tops or an open-necked shirt but he makes it seem like it's the only way a man should dress, and when he has to scrub up he looks great clean-shaven and in a suit. There's no doubt about it, a lot of women would be very interested in a newly single Mike.

'And you wouldn't mind that? Mike being with other women?'

'No, why should I? I'm planning to be with other men.'

'Jean, I don't know if it's as simple as that. There are probably a lot more women out there for Mike than there are men for you.' I hated to be so blunt but it was the truth.

'Of course I know that. Look, I'm nearly forty, I've never been particularly good-looking, I'm very high maintenance,

I'm not a great catch. But, Kate, that's not what this is about. If I meet someone else and we're together for two nights or two months or two years, then great. And if I don't meet anybody, that's OK too. I think I'll be able to grow old with just myself.'

'OK, then.'

We went back to our gin and our half-empty packet of crisps.

'Mike would like to have kids,' she said, after a while.

'Oh, yeah?' I said, a little disingenuously.

'He always wanted children. And I didn't grasp how much I didn't until well after we were married. He was always really good about it. He never made me feel I was denying him anything. But he would really like to have kids.'

And now he could.

'So when will you say all this to him?'

'I'm going to see him straight away. I rang him earlier today. I'll meet him later at the office, when it's quiet.'

'Oh. How did he sound?'

'He sounded OK. A bit relieved. Calm, I suppose.'

'He wasn't calm last week. I've never seen a man so upset.'

'Oh, I know. This must be especially hard for you at the moment. I hope it hasn't rattled you too much.'

'How do you mean?'

'Well, the certainty of marriage and all that. It's a bit off-putting to have marriages break up around you when you're about to get married yourself.'

'Oh, we're fine. We're just back from a holiday in the sun, actually. It was great. We're having a great time.'

'Good. Have ye set a date yet?'

'No, we haven't. We're just about to.'

'Good.'

The afternoon gin was making me sleepy so I suggested we switch to coffee. 'So,' I asked, needing to leave the soul-searching aside for a bit, 'what are ye going to do with the house?'

'Oh,' she said, 'I don't know. Probably sell it. I don't want it anyway.'

'But ye designed that house together. It was your passion for years.'

'I know, but that's changed. I mean, it's a great house – remember, the plans won a prize – but I'm not interested in living there any more. It's too far out. I want something closer to work and town. You've always said there's nothing like living in town.'

'I can't argue with that. I never could understand your obsession with doing up a house.'

'Oh, I know, I was obsessed for a long time, but it doesn't mean anything to me any more.'

'Do you think Mike wants it?'

'Probably not. He was never that keen on living in the sticks. And it was always more my house than his, even though he designed it.'

'Not to be crass, but if ye do sell it, ye'll probably get a truckload of money for it.'

'You're probably right,' she said, with a smile.

The coffee was reviving me. I was definitely suffering from sensory overload.

'Oh, that reminds me,' she continued, after another shot of espresso, 'I need to ask you yet another favour. I know, I know, when will it end? I promise you a share in my half of the house.'

'You'd better!'

'Seriously, could I stay with you for a while until I get myself organized? I won't be any bother, I promise.'

'Of course you can. I'd like having you around for a while. We can have a second go at being sisters together. Stay as long as you like.'

'Oh, thanks a million. Are you sure Keith won't mind? It won't cramp your style?'

I'd forgotten about Keith. 'No, of course not.'

'Great! Listen, I'm going over to Mike's office now. I'd say there's hardly anybody left. I'll ring you later tonight and tell you how it went.'

'Are you sure you're OK? Do you want me to go with you, just for the beginning?'

'No, I'm fine, honestly. I don't think there'll be any problem. But I could do with your help tomorrow when I talk to Mum and Dad. Could you be around for that?'

'Of course.'

She got up and we embraced once more. To look at her, you wouldn't have thought she was about to explain to the former love of her life why she'd dumped him. You might have thought she was about to embark on some very exciting adventure.

So, after hearing what Jean had to say I was curious to know what Mike made of it. I left it a couple of days, and without saying anything to Jean, I stayed at work late one evening and called round to his office when I knew he'd be alone. He was staying at work quite late, these days. I hadn't phoned to tell him I was coming but when I arrived he seemed to have been expecting me. 'Kate,' he said. 'Kate,' he repeated, holding out his hands to me. 'I'm so sorry about the other night. I was deranged. I didn't know what I was saying.' His voice was soft and frayed at the edges.

'It's OK,' I told him. 'You were upset. We didn't take any notice. It's fine.'

'No,' he said, 'it's not fine. I had no right to treat you like that.'

His look was deeply intent.

'It's OK, really,' I assured him. I could see the lines round his eyes and the puffiness beneath. He was doing a good impression of everything having gone back to normal, but it was clear he was still quite rattled.

'Did Jean tell you about our chat?' he asked, with a smile approaching his usual self-possession.

'She told me bits. She said ye were very civilized.'

'Yes, we were. Especially Jean. I've seen her more agitated telling me there's no milk in the fridge.'

I laughed feebly. 'She said you were still a bit dazed but that you were essentially resigned to the whole thing. She said you could see where she was coming from.'

'Where she's coming from?' he mused. 'She's coming from one strange place.' He was shaking his head and laughing. 'She seems to think she's done me a favour. I can now go out and sleep with all the women I've been lusting after for years. I can do unmentionably kinky things to them, I can father their children . . . Yes, indeed, Jean has it all worked out for me.'

'It's not as cynical as you're making it sound. I think she really believes she might have held you back.'

I didn't know if I was defending Jean or trying to pacify him.

'That's the funny thing,' he said then. 'I think so too. And the even funnier thing is that I do see where she's coming from.'

'Oh?'

'I don't mean I'm ready for . . . well . . . whatever it is, but the truth is that . . . maybe some time in the future, it might be nice to have . . . some options. Oh, fuck, I don't know what I'm saying. All I'm saying is that, yeah, some part of me realizes that this isn't entirely a bad thing.'

'Oh.'

'I'm sorry, Kate.'

'For what?'

'For everything. For having to listen to me, for having to listen to Jean. We're working things out, we're fine. You've got better things to be thinking about – like your own marriage. We're just the idiots who fucked it up.'

'She fucked it up, not you.'

'No, no, I did too. Look . . . she's right, I'm not all that surprised. Now that I've calmed down, well, yeah, of course I saw it coming. I just never thought it would actually arrive.'

'What do you mean?'

'Well, I'd known our marriage wasn't right for years. But, asshole that I am, I thought I was being the big man and that I was protecting her. I mean, in the beginning, she depended on me. She really was a bit of a mess in those days. I suppose that was part of what I found so attractive in her. But it waned, you know? I mean, she was still needy, but I was finding it less attractive. But I felt that this was what I'd chosen and there was no backing out. So what if I'd fallen a little out of love with her? I'd learn to live with it. But I suppose I was actually being arrogant, believing she still needed me. That was why I was so shocked when it turned out that she didn't need me, after all.'

'Is that true?'

'That is the sorry truth of our fifteen-year marriage.'

'Is that what you told Jean?'

'Mostly. I didn't labour the bits about her being needy, but she knew it anyway. She's much more perceptive and self-aware than I'd thought.'

'Yeah, me too. We're getting on really well now.'

'She told me.'

'It's weird.'

'Weird is not the word.'

We laughed. It *was* weird, and it would probably get weirder.

'Anyway,' he said, 'enough about me. How are you? How was your holiday? How's work?'

'Work is terrible. I think I want to pack it in.' I was surprised by my outburst. Had I been thinking this already or had it just occurred to me?

'OK, OK,' he said. 'Just how terrible? Are you in any . . . trouble?'

'Trouble? Oh, God, no. At least, I don't think so. No, I just hate it. I've always hated it. I can't pretend to be a solicitor any longer.'

'Right. Well, you've loads of options. You still have a very good degree, and your training and experience won't go to waste. There's a lot you could do within the law field.'

'But I'm so fed up of the law!'

'Well, in that case, you could go back to college for a year. Retrain.'

'At my age?'

'Of course. You're not over the hill yet. You just need to think about what you'd like to do.'

Mike *was* so level-headed. He could make any problem seem clearer.

'Thanks, Mike. I'll do that. And listen,' I added, 'if you need anything . . . or you want to talk . . .'

'Thanks, Kate, but I'll be fine. You have your hands full looking after one half of this mess. Go home and take a rest.'

I went home, where I found Jean in the lotus position on the couch eating a tub of ice-cream and watching *Emmerdale*. Life seemed good.

9

Whenever I wonder what makes Keith such a nice person, I have only to think of his parents. They are incredibly nice people. My parents are good people (though they have their flaws), but 'nice' isn't a word I would use to describe them. My mother is a snob and a bit highly strung and a desperate social climber (I do realize I'm like her in many ways). My father is an ambitious go-getter who loves his family utterly but isn't all that bothered about anybody else. Most people admire them, or are slightly in awe of them, or wish to compete with them, but I don't think anybody thinks they are nice.

Now, Keith's parents *are* nice. Even as I use the word I know it's losing its meaning and that's an awful shame because it's a good word to describe a good thing. I've never underestimated the simple goodness of being nice. People who are genuinely nice – who do nice things for people and say nice things about them and mean it – are generally good people. And while sometimes they might not be the most exciting people in the world, they're better than most of the rest.

Anyway, Keith's parents – good people. We were at their house in Corbally one evening and his mother was excited that we had been invited to a Doheny family wedding. 'Of course, it's a late invite,' Irene explained. 'Breda's wedding's only three weeks away, Keith, but seeing as the family's so big, your aunt Nuala decided not to ask any of the cousins to the main wedding and invite all of them to the afters.

That way no one would be left out. But now, you see,' she continued, sitting down beside us on the couch, 'it seems that a lot of the family that was to travel from America won't be able to make it. There's a dying uncle in Colorado, you see, and a very sick aunt in Utah and the families don't want to travel. You can understand that. And I think there's a conflict with some of the family on the other side, I don't know what it's about, but the numbers will be down there too. So the upshot of it all, anyway, is that Nuala has decided to ask the cousins to the full reception. I'm delighted. You can travel with us and we'll stay the night in the hotel. It'll be great altogether. Of course, that's if ye can go. Keith always has a devil of a time getting off work – Kate, sure you know that, they work him far too hard out there in Shannon. And you're very busy too, Kate – aren't lawyers always busy? But it would be really lovely if ye could come.'

She sat there looking as anxious as if she'd asked us to do something criminal, and could only expect an answer in the negative with a rap on the knuckles. Actually, I was enthralled by the whole idea. Having a very large, over-bearing family myself, I was always curious about other people's. And, I guessed that Keith's family was large and overbearing in a different way from mine. 'We'd be absolutely thrilled to go, Irene,' I said. 'I'm dying to meet all the family.'

Keith was delighted that, for once, he didn't have to persuade me into it. He's very fond of his extended family even though he readily admits that half of them are a bit nuts. But isn't that the way with all families? And he's very, very fond of his parents, and very protective of them. His father is recently retired, having worked all of his life for CIÉ and then Iarnród Éireann. He's a quiet man who likes to let his wife do the talking when the topic of conversation

124

is in her arena and outside his, like family weddings, for example. But if sports or politics are on the agenda, he will argue with the best of them. His mother, I suppose, is a typical Irish mammy, adoring her two sons beyond anything in the world. They and her husband have been her whole life, and it's clear she's enjoyed every minute of it. Keith is very good to them, giving them generous presents and still spending a lot of time with them. They say that a girl should always watch the way a man treats his mother because he will eventually end up treating her like that. If it's true, I'll have a lovely life, if a little quiet.

Ever since our first meeting, after we'd got engaged, Irene and Tom had treated me as if I was already part of the family. Keith's older brother Kevin isn't married either, and they were getting a little worried that there wouldn't be any grandchildren. When I met them I was a little freaked out by how willing they were to believe that I was the girl of their son's dreams and that I would make him blissfully happy for the rest of his life. I didn't think I could take the responsibility. They were such nice people – whatever I might end up doing to Keith, I couldn't hurt them. But they did what people like them always do: they put me at my ease and made me believe that everything would be all right. And each time I met them, I felt confident I could be a successful daughter-in-law.

Having established that we were going to the wedding, Keith's mother was now getting on with what she does best: serving tea and cakes. Every day Keith's parents drink leaf tea out of china cups, poured from a china teapot. Irene bakes a small brown loaf of bread or white scones every alternate day and a Victoria sponge at the weekend. If visitors are likely she might run to an apple tart or a spotted dick. Not having grown up with home baking, I find it the most heavenly thing in the world. Today, Irene has made a bread and butter pudding, soaked in whiskey (the only place you'll find alcohol in Keith's house is in the baking), and served with hot custard made from scratch. Everyone should have a wife like Irene.

'Oh, that's marvellous, dear. We'll have a lovely time, won't we, Tom? I know Keith's been dying for you to meet the cousins. They had such fun growing up together and now they're scattered all over the place. It'll be great for everybody to get together again. I was talking to Nuala only last night, Kate, and she said she couldn't wait to meet you. They're all agog. And ye were so quick with everything – Breda's been going out with Tony for nearly ten years. Of course, they were trying to buy a house for ages but the prices kept getting more and more ridiculous. Ye were so lucky, both of you, to have bought houses when ye did. When Keith was buying his in Clareview we thought it was an awful price – didn't we, Tom? We didn't know how he could afford it – but sure now look at the price of those houses. There was one in the paper last week and they wanted three hundred and fifty thousand for it! Now it was extended, all right, it would have been a lot bigger than Keith's, but three hundred and fifty thousand euros! I suppose you've found the same with your flat? It's on Hartstonge Street, isn't it?'

'That's right.'

'That's very central – that whole part of town has opened up so much. When you're young it's great to be in the middle of everything. Do you find it can be noisy at night?'

'Not really,' I answered. 'I like a bit of noise, anyway.'

I was about to tell her how Keith and I sometimes hang out of the bedroom window at night, watching people pass by and earwigging on their conversations, and how sometimes, maybe if we're a little tipsy, we call out to them, then collapse into bed, weak with laughing. But I remembered that Keith's mother believes vehemently that Keith lives in his house and I live in mine, and while we might pay visits to each other, we sleep in our own beds. And that is how Keith wants to keep it. I used to be impatient with that sort of thing – if a person is of age and living their own life away from their parents, they should be able to do as they please and not have to make up stories about it. I've always been brutally honest with my parents whether they liked it or not. (Well . . . maybe not always.) But Keith explained to me that it was simply a case of considering their feelings. They can't help the world they grew up in, or the strongly held beliefs they can't abandon because their son wants to get it on with his fiancée on a regular basis. They really believe that having sex with someone before you're married is wrong. Well, as Keith reminded me, it's what the Pope believes too. I suppose, in a way, I'm a little envious of people who have a really strong faith. Sometimes I think I have more faith in my night cream than I do in anything else. Anyway, chastity was the story we were sticking with. In Keith's house. My parents were beyond thinking about it.

It was while Irene was wittering on like this that she said something rather startling: 'I was saying to Tom last night, when I got off the phone from Nuala,' she began, 'that we hadn't seen the two of you for ages. Isn't that right, Tom? I was trying to think was there any more news. Kevin was over earlier in the evening – he called into us on his way home from the airport. He was in America for a couple of weeks, Kate, his work had him over there. He said he hardly saw the outside of the place the whole time he was there. He was in Seattle, Kate, that's where the headquarters of his company are. And the whole time they were indoors,

127

working, or travelling to the other factories. Oh! He has a new girlfriend! Another new girlfriend. He always has new girlfriends, Kate. I never knew anyone like him for having new girlfriends all the time. And you won't believe who it is, Keith! It's a sister of Jacqueline Dunleavy, your Jacqueline. A younger sister. Would you believe that? Isn't it a small world, Kate? Oh, listen to me, I probably shouldn't be talking about old girlfriends, isn't it true, Kate, but I was so struck by the coincidence. Now, he said very little about her – isn't that always the way with Kevin? – but sure he was in good form anyway. Will I put a little hot water in the pot? Would you drink another cup, Tom?'

And off she went to the kitchen, leaving the rest of us behind, literally. Now, here was something to think about. Obviously I had no right to be getting on my high horse because Keith had some old girlfriend he'd never told me about. There was the odd dark chapter in my life that I'd never told him about, including the most recent one. We'd had the conversation of the exes, and while mine was highly edited and sanitized, I'd had no idea that his might have been too. To be honest, I wasn't that interested in Keith's old girlfriends. I believed him when he said that nobody had meant anything to him before me, that they were pale imitations, forgettable, inconsequential, but I didn't believe he would actually forget about one of them, not about *his* Jacqueline. I looked at Keith, straight on, believing my face to bear the signs of a mild, bemused curiosity. Without catching my eye, he grabbed my hand, prised a piece of cake from it and whisked me out of the door.

'We're just going for a walk,' he hollered. 'Back in a while.'

Mmm, now what did my Keith have to say for himself?

If he was feeling guilt or remorse, or whatever one feels in these situations, I didn't want him to feel it for too long. I began in a very airy tone: 'No . . . no . . . You definitely never told me about a Jacqueline. Fancy name, Jacqueline. You don't get that many around Limerick any more . . .'

He stopped us in our tracks – we were only a couple of yards down the road – and pulled me to him so I had to look him in the eye. 'You know there's nothing sinister in this, don't you? I'm not keeping anything terrible from you. She really is just an old girlfriend, no skeletons, no love children, no secret marriage.'

I hadn't thought it might be any of those things and now I was sorry he'd been so quick to put me straight. If I'd known this was the kind of mood he was in, I might have had a little more fun with him. 'Really, Keith? No skeletons, no love children, no secret marriage?'

'Please don't make fun of me. Yeah, when we talked about old relationships, I didn't tell you about Jacqueline. I should have – I'm not even hiding anything, for God's sake. I just didn't feel like talking about her at the time.'

I didn't want to make fun of Keith. And he was only acting weird now because lying, or having lied, or even evading a little of the truth was so alien to him that he didn't know how to handle it.

'Just tell me about her,' I said.

'Well . . .' he paused '. . . I went out with her before you, but we were broken up nearly a year before I met you. We'd been together for about three years –'

'Three years!' I interrupted.

'Please don't interrupt me.'

'OK.'

'We'd been going out about three years and, well, we were naturally drifting towards the inevitable. We were both over thirty, we seemed to be very steady, there was no reason why we wouldn't do what several of our friends had already done – go and get married. But there's why I didn't tell you about her – all around that time, before we broke up, I realized I'd been drifting and that I could continue, very easily, to drift into marriage with her. She was a nice girl, we had loads in common, we had good times together, but I knew, deep down, that I wasn't in love with her. You know? I suddenly thought, Well, this is it. She's the one. This is your life. And I didn't want it. I mean, I'd always been the sort of guy who knew he wanted to get married. I'd never seen the attraction in running around and sleeping with girls all over the place. I suppose it's part of the way I was brought up. That's probably why I let things with Jacqueline drift for so long. But when it came to it, I didn't see myself married to her, for good, because that's what it would have been.'

'Oh!'

'Yeah, and when it came to us talking about exes, I didn't want to remind myself, or admit to myself, how close I had come to something that wasn't right.'

'Was she mad as hell?'

'Ahm, yes. Yes, she was.'

'Do you feel guilty?'

'Well, I know I did the right thing but, yeah, I was guilty of stringing her along, of not knowing my own mind. But as soon as I realized it, there was no way I could continue to go along with it. That would have been worse.'

'Does she hate you?'

'I don't know. She probably did for a while. We had endless sessions of thrashing it all out. It totally wrecked my head. But the bottom line was, she wanted to stay together and I didn't.'

'Right. I had no idea you had it in you.'

'Had what in me?'

'The ability to break up with someone like that. Passion, I suppose. I had no idea you had that kind of passion.'

'Well, I have. I have it for you, Kate. All my passion is for you.'

I was taken aback. In fact, what he had told me was far more shocking than any love children might have been. It wasn't the Keith of my imagination. And it scared me. How wrong was I about him? How well did I know him? I liked to believe that he was partly my own creation, and of course that's not true. He is a man with all that passion I never knew he had.

It's not an easy thing for a man to do – break up with a woman who thinks she has a future with him. Some men won't do it and others do it so unsatisfactorily that the women never recover. Keith, it seems, had done it. Daniel O'Hanlon did it. But not very well. The woman is still in recovery.

Things with Daniel started to go wrong when I stopped believing that it was all a perfectly under-control adult entertainment being mutually enjoyed by two equally under-control adults. Things with Daniel went wrong when I started to believe we had a future together. Paris was the catalyst for everything. We were doomed before we ever got on our separate planes from separate cities in our separate lives. Daniel was already feeling the strain of dividing his life and I was feeling the strain of living half a life. I wanted more and he wanted less. It was that simple. In a perfect world we would have continued to see each other occasionally and passionately. We would have loved being together and we would have had enough in between to love being apart. But the world, as we know, is flawed.

After my high-altitude crisis on that first day of our secret romantic tryst, we did go and get drunk. Or, at least, I did. Daniel's beyond that sort of adolescent behaviour. We holed up in a bar on the Left Bank while I drank very expensively for the rest of the afternoon. I don't remember the details very well (that's one of the nice things alcohol can do for you – spare you the memory of your most embarrassing moments) but the afternoon went along the lines of me telling Daniel how much I loved him and how we could be blissfully happy together if only he'd leave his wife, and him telling me that now was not the time to talk about it and of course he loved me but it wasn't as simple as that. I had become the thing he dreaded – an out-of-control woman who could, at any moment, tip the finely balanced equilibrium of his life. I had transformed myself from an easy-going, self-contained, self-fulfilled libertine to a clingy, hysterical wannabe wife. I had really upset his day.

It was over that afternoon. It was only a matter of time before I realized it and he managed to say it out loud. We didn't have sex again. When I was back home and I was left alone in my flat for the last time, one of the most heartbreaking things was that I couldn't remember the last time we had kissed truly passionately, truly blissfully. One of the things he said to me was that I couldn't have expected more from him. I'd known his situation from the beginning. I must have understood it could never be more than it was. I hadn't expected more: I had discovered more, and discovered that I wanted it.

When we got back to the house Keith's mother had cleared away the afternoon tea-things and was wondering if we'd like a bit of cold meat and salad as there was plenty left over from lunch. We assured her that we were still full of bread-and-butter pudding and Victoria sponge and, anyway, we had to be getting back. I had a suit to iron and Keith needed to check on the house in Clareview. We said our goodbyes and Irene told us again how delighted she was that we were coming to Breda's wedding. Just as we were about to go out of the door Tom got up from his chair and strolled out to the car with us.

'Irene can talk too much at times,' he said, 'but she'd never mean any harm.' He spoke quietly and almost into my ear. His words were meant only for me.

'Oh, I know,' I said. 'There's no bother.'

'No, no bother at all. He's a good lad.' With that he turned and went back into the house.

We drove straight back to Hartstonge Street. Keith wasn't really checking on his house and I certainly wasn't ironing a suit. I felt a casual day coming on – it might only be Monday but my mind was feeling Friday. I'd have to lie low at the back of the office and spend a lot of time in the library. I was getting to the point that I really didn't care any more. I was begining to wonder how far I would push it. Would I risk a big show-down with my boss? Would I risk getting fired? Would I risk liberating myself from a job I hated? Was I capable of doing anything else?

I was thinking back over all the opportunities I had had to get off this ridiculous roller-coaster – I could have changed course in college when I saw how monumentally boring law was. Pride had prevented me. I could have not gone to Blackhall Place – but it seemed like the obvious thing to do once I had a law degree. I could have left the profession after any one of the three times I'd failed my professional exams. Pride had got me again. I could have not gone into the cushy job my dad had lined up for me when I got back from my year and a half of travelling. I could have left that job on any one of the days that followed on which I felt like an incompetent misfit. Yet I was still at the firm of O'Sullivan and Woulfe, feeling ever more incompetent and ever more of a misfit.

My conversation with Mike was the first time I had ever seriously contemplated packing it in. The idea was so huge, so scary, I didn't know if I had the courage to go through with it.

As soon as we got back to the flat I ran a bath, pouring into it half a bottle of something blue and fragrant that Clarins promised would soothe away my troubles. It dawned on me as I sat on the edge of the tub that I didn't have any troubles, yet I couldn't shake off the general malaise that had overtaken me on the drive home. I felt as if I'd been drinking on an empty stomach all afternoon, and now I'd sobered up enough to feel tired, hungry and slightly hung-over. What was my problem? Sure, I'd discovered that Keith had had a long-term relationship he'd never told me about, but it wasn't like he cared anything for that girl, and I still had secrets I hadn't told him about and I didn't think there was anything wrong in that. Sometimes you can hear too much of the truth. If anything, I had discovered another aspect to my boyfriend, which made him even more appealing. So why hadn't it thrilled me to hear my fiancé say that all his passion was for me?

Before I had undressed, Keith came into the bathroom. He said nothing, but pulled me off the bath and began to remove my clothes. One by one, he opened the buttons on my shirt and placed his hand inside my bra. Then, as he unclipped the hooks, he undid the fly of his jeans. With my bra on the floor he placed his other hand under my skirt and removed my underwear. He moved very slowly, yet very deliberately. We were backed up against the sink, our mouths locked together, our bodies hardly moving as he went deeper and deeper. It was one of the sweetest orgasms I had ever had and one of the saddest; Keith had never been more present in my body, or more absent from my mind.

10

There are a small number of days throughout the entire year on which the whole business of waking up can be accomplished truly successfully. They are usually during holidays and sometimes on festive days like Christmas, but very occasionally, for no reason, you wake up in the morning and everything runs perfectly.

I had a Wednesday, towards the middle of July, that started like that. I must have got to bed early the night before because I woke feeling as if every cell had been swept liberally with oxygen, the cobwebs and stale air flushed out. The little alcohol detox I had been giving myself contributed, no doubt, to the effect. Keith was already gone and had left his side of the bed almost as if it hadn't been slept in. It led me to reflect that we hadn't had much sex lately. But I presumed that was part of living together, or living together with my sister in the way, and that it was only temporary. I sat up in bed and drew the curtains to allow the morning light to flood the room. It was still early so there was no need to rush into the shower straight away. I could just *be* for a while.

Part of this sense of calm had to come from the fact that I had given notice at work and it had been accepted with a distinct touch of regret on my boss's part. But he wished me well, said he would be sorry to lose me (I had always brightened up the office, apparently) and assured me he would do anything he could to facilitate my 'change of direction'. It was, as they say, a weight off my mind. And to add to that, I had made several enquiries regarding under-graduate and post-graduate courses. It looked as if I'd have a lot to choose from and I'd be able to start in September. Suddenly waking up was a whole other business.

Thus my morning continued. The water temperature in the shower was perfect (always difficult when the ambient temperature starts to rise), and the new shampoo I was trying out left my hair silky smooth and tangle free as well as sweetly fragrant. As I dressed I contemplated the joy I would soon have in climbing into my jeans whenever I felt like it or going all out in some crazy creation I had put together with Lucy. I might even wear a suit from time to time, just to play a role – it was all in the joy of not having to. What I saw in the mirror that morning was a young woman quite happy with herself. Her navy linen trousers and crisp linen blouse, offset with an ethnic necklace, gave the impression of someone at ease with her life choices. She might be in transition, but she was confident of her new direction. I could smile at myself and feel that, finally, I was taking charge.

My mind was also at ease because I had made an overdue visit to Mum and Dad. Mum greeted me with deserved coolness but Dad was visibly delighted and started bustling about with a wine he had just opened, one of the best white burgundies, he said, that he'd had in years. We sat out on the lawn, which was impeccably trimmed, and after listening to news of the aunts and cousins, I told them about my future career plans.

'Well, dear, that's so unfortunate,' Mum said, 'after all the years you were studying, and you have no idea how much your father and I spent. No idea. I hope no child of yours ever wastes money in the same way. Do you know that your cousin Sheila financed the whole of her college courses?

Every penny? Her parents didn't have to shell out a single *sou*! But she's always been a considerate girl. When she was young she used to come in from school and tell her mother to go and have a lie-down while she put on the dinner. Imagine that! And she was only in primary school! But they've been blessed in all their children. Donny, her eldest, takes them both away to –'

Here, Dad cut her off. 'So,' he said, 'you've finally done it. Well done. It was a brave thing to do. Can't have been easy. You won't regret it.'

'Thank you, Dad. I'm really glad I did it, and if I'd listened to you in the first place I wouldn't have had to. And you, Mum,' I acknowledged.

'Honestly, David, congratulating her when she's throwing up her whole career. And what an age to go back to college! Honestly, in our day you were lucky if you got a job at all, not to mind this business of finding careers that suit you. I suppose you'll have that boy supporting you now.'

'If you mean Keith, Mum, then no. I'll support myself. I'll get a part-time job.'

'Oh, well, do whatever you want to. You always do.' With that she charged back into the house. I knew she wasn't really in a temper. She'd bang about in the kitchen for a while, then reappear with a beautifully made-up tray laden with delightful shop-bought goodies.

'It's a good decision,' Dad said, and when Mum was safely inside the house, he added, 'and you know if you need a little bit of help to get you sorted, you can rely on me.'

'Thanks, Dad. And thanks for the offer, but I'm going to try to do this myself. Oh, Keith won't throw me out if I can't find my half of the mortgage every once in a while. I'm sure it'll be fine.'

'And what does he think of it?' asked Dad.

'Ahm,' I fudged, 'he thinks it's great. He's delighted.'

In fact Keith wasn't one bit pleased. We'd had a huge row about it and for the moment we were refusing to discuss it.

'That's good,' Dad said. 'You need to have your man behind you.'

Mum reappeared presently with said tray, china and a plate of assorted Mr Kiplings. She had brushed her hair and reapplied lipstick. This little ritual helps her composure. 'You're very nearly thirty,' she began. 'At your age I had three children and no career.'

I was about to remind her that she had always said raising children was the most rewarding career a woman could have but I figured that now wasn't the time. I'd have to let her say her piece. After all, I deserved it.

'It's about time you started being responsible. And how long has it taken you to tell us? We haven't seen you out here in over a month. If it wasn't for Marion calling to tell us a bit of news, you might all be dead and we wouldn't know it.'

By 'all', she meant Lucy, Jean and me. Ruth checks in daily.

'Jean used to be much better before she moved in with you. We used to see her and Mike regularly.'

Neither would it have been helpful to point out to Mum that the reason she wasn't seeing so much of Mike and Jean might have been because Jean had walked out on Mike, thus ending their marriage, not because Jean was now living under my roof.

'Well,' I said innocuously, 'Jean might be moving out soon, now that their house is sold.'

'Their house is sold?' she snapped. 'When is anyone going to tell me what's going on in this family? Did you know?' she asked Dad.

'No,' he said wisely, although apparently Mike had asked his advice on a few things regarding the sale.

'Well,' she said, biting into a French fancy, 'I'm glad I have other daughters to rely on to tell me news. Did you know that Ruth's thinking of getting a new kitchen? The one she has was never great – it's too small. And she's so creative in the kitchen, she needs space. She was thinking of knocking through to the dining room and making one big room of it, but it's nice to have a formal dining room. It's so civilized. So now she's thinking of extending out the back. They have plenty of room – it wouldn't take from the patio at all. She was here earlier today, you only just missed her. She was getting ideas from my kitchen. She's going to have an architect draw up proper plans and she was wondering if she should ask Mike or not. She'd like to give him the business but he might be embarrassed. She was wondering what I thought.'

Since she paused here, I figured she was wondering what I thought. Which was that Ruth should have her head flushed down the toilet, getting my mother involved in her shady speculations like that. Yet again, I resisted saying what was on my mind.

'Mum, Mike isn't likely to be embarrassed either by Ruth or her kitchen, no matter how small it is. And he's a fabulous architect, so he doesn't need the business. Tell Ruth to do whatever her conscience tells her is right.'

Mum clearly saw my lack of sympathy for Ruth's dilemma, but she didn't scold me as she might. My mother has more sensitivity than her favourite daughter gives her credit for. 'Oh, yes,' she said, after a long pause in which she refilled our cups and started on her second fancy, 'I knew there was something else.'

'Oh.' Was somebody having new wardrobes fitted?

'Yes,' she said. 'Anna's paying us a visit.'

'Anna?' I said amazed. 'Our Anna in New Zealand?'

'Of course our Anna. She's coming with Tommy and the kids in August. It'll be around the time of your birthday. Won't that be nice?'

I had to agree that it would. I hadn't seen Anna in about four years, and that had been at Ruth's wedding so I'd blocked most of it out. She hadn't had the rest of the family with her, either. Wow! It *would* be nice to see her again.

'Did you know about this?' It was my turn to accuse Dad.

'I knew,' he said, 'but family news is your mother's domain.'

'So when exactly is she coming?' I asked.

'The details aren't clear, but some time in late August. You know the way it is with New Zealand – it's the other side of the world so you're losing days or gaining them, I never know which. But I remember thinking that it would coincide with your birthday so I was thinking of having a party for all the family. Though why I keep having parties for you, I don't know.'

'Oh, Mum, that's a lovely idea,' I responded, genuinely enthused, 'but you know what would make it really special – for Anna, I mean? If you kept it to the immediate family. Just you and Dad and the six of us and the husbands and kids. Any more might be too much for Anna. We never get the chance to have time together, just the six of us – it's always something crazy like a wedding where you never get to talk. What do you think?' I was surprised by my own enthusiasm but I'd meant everything I said.

'Well, actually,' returned Mum, 'that's what I was thinking myself.'

'Oh.'

'Yes. And your father agrees.'

141

'Great, then. That's settled. It'll take the harm out of turning thirty.'

'You don't look thirty,' she said, 'and you certainly don't act it.'

I took this as a compliment but decided not to thank her.

Yes, sometimes it's good to touch base with the family and rekindle a little excitement. Marion would be delighted: Anna and she have always been great friends. I was a little surprised that Mum was throwing me another party, especially after my disappointing news, but I suppose she needed an excuse and nobody else was having a significant birthday any time soon. Nor was I bothered about turning thirty, not really. I was about to be married and I was finally starting to take hold of my 'professional' life. I don't think there's very much grey under the swamp of colour in my hair and my skin seems to be justifying the expensive creams I slather on it. All in all, not too bad for a girl at the beginning of the new millennium.

All these pleasant thoughts were swooshing about in my head as I walked the two blocks to work under a brilliant blue sky lightly studded with high cumulus clouds. I was already thinking about getting something new to wear – I hadn't ventured back into Party Dress Land since my last abortive attempt. Lucy might come with me: we could make a day of it.

And so my morning continued. Now that I was leaving, I was finding work pleasant. I even seemed to be manoeuvring my desk-top with improved efficiency and there was a feeling in the air that I might, at any moment, do or say something very clever indeed. However, by lunchtime I needed to get out of there.

One of the things I'd always enjoyed about my job was lunchtime. Because so many of my colleagues' lunches involved taking clients to restaurants, there was a long-lunch tradition. I wasn't usually involved in the client lunches so often I'd slip out to the local Spar, buy a sandwich and stroll up to the People's Park. It was one of my favourite things – I loved to sit there in the middle of all that lush greenery, nodding conspiratorially to refugees from other offices. It was a great way to decompress after a stressful morning.

I had just reached the top of the queue with my Hawaiian chicken sandwich and a bottle of water when I noticed that Mike was at the top of the adjacent queue.

'Hey,' he said. 'Fancy meeting you here.'

'Hi,' I said. 'I thought you had your lunch specially prepared by a team of imported chefs.'

'Oh, I give them the day off on Wednesdays.' He paused. 'Are you in a hurry to get back?'

'Me? No way. I was on my way up to the park. Care to join me? Or are you in a hurry?' I added quickly.

'No, no,' he said. 'I was going to take a leisurely lunch at home. Would you . . . like to stroll up and see the house? It's still a bit of a mess but . . .'

I'd heard from Jean that he'd bought a small mews house on Charlotte Avenue just off O'Connell Avenue, only up the road from me. I'd been dying to call but somehow it didn't seem appropriate with Jean living at my flat.

'I'd love to,' I said. 'I've heard loads about it.'

'Well, great then, let's go.'

We walked up the remainder of O'Connell Street, through The Crescent and on into O'Connell Avenue. He made a point of walking on the outside and each time we crossed the road his hand, unconsciously, I presume, went up as if to prevent me running straight across. I am the world's worst jay-walker; I'd forgotten what it's like to stop and wait.

His house was on a cul-de-sac just off the main avenue. It was at the back of the row where you'd hardly see it from the road. A wrought-iron railing and gate enclosed a small but neat front garden and a winding paved path led to his front door.

'Welcome to my new abode,' he said, somewhat ornately, as he opened the gate for me. 'Don't be too harsh – it's a work in progress.'

'You're forgetting who you're talking to,' I said. 'You've seen my flat. I've been in it for years and it's still the same as it was when I moved in.'

He was wearing khaki-coloured Wranglers, brown Dr Martens shoes and a loose-fitting off-white shirt. He was the essence of casual cool, but as he fumbled for his keys and struggled with the lock, he seemed nervous.

'*Voilà!*' he said, and waved an arm while letting me step into the house before him. It certainly was a work in progress: there were beams sticking out of places they couldn't possibly be meant to stick out from; there was a workman's bench covered with tools; plastic sheeting was strewn about the floor, which was being ripped apart to reveal what seemed to be original wooden boards. The place was a building site. The whole of the downstairs had been made open-plan and the remains of the walls that had been torn down lay everywhere. I couldn't imagine how he was living in this mess.

'You were going to have a leisurely lunch here?' I asked, in not-quite-mock amazement.

'Oh, it's not that bad,' he said, 'or maybe I've got used to it. Upstairs is a lot better. I'm kind of living in one room at the moment.'

'Can you even make me a cup of coffee?' I asked, pretending to be appalled.

'As a matter of fact, madam,' he said, 'I can make you a very fine cup of coffee with my very excellent coffee machine, which is plugged in upstairs. Follow me.'

He led the way up a flight of stairs that definitely wasn't fastened to anything.

'Hold on tight,' he said, 'but not too tight, or you'll make the whole thing sway.'

He held out a hand and guided me up.

Things were a little better up here. It had originally been a three-bedroom house with a bathroom downstairs but he had already converted one of the bedrooms into a sizeable bathroom and in one of the others, as he'd said, he had set up camp. There was a mattress on the floor, surrounded by a desk lamp, a pile of books, a small stereo, and assorted bags that seemed to contain his clothes. How could he emerge from this chaos so well put together? The coffee machine was on the floor by the window, along with a toaster, a kettle and a miniature microwave. A portable TV stood on a shaky-looking chair.

'You see?' he said. 'All a man could want in one small room.'

I suspected he was enjoying living like this. It was probably a nice change from a house that had more rooms than its occupants could use.

'Wow!' I said. 'Very cosy. I don't know why you're bothering to do up downstairs – you need never leave this room. Everybody should live this way.'

'You practically do!' He was grinning broadly. 'Don't think it hasn't been noticed, the way you gather your bits round you on the couch and hibernate for the winter.'

'That's not true,' I retorted. 'I only do that when it gets very cold, or at Christmas. My flat can get *very* cold.'

'Oh, I know, and you can get very comfortable in your

pyjamas and sleeping-bag with your videos. *The Princess Bride?*
Willy Wonka?'

He was really laughing now.

'Hey!' I said. 'I came here to laugh at your house, not the other way round. How did you know about *Willy Wonka* anyway?'

'Oh, you know me, I notice everything.'

'You're a bollocks,' I said.

'Why, thank you. Does that mean you don't want to see the rest?'

'What? There's a rest? How big is this house?'

'Oh, not very,' he said, getting up off the floor where he had been putting on the coffee. 'That's why I decided to convert the attic.'

'Mmm,' I said. 'An attic conversion. Ruth would be well impressed. She's doing her kitchen. Expect a garbled phone call from her one of these days. Or from my mother. Oh, by the way, Anna's coming home in August.'

'Anna? It's been a while.'

'Yeah. Mum's throwing a party for her. Well, for me as well. I don't know if you keep abreast of these things,' I added, rather sheepishly, 'but I have a slightly significant birthday coming up soon.'

'Yes, indeed I keep abreast. I know exactly what age you are. It's the end of everything, you know. It's as well someone's marrying you.'

'Bollocks!' I said. 'But, seriously, will you come to the party? Or would it be, as Ruth might suggest, *embarrassing* for you?'

'No, indeed,' he said. 'For two sisters I can forgo the embarrassment of seeing one sister.' He was still smiling, but not as broadly.

'So, what about this attic?' I said, getting up. 'How does a body get up there?'

'This way, madam.'

He led the way past the other bedroom, which looked like it contained every other thing he owned, and pointed out a hole – that was all you could call it – in the ceiling. He positioned a ladder and told me to climb up.

'I have two options,' he was saying, as he followed my timid steps. 'I can leave it as it is or I was considering putting in a spiral staircase. What do you think?'

'Oh, my God,' I said, nearly falling off the ladder. 'You *have* to put in the spiral staircase. It's always been my fantasy to have a spiral staircase. And it would be much safer than this ladder.' I turned to say this, and he had to put his two hands on my hips to steady us both.

'Whoa there,' he said. 'The spiral staircase it is, then.'

The attic was amazing. Clearly he had started at the top of the house and was working his way down. I had expected a poky, dark little room, but the first thing that struck me was the light. He had replaced both the front and the back gable ends with glass that afforded incredible views over the street on one side, and what looked like a miniature forest on the other. The room was positively alive with light.

'Oh, my God,' I said. 'This is incredible! I'd live here for ever!'

'Glad you like it,' he said, emerging behind me. 'It did take some structural skulduggery, but I think it'll hold.'

He was obviously very pleased with it. There was little else in the room apart from the remains of the structural work so there was no clue as to what he might use it for. 'I was thinking I might make it a workroom,' he said, reading my mind. 'The light is great and it would be very peaceful.'

'Mm,' I said, rushing from one window to the other, 'of course. But you know what I'd do with it?' I was beginning to lose the run of myself. 'I'd use it as my bedroom. Imagine waking up to that view, or going to sleep with it. You'd never have to close your curtains – you wouldn't even need curtains.'

He nodded and said that was something he hadn't thought of.

'You've done an amazing amount of work,' I said. 'It must have taken ages.'

'It was a good distraction,' he said. 'And I do have a few contacts in the building trade.'

Perhaps it was the altitude, but I was feeling a little light-headed. I decided to change the subject.

'I've been a little busy myself,' I said, moving away from the intoxicating windows.

'Oh?'

'Yes,' I said. 'I've quit my job.'

'You have?' He seemed amazed.

'Yes, I've actually done it.'

He came over to me and wrapped his arms round me. 'I am absolutely delighted.'

I was rather taken aback by the warmth of his response.

'It's a brave thing you've done,' he said, placing me in front of him and fixing my eyes with his. 'There's hope for you yet.'

'Hey, what do you mean by that?' I was glad to get a note of mock-anger into my voice because I'd been afraid it was starting to wobble.

'I'm so thrilled you did it. I didn't know you had it in you.'

'I didn't either. But I guess I do now. It was good talking to you that day – it really helped.'

'I only told you what you knew already.'

'Yes. But it was good to hear it.'

'Well, I'm glad if I helped you out. It can be hard some-times to find what you really want.'

There was silence for a moment until he said, 'Come on, let's take the coffee outside and I'll show you the garden.'

The garden was a gem. It wasn't very big but it didn't need to be. There was an old wrought-iron table and chairs on a small patio that opened from the house by what would eventually be french windows, and the rest was grass with neat little flowerbeds round the edges. Trees – birch, elm, beech – surrounded it, which gave the space complete privacy. They were on the other side of an old creeper-covered wall so they gave shelter without smothering the garden. From any angle, you would have had no idea that you were in the middle of the city.

I sat down while he went to get the coffee.

When he came back he put prospectuses for the local colleges on the table in front of me. 'I thought these might be useful. There's a lot to choose from. I was surprised by how many courses they're running now.'

'Thank you,' was all I could muster, as I leafed through the glossy pages.

'What does Keith think of your plans?'

'Oh, ahm . . . he's thrilled.'

Keith and I still hadn't discussed it any further. My plans had become a rather large elephant in my compact little flat.

'It's all go, then.'

'Yeah, all go.'

We had been silent for some time when I became aware of him placing his cup on the table.

'I've missed this,' he said. 'I've missed our chats.'

'Oh, me, too,' I blurted out. 'I was afraid that, with Jean living at my place, you wouldn't feel comfortable calling and I wasn't sure if I could come and see you. Jean and I are getting on so well now and I suppose I didn't want to seem disloyal. It's all a bit silly, really.'

149

He was smiling again, but this time there was a slight quiver at the edge of his mouth, almost as if he wasn't sure he should be smiling.

'It *is* a bit silly,' he said, 'but there's no reason why we can't be friends. I've known you all a long time, and as long as Jean and I can keep it civil, there shouldn't be a problem.'

'No,' I said, ridiculously delighted. 'You know she's seeing someone?' Jean's boyfriend of nearly two weeks wasn't a secret but the minute I'd said it I knew I shouldn't have.

'She told me. She asked if I minded. I said I didn't.'

'Really?'

'Yes. Why would I? It was why she left.'

'But you really don't mind?'

'No.'

'Are you seeing anybody?' I didn't know where the question came from.

'No, Kate, I'm not.'

'I'm sorry. I don't know what made me ask that.'

'It's OK.' He took my hand in his. 'This is probably hard for you, seeing a marriage break down as you're about to get married. But just because it didn't work out for us, it doesn't mean it won't for you and Keith. Trust yourself.'

'OK.'

'Forget what other people think you should do, forget even what you think you should do. Trust your instincts.'

'OK.'

Later, as I was walking home from work a text came in from Keith suggesting we meet for an early dinner in La Cuchera, as he had to go back to work again. His new product was misbehaving and he had to go and give it a good talking-to. I texted back that that would be fine – I'd meet him there at six, which would give me the opportunity to have a soak in the bath and either think or not think about things. I seemed to be doing that a lot lately – desperately trying to soothe my permanently throbbing head. Soon everything would calm down and life would be simple again. But when I tried to remember the last time life had been simple I drew a blank. I did recall a pleasant afternoon playing hooky from school some time in Fifth Year – but surely there had been something since then?

After my bath I decided to dress up. I'd make one more attempt to get Keith to understand what I was doing and I figured I might as well use my full armoury. It was true that he'd been working very hard lately, but I felt he was being particularly obtuse about my decision to give up the law. I hadn't been so happy about anything in years and I didn't see why he couldn't share in that.

I put on a new pair of white cotton cropped trousers and a fancy low-necked top to gizz them up. I played about with my hair and managed to get it to do something it hadn't done before, which was either a great success or a ridiculous mess. I had got a little colour from my misspent afternoon so I enhanced it with a touch of bronzer. I must have looked all right because as he watched me walk through the door of La Cuchera and saunter over to his table, he emitted an audible sigh of approval. 'You look great!'

'Thank you.'

'I'm a mess. I came straight from work.'

'No, baby, you look fine.' In fact, he looked very tired.

'But you really look great. You do know I have to go back to work?'

'I just thought we'd make the most of the time we have.'

'Great!'

I sat down and perused the menu. He did the same, but I don't believe either of us was reading a thing. 'I want to talk to you, Keith.'

'I know. Me too.'

'I want you to be happy for me. This is a really big deal, you know.'

'That's why I thought you might discuss it with me first.'

'I tried to.'

'After you'd handed in your notice.'

'I had to just go and do it before I lost my nerve.'

He was shaking his head.

'You know how much I hated working there,' I continued. 'You know how wrong it was for me. I should never have been a solicitor.'

'I always thought you were exaggerating.'

'Well, I wasn't.'

'And this is it? You've packed in your job . . . and you're going to college?'

'Yes.'

'Kate, I'm sorry if I don't seem supportive but I wish you hadn't excluded me.'

'I didn't exclude you. I told you straight away.'

'We're engaged, Kate, we're starting a life together. We should talk about things like this.'

'I know,' I said. 'I'm sorry, but this is something I started on my own and I have to fix it on my own. You've no idea how miserable I was. And, anyway, this isn't going to affect anything. We're still getting married.'

'It's such a big decision.'

'Not really. Loads of people change direction in their careers.' I took his hands in mine. 'I feel really good about this. It's like a weight's been lifted from my shoulders. Now we can move on. We can set a date for the wedding. We can go and look at houses.'

I wasn't getting any reaction.

'I suppose,' I added, 'I should have made it clear to you just how miserable I was.'

'Yes, you should.'

'You see, I think you think I was more of a solicitor than I really was. Ask anybody else who knows me and they'll tell you I was really bad at it. Ask my boss!'

'Look, Kate, if this is what you want then of course I'm behind you, one hundred per cent. But if it's just a whim . . .'

'Oh, my God, Keith, this is *not* a whim! This is the biggest thing I've done in my life and I'm actually very proud of it. I'm —'

'OK, OK,' he said, reaching out to take back my hands. 'It's OK. I'm with you, I support you . . . I'm happy for you.'

'Thanks. And I am capable of doing things on a whim but, believe me, this isn't one.'

'I do believe you. Now, let's eat. I have an appetite after all that.'

I felt a lot better now that it was over, but I couldn't help thinking it shouldn't have been so hard. I started to chat about the courses available (I'd taken a quick look at the prospectuses Mike had given me) – there was one in Arts Management and another in Human Resources that looked interesting. In the meantime I was going to check out what kind of low-input part-time job I could get. I was even thinking of doing a bit of waitressing – that was how I'd got by in my former student days and I'd always enjoyed it. In fact, I'd enjoyed it far more than anything else at college. Keith listened attentively, as he always does, but I felt he wasn't heeding anything I was saying. I let it go. We'd said enough for one day.

He had been busy looking at houses again. He told me

about several that had just come on to the market, all within walking distance of town. Two were close to Mom and Dad's, so that and their high price-tags put them in the doubtful box, but there were another two on the South Circular Road that seemed promising.

'They're also quite pricey,' Keith said, getting into his stride, 'but if we sell both our places we will have a lot of leeway.'

I still wasn't sure I wanted to sell my flat, but this wasn't the time to bring it up. Speaking of houses, I told him about Mike's new place and the work he was doing on it, but he didn't seem very interested. I owed him a trip out into the field, a trudge through what the property market had to offer, so we consulted our diaries (mine was blank) and made appointments to view.

It was a pity he had to rush away again so soon. My pizza was delicious and the half-bottle of Valpolicella we'd ordered (I'd drunk most of it) had put me in the mood for another. But he had to go. He promised he'd make it as short as possible and I promised I'd wait up.

Once I was back in the flat, alone again – Jean was out with her new man – I decided to reward myself with a little glass of a powerful Shiraz she had left lying around. After all, it had been a very good day and I was, on the whole, behaving very well. Then I treated myself to a second little glass and so, by the time the buzzer rang some time later but nobody was there, I wasn't bothered. And when my doorbell rang again a little later, I didn't think it strange at all. However, when I opened the door to Daniel O'Hanlon, you could have knocked me down with a feather.

I I

I hadn't been expecting it. If pressed, I'd have said that I never expected to see him again. He'd been wiped from the universe, and while I might bump into his wife in the odd department-store changing room, he had ceased to exist. Yet there he was, standing in the doorway to my flat, one hand resting on the upper jamb, the rest of him sort of hanging in the door frame. If I'd had time to register who he was I would have closed the door. I wasn't interested in starting all that again, but he had stepped inside before I was fully aware that he, Daniel O'Hanlon, was standing in front of me.

Then I tried to get out of the door myself, but that wasn't going to happen. He shut it and wedged himself in front of it to prevent me going anywhere. He looked wretched. His suit was crumpled, as if he had been wearing it for several days without a pressing. His shirt was wide open at the collar and seemed grimy. His skin was greasy, his hair matted and thin. It took me only seconds to get a picture of a man under duress. I was trying to push past him but he grabbed my arms and pinned me against the wall. Immediately he let go, holding up his hands in surrender.

'Sorry, sorry,' he gasped. 'I just want to talk for a minute. Just a minute. Then I'll go, I promise.'

'I don't want to talk to you,' I said firmly.

'Just for a minute.'

'I have nothing to say to you.'

'I needed to see you,' he said. 'I've missed you.'

'Please go, Daniel.'

'Just hear me out.'

'I'm not interested in anything you have to say. I'm engaged now. I'm getting married.'

'I've missed you so much. You're beautiful, Kate.'

He made a pathetic picture: a middle-aged man in need of a wash and a shave, spouting garbage to a woman who had no use for him.

'Daniel, there's nothing to say. We're finished. We were finished that day when you dumped me. So turn round and get out of here, or I'm calling the police.'

'I love you, Kate.'

'I'm calling the police. And your wife. I'm calling your wife to come and take you away.'

'My marriage is over, Kate. It was over from the day I met you.'

'That's bollocks and you know it. Go on home to your wife,' I shouted. 'Go on home to your wife and your new baby.'

'It's over, Kate. It's you I love. It's always been you.'

'Bollocks.'

'Don't say that. It's true. I love you. I'm leaving her.'

'Look, Daniel, you can leave your wife all you like, just not on my account.'

'We can have a life together, Kate. I should never have pushed you away.'

'You didn't push me away,' I almost spat at him. 'You dumped me in no uncertain terms. You dropped me, just like you picked me up in the first place, on a whim. I don't know what's going on with you at the moment, maybe you're not getting enough sleep, but I'm wide awake, and I'm more than capable of telling you to fuck off out of here or I really will call the police and your wife.' I felt weak by the end of my tirade.

'Come on, Kate.'

'No!'

'Come on.'

'Look, Daniel,' I said, finding a calm note, 'I've moved on. I'm getting married soon. I –'

'OK, OK,' he said. 'I'll go. But you have to give me one thing. You have to admit that what we had was good.'

'I'll admit nothing.'

'Oh, come on. I bet what you have now with this guy isn't a patch on what we had. You don't often find passion like that, Kate.'

'It wasn't passion, it was lust.'

'It was love, Kate. When it was good, it was love. You know it was.'

'Daniel, please, go away.'

'Kate, don't settle for second best.'

'It is not second best!' I exploded. I was nearly choking I was so angry. 'What I have with Keith is a million times better than – than our sordid affair.'

'I don't believe you.'

'Believe me.'

'OK. Whatever you say. But believe me when I say I still love you. That I still want you.'

'I don't care. I don't feel anything for you and I'm amazed I ever did. Now will you please get out of my house?'

'All right, I'm going.' He began to walk away, then added, 'You know where I am.'

He went slowly down the stairs, looking back one more time before he disappeared round the corner.

I watched him go, then closed the door and turned the lock. I was shattered. I reached for one more glass of wine, but even the smell of it made my stomach heave. I dashed into the bathroom and vomited. It was pure revulsion. I crawled out of the bathroom and straight into bed.

But, of course, I couldn't sleep. How could I after what had happened? My head was pounding, my hands were trembling, my very core was aching. I still couldn't quite believe that he had really been here, that Daniel O'Hanlon had come back into my life and apparently wanted me back in his. Yet the most surprising thing was how much I had hated the sight of him. Not for one second did I see the man standing in my doorway as anything other than a very old, very sorry mistake. I had loved him once, or thought I had. Now, there was nothing of that and I was still too angry to work out what had been left behind.

How dare he come here and think I'd want him back? How dare he tell me that what we had was special when it was only more of the same story that suave older men and foolish younger women had been playing over and over since time began? And how dare he presume to comment on what Keith and I had, let alone criticize it?

Whenever I've felt strong enough, I've wondered how I got to be in that position with Daniel – how I went from being happily in control and at ease with our scenario to a blubbering mess that couldn't have all the things she thought she didn't want. Somewhere along the line my expectations changed. In the beginning I had everything I desired. He was good-looking (the word 'dashing', however ridiculous, always seems apt); he was successful (at the very thing I was failing at); he was charming; he was passionate, although sex with him was probably never as good as I thought it was but fuelled by the most powerful thing about him – that he was forbidden. It must be the simplest and most potent aphrodisiac, but I never thought I was simple enough to be fooled by it. I used to congratulate myself on having escaped the boring norms of everyone around me. They might do the conventional thing, they might perpetuate their bourgeois existence, but not me. I would be different. I wasn't afraid to live on the edge.

But that wasn't the reality at all. The reality was that I spent nearly a year of my life in hiding. Hiding from my family, hiding from my friends, hiding from myself. When I look back on it I seem pathetic. I don't know if the worst part was my arrogance in thinking I was so different from everyone else, or my weakness in failing to grasp that what I was doing was wrong in so many ways. It doesn't matter. What matters is that it is over.

And I had escaped. Into a safe, stable relationship with a man who would look after me and never hurt me.

And I had spent the evening arguing with him. Keith was right: I should have discussed leaving work with him. I wasn't treating him as he deserved by carrying on as if his opinion didn't matter. And no wonder he had concerns, given the way I'd presented him with a *fait accompli*. I could be flighty and selfish and unthinking, and Keith deserved better. He deserved a wife as committed as he was.

So, there and then I resolved to stop mucking around and just get on with it. What was my problem? I was about to get married. I was about to embark on the next phase of my life with the man I loved. I was lucky to have so much.

By the time he came home that night I had been asleep for a few hours but I woke as he was getting into bed. He was big and safe beside me. He was everything I wanted.

The following morning I woke when he did. He had to be in work for eight so I usually just rolled over when the alarm went off. But that morning I wanted to get up with him, make him coffee, see him out the door.

159

'What's up with you this morning?' he asked. 'Usually a grunt is the most I can hope for at this hour.'

'Nothing. I'm just happy.' He looked puzzled so I added, 'You don't have to worry about me, you know. I'm not as dumb as I look.'

'Don't play that game, Kate, it doesn't suit you.'

'What do you mean?' I'd been quite pleased with myself and my airy tone.

'You know.'

'What?'

'Kate, you're not dumb at all but sometimes you'll happily play the fool. I don't like it.'

I was more than a little put out. That was not how I'd intended the morning to go. 'I only meant,' I said, 'that you don't have to worry about me. I love you. Everything will be fine. Trust me.'

He softened. 'OK.'

'Anyway,' I said, 'I wanted to check with you about the house appointments today.'

'The first one's at four o'clock. I should be able to get away early.'

'Will I meet you there? I have the address so I know exactly where the house is.'

'OK. I'll ring you if there's any change.'

Maybe it was because I didn't usually have conversations with Keith at this hour of the morning but he definitely sounded different. 'Keith?'

'Mmm . . .'

'Are you OK?'

'What?'

'Are you OK? You seem very distant.'

'No, I'm fine. I'm just tired. I'm seeing a bit too much of work, these days. That's all.'

'We could do with getting away,' I said, the idea suddenly popping into my head. 'What about next weekend? There's nothing else on, is there?'

'No, but don't make any plans yet. I'll know better at the end of the week how work is fixed.'

'OK.'

'It's just a busy time, Kate. It'll be over soon.'

He kissed me moderately warmly on the lips and then he was out of the door before I even had a chance to put the kettle on.

Since I was up I used the time to ring Mum and ask her if we could call over that evening. I wanted to pick a date for the wedding and there was no point in getting the calendar out without her approval. She said she'd love to see us as long as we didn't mind having salad for dinner – they were on a health regime. Once that was sorted I made coffee for Jean, who was in need of something to kick-start her day, but she was out the door before I had a chance to tell her about the previous evening. As I left the flat in my neat little pinstripe, having breakfasted on bran flakes, I determined to be sensible and efficient. I needed to be. I had a wedding to plan, after all.

Our house viewing didn't go as well as I'd hoped. I thought one house was great but Keith preferred the other. The one I liked was a real fixer-upper. An old couple had been living there for nearly fifty years and nothing much had changed in that time. The potential was obvious, though. Structurally, the house seemed sound but it would benefit by breaking a few walls here and there. Of course, absolutely everything would have to be stripped out – wallpaper, car-pets, shelving, kitchen and bathroom units – but given the house's great location and perfect situation at the end of a row of similar red-brick Victorian villas with a fabulous walled-in garden at the back, it seemed perfect to me. Keith couldn't see the point of bringing all that work on ourselves when we could buy a house that was ready to move into.

'But we want to put our mark on the house, don't we?' I implored. 'Otherwise we might as well stick with what we have. I thought that was what you wanted.'

'It is, but that doesn't mean we have to go into the demolition business to do it.'

I hate it when he's sarcastic.

The house he preferred had been built in the last twenty years and while it was perfectly nice I didn't get any feel from it. He said we could make a 'feel' in the way we painted it and filled it with our things, but I wasn't as excited by a little painting job as by the prospect of totally overhauling the other house.

'But, Kate, neither of us knows anything about that kind of thing.'

'We could learn.'

'It's very time-consuming and it can work out expensive.'

'We're not in a major hurry and the asking price is much lower than the other one.'

'It would want to be.'

We agreed to think about it and maybe come back and see them again later in the week. The locations, on the South Circular Road, were ideal, and even though they were expensive we knew we could probably manage it. I asked Keith if he was worried about meeting the mortgage if I wasn't bringing in that much money and he said, no, absolutely not, he wasn't worried about that at all. I had to take him at his word.

Next stop Sycamore Lodge.

Mum and Dad were out in the garden: she was reading and he was tidying some flowerbeds. They looked very companionable, the two of them, the perfect picture of old married contentment. In truth, they'd just had a row and had come into the garden to cool off. Mum hates reading out of doors: the glare strains her eyes and she won't wear sunglasses because she thinks they're common.

'Hello, there,' we greeted Mum in unison.

'Oh, hello, dears,' she said, squinting at us. 'Is it that time already?'

'It's nearly quarter past,' I said. 'We got held up arguing over the houses.'

'Oh, well, your father just keeps on working. He works all day and then he comes home and starts working again. I have absolutely no life . . . Oh, sorry, Keith, dear, you don't want to be listening to my woes. So, you were arguing over the houses? Kate needs to be told what's what, Keith. She's always being awkward for the sake of it.'

'Oh, Mrs Delahunty,' Keith can never get up the nerve to call my mother by her Christian name, no matter how much she tells him to, 'we have to argue. It's the only way we know what we want.'

'Don't be silly, Keith. You know best in these things.'

'Mum!'

It never ceases to amaze me how she can come out of a row with Dad about how nobody listens to her and nobody cares what she thinks to tell another man to do exactly the same thing to her daughter.

Keith could sense the temperature rising so he admired the garden. Dad did the work but Mum was proud of it too. She just wished the work had been done by a gardener.

'Both of the houses we looked at had nice gardens,' Keith said. 'I could really see myself doing something with them. I must get a few pointers from Mr Delahunty on the best way to start.'

163

'Oh, David will know what to do.'

At this point Dad joined us and took Keith off to show him something he had done with a creeping rose that was quite spectacular. Dad was fond of Keith; I think he found his company soothing.

'Lucy was here the other day,' Mum said, as soon as they were out of earshot. 'She brought a friend with her.'

'Oh?'

'Yes, a very nice girl. Iris – Iris Considine. I think I knew her mother at one time. They used to live near us in Ballykeefe. She was a lovely girl, very nice manners.'

'Oh, Iris . . .'

'It was nice of Lucy to bring her. I don't know why you all stopped bringing your friends round.'

'So,' I asked, all innocence, 'what was she like?'

'Iris? I told you, a lovely girl.'

'Right. Did Lucy have any news?'

'She's worse than you – she never has any news. But she was looking well. I worry about her sometimes.'

'Oh, Lucy's fine, Mum. She can take care of herself.'

'It's not a question of that, it's more . . . Well, I never know if Lucy's happy. Out of all of you, she's the hardest one to read.'

'Oh.' Had I misjudged my mother? Was she really taking that much notice? 'Mum,' I said, after a while, 'Keith and I came over to talk about dates for the wedding. We wanted to make sure we didn't clash with anything else that was going on.'

I was amazed by my own consideration, but in fact I was just eager to start talking about the wedding. When I'd mentioned the idea to Keith he was decidedly less excited than I'd thought he would be. 'What's the matter?' I had asked. 'I thought you were dying to get this sorted.'

'I am,' he said, 'but I have a lot on my mind at the moment with work. I'd rather think about it when I'm less hassled. Why don't you have a chat with your mother? We can go from there.' I had agreed, but I wasn't happy about it.

Mum, meanwhile, had loads to say on the matter.

'Well, I presume you're thinking about next summer. I don't agree with winter weddings, not when people have to travel. Summer is the time to get married. Now, June can be lovely, but the weather's dicey and, besides, your father's always busy in June. July, I like, but you have a cousin getting married next July. Then August can seem a long time to wait once the summer arrives but it . . .' She wittered on and on with her non-objections to all the possible times for getting married.

Maybe Keith was right and this wasn't a good time to talk about it. I changed the subject and enquired after the rest of the family, which I dread doing because you never know where it will lead. But it seemed everyone was doing well at the moment; no aunt was having a menopausal crisis, no cousin had been caught doing anything newsworthy, no uncle had done something terrible to an aunt.

The news of Anna and her trip was positive and Mum had been planning the party. She was going out on an optimistic limb, she said, and had decided to have it outside. She was hiring a marquee and borrowing a barbecue from Marion and Nick. She already had outside lights from last Christmas (Mike had set them up) and she was going to invest in a couple of those patio gas heaters that everybody was talking about. She was as animated as I'd seen her in a long time.

When Dad and Keith joined us, after an extensive tour of the garden, I could see that Dad was tired. It reminded me to ask them, tentatively (they both hate getting bulldozed into anything), if they'd thought about a holiday this year. They spoke together, almost as if they'd prepared speeches. Mum's excuse was Anna coming home and the planning that needed to be done for her visit, and Dad went on about holidays being more stressful than staying at home. I gave up and suggested they think about it again in September when everything would have quietened down. We went inside, where an elaborate table was laid with salad for three and steak for one.

That evening we were silent on the way home; perhaps I should have been more concerned that Keith wasn't as enthusiastic as I'd expected, but I was preoccupied. I'd convinced myself that I was over Daniel's reappearance, but I couldn't stop thinking about him. About him and us and Keith and me and what it all meant. I was over Daniel, of that much I was sure. I regretted ever having got involved with him. I regretted the pain it had caused his family but mainly I regretted the pain it had caused me. Then, for the first time, I wondered if my relationship with Keith was built on running away from Daniel. After all, they were the polar opposites of each other. Daniel was exciting, dangerous, callous and possibly amoral, while Keith was safe, solid, loving and profoundly moral. Having played the *femme fatale* with one man, was I now merely playing a different game with the other? It had been so easy to run from Daniel, and the memory of all I was (and was not) with him, to the security of a man who would make me a better person if I just breathed the same air he did. And, yes, I did love him – I couldn't be planning to marry him if I didn't love him. But did I love him more for what he could be for me than for what he was himself?

And why, after all I had told myself, was I still unable to shake certain thoughts (terrible, terrifying, irresistible thoughts) from my mind?

12

The following Saturday I had a lunch date with Colette. We hadn't seen each other in ages but we could go for years without and then, as they say, pick up where we left off. Yet meeting her now, after only a couple of months, I couldn't remember where we had left off. I couldn't remember what I had told her and what I was keeping to myself. It felt odd and not very pleasant because I was used to being open with her.

We met in Poons, the new rooftop restaurant on top of Limerick's oldest department store. It was large, white and airy and made me think of places like Harvey Nichols and Harrods (especially when I looked at the prices). She still looked wonderful. If that was what having kids and running a household did for you, I might just sign up some day. In fact, part of our lunch date was to include a trip to the beauty parlour, which Colette does regularly, for a facial and a massage.

'Utterly inessential,' she says, 'but absolutely necessary.'

Whenever she has a day out, she reverts right back to the Colette I knew as a teenager. I don't know if it's an unconscious loosening of her present life as soon as she's away from it, or something she does especially for me so I won't be bored by the things I don't have. Either way, it means I love being in her company.

'So,' she began, as we took our seats by a breathtaking view of the Shannon, 'what's all this I've been hearing about your wayward sisters leaving their husbands and becoming lesbians?' In fairness, the texts I'd been sending her in an attempt to maintain contact must have been tantalizing.

'Oh, you know, run-of-the-mill stuff for my family,' I said.

'Go on, give me details. Jean left Mike. How could she do that? Mike's gorgeous. I used to have a crush on him at one time.'

'Did you really?' I said quickly. 'When?'

'Oh, for ever ago. When we were kids. But go on . . .'

'Well, I've told you most of it. She wants to go it alone. She . . .' And I proceeded to tell Colette everything as I had become aware of it, from dealing with a devastated Mike to his and Jean's now, seemingly, amicable separation. It didn't seem all that sensational in the retelling.

'And it's for good, no trials or anything?'

'Oh, it's for good. The house is sold and Mike has already bought a new one. I don't think Jean could cope with a house purchase at the moment. She's happy staying with me and I like having her around. That's something else new – we're the best of friends now.'

'And you two used to hate each other.' She paused a while. 'I always did think it was strange they never had kids – not because I have them but, you know, most couples do, eventually, if they can.'

'Yeah, but I believe her when she says she never wants children. I mean, if you were going to have a baby with anyone, wouldn't you have one with Mike?'

'Yes! Apart from the obvious good genes and that he'd be an absolutely brilliant father, you wouldn't have to lift a finger. He'd be the kind of guy who'd do the night feeds and the sterilizing and the nappy changes . . .'

'All the burping and mopping up . . .'

'All the bathing and powdering . . .'

169

'He'd even breastfeed if he could . . .'

We were laughing wildly now. That's another great thing about Colette – she's as straight as can be most of the time but she has a great quirky side too.

'I still can't get over it,' she went on. 'I mean, I know it's nothing new or anything – I hear about a couple breaking up every day – but I never expected it to be them. I always thought of them as one of those couples who seem to have nothing in common yet they're devoted to each other. Whatever brought them together in the first place would last for ever. You know what I mean?'

'Yeah. I always thought something like that about them too.'

'So he's doing well, then?' she asked. 'Any new women on the scene?'

'Don't appear to be.'

'He's a great catch. I'm almost sorry I'm happily married.'

'Yeah . . .'

'And Lucy? She's a dark one. When did all of this come about?'

I could tell that Colette was trying not to appear too gossipy but she couldn't help it. Unlike the break-up, going gay was not something she heard about in her circle every other day.

'Lucy is so happy with herself, these days. I mean I agree with you, she took her time, but I dare say it's not the same for everyone. Some people know all their lives that they're gay, others, obviously, realize slowly. I was talking to her only last night and she was telling me more about this woman who sort of helped her along the way. Initially she said she didn't think it was any more than a very good friendship. She thought of Iris as a mentor, but that's all changed now and they're something of a couple. She says she can't get over how different it is to be in a relationship with a woman. Everything is different, she says. There are no games, no competitions, no decoding of what the other is thinking, and the sex is just so relaxing.'

'Relaxing?'

'Yeah, I think she meant everything around the sex, not the sex itself, which I imagine is far from relaxing. Actually, it sounds like it might be a lot of hard work. But, you know, there's no big song and dance about it. I think she meant they both want the same thing.'

'Well, good for her. I'm glad things are working out for Lucy. She's an amazing girl, but she always seemed to be missing something.'

'Oh, God, aren't we all?' I hadn't intended that to sound as desperate as it did.

Colette looked at me quizzically. 'So, have you not found it yet?'

'What I'm looking for? Oh, God, Colette, I don't know what I want. You won't believe it, but Daniel's back.'

'What? Back with you?'

'No, no, God, no.' I had to shake my head to rid myself of the notion. 'No, he's just back hanging around. Calling to the flat, ringing me at work.'

'And what does he want?'

'Oh, to start things up again. It seems that now the fifth baby is born, things are a little hectic in the O'Hanlon house-hold. He's obviously not getting any at the moment . . .'

Our waitress had been hovering for ever, so it was time we looked at our menus and ordered something.

'Are we drinking wine?' asked Colette.

'Definitely,' I answered.

'That man should be taken out and have his balls cut off,' she said matter-of-factly.

I smiled. I told her about the first time he'd called to the flat and the wreck I'd become at the sight of him.

'And he's been back since?'

'Twice! Thank God Keith has never been there.'

'What did you say to him?'

'Well, after the first time, I was a lot calmer and better able to put it clearly and succinctly to him that I never, ever wanted to see him again. I was actually a little surprised at myself. I thought that, maybe, after everything we'd been through – and I really did believe he was the true love of my life – that there'd be something, some tiny regret maybe that it couldn't have worked out. I mean, there he was, on my doorstep, offering me everything I'd wanted less than a year before.'

'But there was nothing?'

'Nothing but revulsion.'

'Strong word.'

'Strong feeling. I wasted so much of my time and energy and love on that man, and he's just not worth it. Any man who would cheat on his wife and kids has to be scum.'

The waitress arrived with our starters and two glasses of cold wine.

'Well, that's got to be good. I mean, if you'd been having any doubts about yourself and Keith . . .'

'The truth is I've been having doubts about myself and Keith since the very beginning. I only said yes to him because I couldn't work out how to say no. And if I had said no, that would have been the end and I didn't want it to end. Being with Keith is so relaxing.'

'Almost as if he was a lesbian.'

We laughed.

'It's not funny, you know,' I continued, wiping away the

wine that had come down my nose. 'Here I am trying to sort my life out and you're just mocking.'

'I'm not . . . I'm all for the two of you getting married. It should settle you down no end.'

'I know, I know. And it has. And being able to close the door on Daniel like that has clarified for me how I feel. I mean, if I had any doubts . . . and marrying someone is a big deal . . . and I really do love Keith . . . but still, you know . . .'

Colette paused in the consumption of her goat's cheese and bacon tartlet. 'Kate, what is it you're trying to say?'

What was it I was trying to say or not say? What was it I couldn't (couldn't possibly) say out loud – almost couldn't even think?

'Oh, nothing. Keith and I are about to set a date. Maybe I'm a little jittery about it.'

'You know, Kate,' she said seriously, 'if you're jittery at all . . .'

'I know,' I said. 'I know.'

'Look,' she said, putting her knife and fork on the table, 'it's all about expectations. Yours and his. Every marriage is different. Some of them seem normal enough, some of them probably are normal enough, loads of them are bizarre. But the thing is, none of that matters. If one marriage works one way, the next one works in a completely different way. It depends on what the two of you want out of it. Look at me and Brian. We met, we liked each other, we had fun, we enjoyed the sex, we were getting older, we decided to get married. And it's good, it's very good, but it wouldn't be for everybody. I'm sure plenty of people look at the two of us and think how boring it must be. And sometimes it is, but most of the time it's just getting on with life in a fairly smooth way. I couldn't take all the dramas of your life, and with Brian I'm unlikely to have to. That's what I wanted, and it's what Brian wanted. We like our jobs, we like our kids, we like each other, we like our house. It's not very complicated and it works.'

I was listening intently, almost as if Colette was giving me a grind the night before the Leaving Cert on how to pass without having done any work. I was desperately trying to learn something.

'Now for you,' she continued, 'from what I know of Keith, I believe you could have the very best kind of drama-free life with him. He adores you. He can't quite believe you're his – his in the good way, of course. And he does everything he can to be all that you might want him to be. In fact, you're incredibly lucky to have him. He's intelligent, considerate. He has integrity. He's one of the good ones. However,' she took a deep breath, 'you have to work out if that's what you want. If it is, you'll be as happy as you're willing to be. If it isn't, don't do it. If you believe that there's something or someone out there who's better, don't do it. But you must be willing to accept you might be wrong. You're not the kind of person who would be happy on your own – that's not you. But you haven't been with someone yet who has truly made you happy. I don't think it's a question of whether or not you love Keith – I think you do – but you can love him all you like and still be miserable married to him. Then pretty soon you won't love anybody any more, not even yourself.'

She was finished. I hadn't expected a lecture with my lunch and it was giving me indigestion. It wasn't a lecture, though. It was sound advice.

'I know you're right,' I said at last, 'but I feel incapable of truly knowing what I want. Oh, God, I'm so bored with myself. I want to run away and start all over again. I want to –'

She stopped me. 'Well, you can't. Deal with what you have here. You don't have it bad, you know.'

'I know.'

'And besides,' she continued, 'you *are* starting over again. You're finally chucking in your job and doing something new. Grow up. Stop being so melodramatic and just get on with it.'

'OK.'

That was it. There was no way now that I could talk to her about the thing I couldn't talk about. And she was right. It *was* time I grew up and behaved like an adult. I knew I could be happy with Keith. I was even beginning to see that I could make him happy too. Life *could* be simple.

Our main courses arrived and we spent the rest of lunch talking about former classmates. Many were married, and two were separated. The girl who had had a baby in Fifth Year had just had her fourth with the same guy, and the girl who had had a baby in Sixth Year had a high-powered job with the UN. There was one confirmed lesbian and one pending. (There was a story doing the rounds that she had left her husband for her husband's secretary but it was still only a rumour.) Of the three other girls who had done law with me, one was at home with the kids, one was travelling in South America and the other was starring in *Fair City*. Ironically, she was playing a lawyer.

Colette was the only one I was still in touch with, but she had a way of finding out about everybody else. It was always weird hearing about them because I couldn't picture them as anything other than the schoolgirls they used to be. How can somebody in a dull grey skirt and a black blazer do anything like work for the UN or appear on television? In a way I couldn't stop seeing myself as the cocky schoolgirl who always thought she knew more than everybody else. Colette was right: it was time to get over my teenage *angst* and get on with being a grown-up.

I hadn't been particularly happy in my teens, yet it seemed I wasn't able to let them go. I remember Mike saying to me one day that I should slow down and enjoy the innocence of schooldays. He'd said I had the rest of my life for everything else but I would never experience true simplicity again. I laughed in his face. Oh, hindsight, and all of that.

As we were swallowing the last of our wine, I suggested to Colette that we cry off the beauty parlour. I wasn't in the mood to prostrate myself on the beautician's table while she smathered my face with some gunk, all the time tut-tutting about too many late nights. And all to the painfully relaxing sound of the Pan pipes. I thought it might lead me to violence. Colette didn't mind; she said she might fall asleep anyway so it was better we did something active. I suggested clothes shopping. That big family wedding of Keith's was coming up and I still had nothing to wear. I needed to do him and all the Dohenys proud, so something classy and expensive was called for. Colette agreed, and we headed towards some of the more up-market boutiques in the hope of finding something classy and expensive at half price. It was while we were trudging from one to another that we passed a bridal shop. We looked at each other at the same time with exactly the same idea.

'Well, you are getting married', she said, with a cheeky grin, 'and you know what? I think it might be time Brian and I renewed our vows.'

We rang the bell and asked to see what every bride desired for spring/summer.

It took longer than it should have for the girl to open the

door. She was in her mid-twenties and wore an expression of superiority that was much too old for her. Her outfit was in keeping: a pale green pencil skirt and white blouse with pale green piping round the collar and sleeves. It was like something my mother would have worn in one of her frivolous moments. 'I'm sorry,' she said. 'Do you have an appointment?'

I was tempted to say that we had and turn the superior tables on her for her sloppiness but I wasn't thinking quickly enough. 'No,' I said, in a tone of grave dejection. 'Do we need one?'

'Well, it's usual to make one. We can get very busy and we like to be able to give our customers our full attention.'

The shop was empty.

'Could you possibly make an exception for us?' I asked, most insincerely. 'You have come highly recommended to us and we're only in Limerick for the day . . .'

She gave us an unsubtle sweep with her disapproving little eyes and decided that, well, maybe she could let us in. Colette and I have an unspoken principle: we never go into places that let us in only reluctantly, but we also surmised that we might have a bit of fun and it would be a shame to miss out on that for the sake of a principle.

Once inside, we could see the second part of the 'we' she had mentioned: a woman, probably in her late forties, dressed in black and wearing the same withering expression as her young associate. As it turned out, the pale green girl was the daughter of the shop owner and the woman in black was the owner's friend, who wished she owned the shop. They were no nicer to each other than they were to us.

We gave our respective stories – I was to be married next August and wanted something a little different; Colette's ceremony was to be at Hallowe'en and she wanted something

177

quickly. As we stood in the middle of the poky shop, I was briefly amazed, given my love of clothes and shopping, that I hadn't done this before. But once they started bringing out the dresses I realized that maybe, at a subconscious level, I had known all along what a horror it would be. Because I had asked for something different, I got the dresses that weren't white or off-white. There was a gold monstrosity with a bodice that would have strangled me, a beige creation that looked like a cup of cold coffee, and a red and white strappy number that resembled something one of the Ugly Sisters might have worn. There were dresses with blue bits and dresses with green bits (the bridesmaids' dresses could be ordered to match the blue bits and the green bits). They were all horrible. I couldn't imagine going to a fancy-dress party, let alone getting married, in any of them.

Colette was having more luck. They had last season's sample dresses on sale and she looked quite good in nearly all of them. There was a long, flowing chiffon dress that looked particularly dreamy, which I thought she should buy anyway. It was the kind of thing I could imagine wearing round the house when I felt blue. She wasn't tempted, though. She told the girl she'd keep it in mind but she still had a lot of looking to do. The two women glanced at each other as if they'd expected as much.

I was beginning to feel that this wasn't as much fun as I'd thought it would be, but since I was there, I thought I might as well try on one of the dresses. The gold was pushed forward. It took me for ever to get into it – it was constructed of three bits that had to be wound intricately round each other and some very complicated lacing at the back – but when it was on and I could view myself in the flatteringly lit and ever so slightly elongating mirror, I was glad I'd made the effort. I looked as hideous as I hoped it was possible for me to look. The gold drained my face of colour and even imparted to it a sickly shine. The shape did something frightening to my figure – it made me look like a cross between a prepubescent girl and a woman in the late stages of pregnancy. Surely no bride, no matter how deranged, wanted to look like this?

'It's beautiful on you,' said the young girl, gravely. 'It's really different.'

'Yes,' I said, equally gravely. 'It's very different from the sort of thing I usually wear.'

'You're a picture,' Colette chimed in. 'Keith would die if he saw you.'

'Oh, is Keith your fiancé?' the girl asked.

It was too tempting to say that, no, he wasn't my fiancé, he was my fiancé's brother, with whom I was having an affair. But I didn't. 'Yes,' I said, 'and he'd love to see me in this.'

Colette insisted I try another, even though I was rapidly losing my taste for this particular game, and pulled out a fake Vera Wang that was all satin and shiny bits and yards of material flowing in every direction. There was a veil to go with it, which rested neatly on my head and brushed lightly against my bare shoulders.

'You look gorgeous,' gasped Colette, when she saw me in the ensemble. 'You're absolutely *stunning*.'

There wasn't a note of insincerity in her voice.

I *did* look gorgeous. That was the amazing thing. I looked like those brides you see in magazines with their airbrushed smiles and their perfect hair and the to-die-for dress. Those brides who fill page after page of expensive glossy magazines so that young women in love can imagine how they'll look on their big day. Those brides who, not for one minute, not for one second, do you believe in. Those brides you know are faking it for the camera.

'Come on,' I said to Colette. 'Let's get out of here. I don't feel well.'

13

It was the end of July and it had been raining all day. I hadn't anything to do, so I'd stayed at home watching, listening, feeling the rain. It was soothing. I had a lot to think about and the rain was a gentle accompaniment to my disjointed thoughts. I had the notion that if it didn't stop raining, I might never go out again. It seemed as good a way as any to spend the rest of my life.

I was still wearing my pyjamas but I'd taken the time to shower and even put on a little makeup. My hair was in a style that looked much the same whether I was just out of bed or had spent an hour rubbing half of Boots through it. If someone called to the door unexpectedly I wouldn't have to pretend I wasn't there or make a mad dash to the bathroom. I didn't see why I couldn't continue like this for several days, whether it stopped raining or not. The phone was off the hook, but that had been an accident. My mobile was out of battery and my charger was somewhere under the couch or behind a chair. But nobody was likely to call.

Jean had moved out, although she was offering to come back for a little while. I was doing my utmost to assure her that there was no need. She was sharing a flat with a girl she used to work with and so far she was delighted. It was in a new development of luxury apartments with high ceilings and balconies facing the river. She was considering buying one if the opportunity arose. Her friend had been single for years, had no desire to be otherwise, and Jean found her easy company.

At the moment I couldn't conceive of sharing my space with anyone. It was necessary that the air around me remained empty of other people's thoughts and opinions. Even the physical presence of another person would have been too much. I couldn't remember when I had last spent so much time on my own. Usually I can't wait to fill every available corner with noise. Perhaps this quiet was timely.

However, I was running out of food and I wasn't sure that my stomach was up to the sort of thing I could order in. All the cereal boxes were empty, the last consumed without milk. Bread was long gone. The last of it had been consumed with a side of mould, which I chose to ignore. Cheese, eggs, cold meat had disappeared in a rather tasty omelette the night before. There was some pasta but the only sauce was a year out of date. I'd have to make a decision on that soon. Two tins of tomato soup looked likely to be my lunch. When I remembered that I could enliven it with a dash of vodka, it seemed more appetizing. I was rather enjoying the sense of being under siege and testing myself to find out how long I could survive without the outside world. It was a game, though, and like so many other games, I was too old for playing.

Of course, there were good things to think about. Lucy had called over one evening and announced casually that she was pregnant. She wasn't in the least bit fazed by it. Even before she and Iris had decided they wanted to do it together, she had been happy to have the baby on her own. She was simply thrilled to be pregnant. The father was Luke, the sculptor, who had remained friends with Lucy after their sort of relationship sort of broke up, but he had no interest in being involved with the child. He told Lucy he was delighted if that was what she wanted, and sure, he'd probably like to see the baby when it was born, but he was thinking of going to Australia and he mightn't come back. Lucy knew that even someone as laid back and out of it as Luke might get himself sorted in a few years' time and want to be part of their baby's life, but she said she'd deal with that if and when the time came. 'And besides,' she had said, 'I'm not going to pretend to my child that she doesn't have a father. I'll tell her everything. In fact, it would be nice if he did want to be part of her life later on. I know Luke. He won't stay in Australia. Either he'll never go in the first place because he won't be able to find the money, or he'll go and be back within six months due to some minor crisis.'

When I asked Lucy how this fitted in with her being a lesbian, she smiled. 'Well,' she said, 'you know the way you have to be sure. It seemed that one of the ways to try to be sure was to sleep with a nice guy. After Luke, I was fairly sure I didn't want to sleep with any more men. I mean, whenever I slept with a guy before, I didn't think I might be gay, so I didn't think that was the problem. I just thought I wasn't all that into sex . . . yet I knew I was.'

When I asked her why she hadn't used a condom she said she hadn't had one.

'Well, I hadn't needed one in ages and Luke isn't the kind of guy who carries them in his wallet. Yes, I know it was irresponsible, but I knew Luke was healthy and I didn't even think about getting pregnant.'

It didn't seem to matter how it had happened: Lucy and Iris were moving in together and they were having a baby. They were as happy as any expectant parents would be.

Mum and Dad were taking the news very well. Dad said it was always a blessing to have another grandchild and even if the father wasn't going to do the decent thing he would ensure that Lucy and the baby had every support they needed. Lucy knew he meant it. When we were growing up and Mum did her no-sex-before-marriage routine and warned us of the evils of becoming pregnant without a husband, Dad took us aside afterwards and told us that, no matter what happened, we could always come home. Over the years Mum had softened; I had heard the lecture a lot less frequently than Jean and Marion, and now, when Lucy told her she was pregnant, she said that with six daughters, it was surprising there hadn't been more children born out of wedlock. We all agreed that she was delighted with the news. The fact that Lucy was moving into Iris's house went uncommented on.

And then there was Iris. Of all my brothers-in-law, only Mike could rival her for looks or conversation. Lucy was keen that we meet her formally and that Iris meet us and realize we weren't all latent homophobes preoccupied with doing up our kitchens. (They had bumped into Ruth in town.) So I volunteered to play host to the select few – Lucy, Iris, Jean, Marion and me. Keith said he'd leave us girls alone for the evening – he had to work late anyway and he'd spend the night at his place.

I was quite pleased to be doing the party thing as it had been ages since I'd entertained at home. Keith and I had kept meaning to have dinner parties where we would mingle our friends over some good food and wine, but we'd never got round to it. We could never decide which friends would go with which. I think each of us was privately afraid it would be a disaster. It was easier to order a takeaway and talk about it.

I was, therefore, in the mood to make a bit of a fuss. There was no worry with the liquor part of the evening, I knew I wouldn't disappoint there, but I wasn't much of a cook. People kept telling me that all you needed were good ingredients and a simple recipe, but somehow that wasn't enough to turn me into a domestic goddess. I did have one idea but I wasn't sure if it was entirely above board. However, by the evening before the proposed dinner I'd had no further ideas, so I decided to risk it. I rang Mike to ask for his help.

He was at home. If he hadn't been I'd have put the phone down without leaving a message. It was one thing to be cheeky in person, quite another to leave a cheeky message.

When he answered I almost hung up. Mike was very busy and our family was always pulling and dragging out of him. But he'd said we could still be friends. And friends called on one another when they needed help. I could probably muddle through on my own, but it wouldn't be half as good – and it was certainly cheeky to ask him to help prepare a meal I couldn't invite him to. Or could I? No, it wasn't my place. I was only the nominal host. It was Lucy's party and, besides, they would probably prefer if it was just the girls. Oh, what the hell? I thought. I'll just ask him.

'Hi there!' I said cheerily. 'It's Kate.'

'Oh, hi, Kate.'

'Yeah . . . Listen, Mike, I was wondering if I could ask you a favour?'

'Sure, no problem.'

I went straight for it. 'I'm having Lucy and the girls over tomorrow night so we can introduce Iris to the good part of the family. Now, I know she wouldn't want me to go to any trouble but I kind of want to. The only problem is I don't know how to make anything other than spaghetti Bolognese and the only –'

'I'll give you a hand,' he said. 'I'm nothing great myself now either, but we'll pull something together. Have you got a paper and pencil there? I'll give you a shopping list for tomorrow. Are you ready? OK, start with . . .'

I grabbed a Biro and an old envelope and scribbled furiously.

I had to visit four different shops to get everything on Mike's list – he was very particular about where the ingredients came from – but by four o'clock the next afternoon I had everything ready. He was punctual. He had brought a few things of his own – fresh basil from his garden, some particularly good olive oil, a few utensils that he said would make everything easier and a pile of CDs – 'I know how bad your CD collection is. We'll need something to work to.'

He looked really good. The fine weather and all the time he was spending out of doors had given him a colour, which was well set off by his blue jeans and a pale blue T-shirt. His hair was longer than it had been in ages, and because he had taken holidays to work on the house, he had more than a few days' growth in his beard. Yes, he would definitely be snapped up quickly . . .

'I hope you've got your apron on under there,' I said, rather foolishly, as I opened the door to him.

'In my back pocket,' he said, ignoring the feeble joke.

'Listen,' I said, 'I really do appreciate this. I know it's a bit much asking you to help out, especially when –'

'Stop apologizing. I like this sort of thing. I haven't been doing much cooking lately, so it's nice to have the excuse.'

'You'll have to have a big house-warming party when you've finished your house.'

'You betcha. Now, to work,' and he ushered me into the kitchenette where he surveyed my shopping. 'Excellent! Now, the first thing to make is the marinade for the chicken . . .'

We worked steadily all afternoon; he explained what he had in mind and made suggestions as to how we should

186

proceed. I could see that he was being careful not to take over – he might have had some notion that I was territorial about my kitchen – but all I wanted was to take his instructions and do my best to get it right. He was a patient teacher; when I began to chop the basil he put his hand across the knife and told me you always tear it or you'll damage the flavour. I'm sure everybody knows that but he didn't make me feel like an eejit. We glided through my tiny kitchen as if it had been built for Gordon Ramsay – in fact, I began to feel so expert that I did a TV-chef parody. He laughed and said I'd missed my calling. We were moving happily to the Steely Dan and Jamiroquai he had brought; I couldn't remember when I'd last had so much fun in anyone's kitchen.

Before he left he made sure that everything would run like clockwork. The starter was a tomato, buffalo mozzarella and basil salad, which had only to be plated. While we enjoyed the piquancy of the basil set against the sweetness of the tomatoes and the roundness of the cheese, the main course would be tenderizing nicely, while filling the room with a divine aroma. Mike said there was nothing to beat really good corn-fed chicken on the bone for simplicity and succulence. (I think he was pulling my leg a little with all his chef talk, but I didn't care. My meal was going to be fabulous.) The marinade – white wine, balsamic vinegar and the juice of two oranges – would thicken in the cooking and make a sumptuous sauce. The vegetables were as simple as possible: boiled baby new potatoes, with steamed broccoli and mangetout. Apparently all that the lightly cooked vegetables would need was a little extra seasoning and a sliver of real butter. The dessert, a strawberry fool, I would whip up while everybody was digesting the chicken and engaging in scintillating conversation. And to finish: a cup of excellent coffee and squares of fine dark chocolate. Surely Iris would think we were a marvellous family and fall in love with us all.

When everything was in hand and the washing-up was done Mike produced a bottle of wine he said would go well with the chicken or, he said, we could open it now and have a self-congratulatory glass. We opened it. It was a pinot noir, he said, from the Irancy region in France, a much lighter wine than the rich, plummy reds we usually enjoyed. Its very lightness, he said, made it perfect for drinking on its own.

We sat in almost silence; he reclined on the couch, his feet propped on a magazine on top of the coffee-table, and I sat with my feet tucked under me on the armchair. The wine was perfect, deep and flavoursome, but it wasn't going to knock me out before the evening had begun. At one point Mike closed his eyes; he seemed as satisfied as I was with our afternoon's work. There wasn't any need to talk. It was almost as if, for those few moments, only the two of us existed and there was calm in our universe. I remember such moments, years ago, when Mike and Jean would be over in our house for some family occasion or other. I was probably in college at that stage and particularly disdainful of everything that went on at home. Jean would arrive in a flurry and rush off to find Mum, dumping Mike along the way. He would usually find me in the sitting room, or the conservatory, stealing a glass of wine, and join me without needing to go through the customary formalities of how I was getting on at college or wasn't Christmas/Easter/ Hallowe'en all a bit crazy. We would sit together, sipping the wine, and before we knew it, we'd be laughing about something silly one of us had said. I have always felt so at ease in Mike's company, yet there's the sense that we're on the edge of something very exciting.

Now, suddenly, he turned to me. 'I've really enjoyed this afternoon,' he said.

'Me too.'

He looked as if he might be about to say something more but he finished his wine and said it was time he went.

'You should stay. It wouldn't be a problem, and after all the work you've done . . .'

'No, no, this is definitely just for the girls. We'll do it some other time when it isn't a girls-only evening.'

'Yes,' I said, 'we *will* do this again, that's a great idea.'

He was walking out of the door when I remembered the kitchen equipment and his CDs. 'It's OK,' he said. 'Hold on to them for a while. Your stereo and your kitchen are crying out for something new.'

'OK, but I'll drop them back soon. You might want to do some entertaining yourself.'

'No hurry,' he said and laid a hand on my shoulder and kissed me. It began as a kiss on the cheek, the way we'd always kissed, but just before our faces touched he turned so that the edge of his mouth brushed the edge of mine. It might have been an accident, but it felt as if he'd intended it all along. It was like the prelude to a deeper, longer, more passionate kiss. It was only a few seconds but it was unmistakable.

He didn't catch my eye again and practically ran down the stairs.

The dinner was a great success. From the moment Iris stepped through the door she was at ease and soon it seemed that she'd always been part of the family. She was easy-going by nature – it would take a lot to faze her – but she appeared genuinely relaxed with us. And it was obvious she was stone mad about Lucy. I don't think she took her eyes off her all evening, and everything she said was in some way a compliment to her. Marion had expressed concern to me earlier that she might be very domineering, given that she'd been such a driving force in Lucy's coming out, but that didn't seem to be the case. She was strong, certainly, but no stronger or bossier or more overbearing than the rest of us could be. In fact, she was very nice.

In appearance she was striking. She was roughly the same age as Jean, but she had the demeanour of someone much older. Her skin was soft and peachy and smooth; she was wearing hardly any makeup apart from a little eye-liner and maybe lip balm. Her hair was silvery grey; the grey was her own, the silver was courtesy of her hairdresser. 'It suits me to look my age,' she said. 'I was never girly.' And neither was she womanly exactly, but that's not to say she was manly. She was wearing wide-legged black linen trousers with an oversized white shirt and a thick ethnic belt. Her shoes were indeed comfortable but they were also attractive – soft leather mules in a medley of criss-crossed colours. If you were to take her appearance as a whole you would have to say that she was rather Diane Keatonesque. Everything about her gave the impression of someone comfortably in control of her life.

She was full of interesting conversation too. She had been running her own firm of auctioneers and estate agents for more than ten years. It was small but highly successful. She specialized in leasing and selling office spaces but she'd handle anything if it was profitable. She had us in stitches as she told us stories of her experiences over the years. 'You wouldn't think property could be funny,' she said, 'but I've had some of my best laughs over a sale.'

And so the night proceeded, with Mike's excellent dinner and Iris's entertaining anecdotes, and the odd bit here and there from the rest of us, who were happy just to eat and listen. It was then that Jean first told us about her new flat-share. She was trying to fix a night for her house-warming. 'I'm warning you in advance,' she said, 'that there'll be no food at my party, apart from Pringles and maybe a dip. It'll be another ten years before I'm up to the whole dinner-party thing. Well done, by the way, Kate. Every-thing's surprisingly excellent.'

'Actually,' I had to admit, 'I didn't do this entirely by myself. Mike helped me.'

'*Mike* helped you?' my sisters chorused.

'Yes. It wasn't a secret or anything – I wasn't trying to pretend I'd done it all myself. I was just waiting for the right moment to tell you.'

'I thought I recognized something about this meal,' Jean said. 'The basil and the chicken and everything. He was always trying out new things on me but eventually I had to ban him from cooking. I was going to get way too fat. I'm bad enough as it is.'

'You're not fat. You look great. In fact, I think you've lost weight.'

'I haven't,' she said, straight away. 'I've put it on. But I'm dressing better and that makes the difference. In fact, I should have let Mike cook for me – he'd probably have kept me thin. It's all this drinking and eating junk that's doing the damage. But what the hell? You only live once.'

'So Mike came over?' Marion asked.

'Yeah,' I said. 'Well, I wanted to make a bit of an effort for Iris, and I'm not great in the kitchen. Mike didn't mind – he enjoyed it. At least, he said he did. Shouldn't I have asked him? Was it very cheeky of me?'

'Hold your horses,' said Jean. 'That's what he's there for. He's always had a soft spot for you, anyway. Why wouldn't he help you?'

191

Suddenly Iris cut in. 'Mike is your ex-husband,' she said matter-of-factly, but she was looking at Jean with a degree of expectation.

There was silence for a while. Somehow, none of us had thought of Mike in that way. An ex-husband was such an alien thing, such a grown-up thing, certainly not part of our lives.

Then Jean spoke. 'No,' she said, 'not my ex-husband. He's my present husband, and a very excellent husband he is too, although I did leave him last May. I'm sure Lucy's told you the details. He's one of the best men I've ever known and I went and walked out on him.'

'Does that mean you regret it?' asked Iris, again matter-of-factly.

'No,' answered Jean, without a hint of hesitation. 'After marrying him in the first place, leaving him was the best thing I ever did. I don't know about marriage. I'm not sure about the for-as-long-as-we-both-shall-live bit. I mean, I'm sure there are people who are lucky enough to find exactly the right person for them, then live happily ever after, but it's got to be rare. For most people, you get married because (a) you're way too young and you got carried away and maybe you're pregnant, although that doesn't seem to matter any more, or (b) you're way too old and you're desperate and it seems like the whole fucking world is married and having disgusting wailing babies, or (c) you're simple-minded enough to believe you can make it happen by sheer strength of will. You alone can turn something ordinary and banal and boring into the marriage of the century, the marriage of the fucking millennium.'

It was clear that Jean was drunk. Very drunk indeed.

'Weren't you happy in your marriage, then?' asked Iris, not in the least put off by Jean's tone.

'It wasn't that,' said Jean, pulling herself up in her seat. 'I was happy in my marriage. I just wasn't happy in myself. Maybe if I met Mike for the first time now, or in a year's time, I'd fall in love with him and we'd get married and it would last for ever. But that's not going to happen. I'm a different person, and mainly he's a different person. It's much more a case of he shouldn't have married me than I shouldn't have married him. I should have married some guy who was already married to his job and played golf and did scuba-diving and went on business trips and did every fucking thing he could to get away from me. That would have been perfect. Or I should never have married at all. But Mike really wanted a marriage. He wanted it to be like it should be. He wanted sharing and equality and romance and evenings in by the fire and evenings out in nice restaurants, and I just wanted, I just wanted . . . to . . . behave as if I wasn't married. I don't mean I wanted to go off with loads of men – *and I never cheated on Mike* – I wanted to be like the aborted student I was when I met him. If I'd never met him I would have messed around for years and maybe have met someone, maybe not. But even an eejit like me can recognize one of the good ones when you meet him. I don't know what the fuck he saw in me. I suppose there must have been something, but whatever it was it didn't last. He desperately tried to hide it, but he fell out of love with me . . . I don't know when exactly . . . but there was a long time when he was faking it.'

'Do you resent him for that?' asked Iris.

'No. He faked it because he thought that was what I wanted. And it was. For a long time. And he would have continued to pretend, very expertly, that he still loved me for as long as I appeared to want him to. And I love him for that.'

Nobody had expected so much talk out of Jean and now that she was done she sank back in her seat and appeared to fall asleep. Iris remained composed, as if it was normal for her to provoke such outbursts.

Only Lucy seemed somewhat uncomfortable. She turned to Marion rather urgently. 'But you have a great marriage, don't you, Marion, and it isn't like any of Jean's stupid categories.'

'Yes,' said Marion, 'but we work at it. We're lucky that we suit each other, but we still have to make allowances for our individuality.'

'But ye really, really love each other?'

'Yes, we do. And that probably is the bottom line. As long as you're not leading some insane lifestyle, you can get over most things if you truly love each other. Don't blame Jean – she's right about one thing. She shouldn't have got married. She never liked sharing anything – not her toys, not her room, not her sweets, not to mind her life. She's better at it now, but that's only because she's lived with such a selfless man for so long. Don't be worried. For ever can work.'

'I'm not worried. We're very stable.'

Iris, not disturbed by this either, took Lucy's hand in both of hers and squeezed gently. 'And, besides, we can't get married. Thank God. I'd never want to go through that rigmarole. If you love each other, you stay together. It's as simple as that.' Then she turned to me. 'You're getting married soon, I believe?'

'Yes,' I said, 'probably next summer. We're in the process of deciding on a date.'

'Are you excited?'

'I suppose I am,' I said, although it was an unusual question, 'but we got engaged ages ago and that's where the

194

real excitement was. I'm sure it'll all heat up again once we're booking things.'

Suddenly it felt odd to be sitting with my sisters and one sister's girlfriend, talking about marriage. It surprised me to hear Jean talking about her marriage to Mike almost as if she hadn't been involved. I liked his idea of a marriage, though — it was hopefully what I would have with Keith. Evenings in by the fire and evenings out in nice restaurants . . . I could see how it would go. And then I saw something else, something I really couldn't ignore any more . . .

Then there were some less pleasant things to think about. Like the rather uncomfortable trip with Keith to his family wedding. And the silly row we had about the roles of brides-maids and best men. And then there was my last day at work, which had turned out to be one of my best days at work but it was followed by the realization that I was now unemployed and had no income and that I was going to be a student again, which I hadn't enjoyed very much the first time round. I still knew I was doing the right thing but I needed someone to remind me of it constantly or I'd fall into a deep afraid-of-change depression.

Oh, yes. There was also the fact that Keith had dumped me. I needed to think about that, too.

14

Keith kept staring at the hat box and insisting it wouldn't fit in the car.

'Of course it will,' I said. 'It's just a little hat box.'

In fact it was a very large hat box, outsize almost, but there was still no reason why it wouldn't fit somewhere in his generously proportioned Ford Mondeo.

'Can't you take the hat out and leave the box behind?'

'No way! It would get crumpled – it would get completely wrecked. And it's not even my hat, it's only hired.'

'You've hired a hat?'

'It's what everybody does for weddings. Hats are far too expensive for just one wear.'

I was getting quite annoyed with him; I had made a real effort with my outfit. I wanted his family to look at me and think, Wow! Keith's done well for himself. And it *was* fabulous – a long purple dress that hugged the body with a long deeper purple coat in the same fabric to drape over it. I had decided on the big hat, even though hats were on the wane. But that was merely fashion. I've always loved hats and there's nothing like a great big hat to make a great big statement. So I chose a large wide-brimmed one that picked up the colours of the dress and the coat and sent out an air of elegant mystique with every feather that dived from its crown. It was a fucking great hat and Keith was dismissing it as if it wasn't important. I wasn't having it.

'Look,' I said, 'it can go in the boot. You won't even have to look at it.'

He sighed loudly. 'There'll be nobody else wearing a hat.'

'I don't care!'

'I'm only trying to help.'

'Well, you're not. Look, I'm going for a walk. I'll see you in a while.'

'Good! You could do with cooling off.'

'Would you like me to tell you what you could do with?' I stormed off.

This whole family-wedding business was a strain. I thought Keith wanted me to make a fuss of his family – after all, he had been exposed to so much of mine, and I was curious about his. But as it drew closer he seemed less and less keen on the whole thing. If it weren't for the fact that his mother could talk about nothing else every time he saw her or spoke to her on the phone, he would probably have cried off. They had wanted us all to travel together but Keith was adamant that that wasn't a good idea. He was torn between saving his father the drive and saving me the over-exposure (so he claimed). I tried to tell him I didn't mind, but he wouldn't listen. Eventually his brother agreed to drive their parents. I thought that would put him at ease but he still seemed bothered about something. I was weary of trying to work out what it was.

I headed in the direction of O'Connell Street; something was drawing me once more to the front steps of O'Sullivan and Woulfe. It was right to move on, but I couldn't deny what a large part the firm had played in my life. Mostly it was a lesson in denial and how to deal with a mild-to-middling case of self-inflicted misery but there had been the odd good time. At least, that was how I was choosing to remember it.

They had given me a bloody good send-off. At three o'clock on my last day (the hour when I habitually shut

197

down mentally) my boss came into the office area and announced to everybody that in honour of my leaving we were going to have a party. Then he rolled in the drinks trolley – several bottles of moderately good wine and a truckload of beer, followed not too much later by the food trolley with drumsticks, cocktail sausages and sandwiches. He wasn't being mean, just lacked imagination. Once we'd all had enough to loosen us up he made a speech about the bravery in trying new things and the excitement of taking on a new challenge. For a moment he sounded almost wistful and his gaze was fixed on something indefinable at the end of the room. He quickly sobered up – he probably made a mental tot of his salary and decided things weren't so bad after all. However, I believe his sentiments were genuine, and when he held my hand and kissed me, then presented me with a substantial Brown Thomas voucher, a lot of warmth emanated from him. If I had met him in any other circumstances I'd probably have liked him.

He set the tone for everybody else; even people I knew had never liked me were full of good wishes and sadness that I was leaving. I wondered if I'd underestimated them, but when I saw them eyeing up my desk (and its prime location by a window *and* a radiator) I decided to let my original judgement lie. They weren't bad people; they just weren't my sort of people. Whatever my sort was.

Of course, I'd had one or two allies – Denise was always good for a laugh even though she got on my nerves most of the time, and there was an older woman who proffered advice when it was most needed – but the truth was that I wouldn't be seeing any of them again. It was a sad thought that such a huge part of my life would close so finally, but I was moving on.

Facing the closed doors of the building now (it was

Saturday), I sighed and continued walking. The only place to go was to the shops, and for once I wasn't in the mood for that. I was in the mood to get the car packed and moving. Passing a flower shop I decided to buy Keith a button-hole; it had struck me as the sort of thing he would appreciate. The florist was all chat about weddings and where the one I was going to would take place. She made a lovely button-hole and charged me very little. 'Enjoy your day,' she called, as I went out of the door.

By the time I got back to the car, parked on the street outside my building, Keith had it piled with our luggage, including my enormous hat placed carefully on the back seat. Before I had a chance to say anything, he apologized. 'I'm sorry,' he said. 'It was my fault. I was being a bollocks. Your hat's lovely.'

'Great,' I said. 'Just wait till you see it when I'm wearing my new outfit. Or, better still, wait till you see it when I'm wearing nothing at all . . .'

Somehow the image of me naked except for my hat didn't have the desired effect.

'Come on, let's get going,' he said. 'We have to drive some of the worst roads in the country and it's in the middle of bloody nowhere.' His relations lived in the heart of rural Clare.

'OK,' I said. 'Just don't drive too fast. My hair's in a state of ruffled perfection and I don't want to ruin it.'

'Get in,' he said. 'Isn't the bloody hat going to cover your hair anyway?'

I couldn't argue with that.

The drive was probably the most pleasant part of the trip. He seemed a bit more relaxed, the weather was good, the roads were surprisingly quiet and Steely Dan were excellent company. I sat back and allowed my mind to wander but not too far. I had decided recently that it was possible to spend too much of your life daydreaming. If you want to make a success of your present and have a hope of a future, you have to live fully in your present. Keith was my present and he was going to be my future. He was real and solid and wonderful, and it was about time I appreciated that. I wanted to talk to him about college, but he never seemed keen to sit down and hammer it out with me. I was excited about all that was to come but also quite apprehensive and I needed to feel he would be there to guide me through it. He had assured me that work would quieten down soon and that we might take a holiday, even go back to Los Almiras where everything had seemed so simple. But weren't patience and understanding part of a grown-up relationship? If he was going through a rough time I should support him by not making demands on him, by thinking of him and not myself for once. Then he would do the same for me. I hoped he'd get sorted out before I went headlong into something I knew would freak me out, even if it was in a good way.

I worried about what happened to couples when both parties were needy at the same time. In my innocence, I had always presumed it was only the woman who needed looking after because that had been my experience, but now I had discovered that men needed just as much care. They might be a lot less obvious about it but they could have their mini-crises, just as we did. Keith wasn't throwing any wobblies at me, but it was clear that he needed something from me – and mainly for me to give him space.

The family's plan was to call first at the homestead to see everybody before the wedding, then continue to the hotel to change for the church. I thought it was a crazy idea, involving loads of extra driving, and an invasion of a bride who would probably prefer to get ready in peace. But apparently it was a tradition among them to do this house-visit thing. And it wasn't even as if champagne and whiskey would be flowing: most of the family were teetotal. Keith explained that it was a way for the family to be private together before the wedding was opened up to the public. Which might have been all very well if they were celebrities, I thought, but didn't say. If that was what we were doing, it was what we were doing.

His parents were there before us, his father talking quietly to the bride's father in the kitchen, his mother flapping about with a pot of tea. There were people everywhere, mostly just sitting around as if they were waiting for somebody to call them for dinner. They looked hungry too, which reminded me that I'd only had a slice of toast all day. I wondered if it would be possible to get a bite somewhere before the whole thing kicked off.

The bride was still in her dressing-gown, curled up on an armchair in the living room, smoking. Only the pile of curls on her head gave any indication that she was, indeed, the bride. I had never seen one so relaxed.

Jean had been the worst: up at six that morning, pacing the house, banging doors, having sneaky cigarettes behind the trees at the foot of the garden. I don't think she was nervous, at least I didn't think so at the time, it was more that she'd thought that was the way a bride should behave on the morning of her wedding, or that because this was the morning of her wedding she could get away with behaving like that. Everyone wanted to tell her to calm down and cop on but you can't do that to a bride just hours before she gets married. She kept it up at the hairdresser's and the beautician's, to such an extent that the stylists were on the verge of taking her aside and telling her it was OK, she didn't have to go through with it if she didn't want to.

It was only when she arrived at the church and saw Mike waiting at the altar that she calmed down. I remember it distinctly: Marion (her only bridesmaid), the flower-girl (a neighbour's daughter) and I were lined up at the back of the church. I shouldn't have been there but nobody had told me not to be, so I stayed. I believed I'd been forgotten. She almost charged into the church, leaving Dad behind and kept going until she had Mike in her sights. She even waited for him to turn round, to be sure it was him. Then she smiled, went back to take Dad's arm and said we'd better get things moving, she was late enough already. I ran up to join the family (and be scolded by Mum) and winked at Mike to let him know she had arrived. He winked back, and then the music started. She was fine for the rest of the day – no more skittishness, no tears. She didn't even get drunk. She just seemed relieved.

I decided to take a wander outside. The house was the result of several generations of unplanned and badly executed additions and alterations. The original one-storey cottage had been obliterated. It wasn't going to win any prizes in *House & Garden* but the overall feel of the place was warm and welcoming. The yard was still in evidence and several of the outhouses, but none of it was in use now as the land had been leased to a neighbour. The parents were too old to farm it and none of the children had any interest. They had gone off to college, to jobs in cities, and to houses with three bathrooms on suburban estates. It was sad to think that not only the farm but almost the entire way of life had become redundant.

As I continued to amble round what remained of a couple of hundred years of one family's existence, it occurred to me that Keith would probably have taken to the farming life. Not that he had ever expressed a desire for it, but I could see him getting satisfaction out of a day spent on the land, bending it gently to his will. He would have cared about his animals but without being sentimental; he would have worked hard but enjoyed every moment. And he would have loved to pass it on to the sons he would have by the willing wife at his side. I stopped myself. I had sworn off idle daydreams, even if they were somebody else's.

Keith was right about there being nothing here. We had only passed two other houses for about ten miles before we'd reached his relatives' place and it didn't look like the land could support many more. It had a kind of eerie beauty, though; it wasn't exactly moorland but there were pinks and purples reminiscent of the Burren. I could almost imagine Heathcliff and Cathy scaling the landscape. But that was just it: it was romantic as I looked at it now in the height of summer, but it would be a different story in the middle of winter when somebody needed a doctor, or a bag of chips. I didn't need to muse on it any longer. I was a city girl through and through – there was no question about that. It was still nice, though, to be able to appreciate an alternative.

The only thing marring my appreciation of the scene was my growing awareness of my empty stomach. I couldn't ignore it any longer. I needed to eat. I decided to go back to the house and find something to keep me going. Surely all country houses were full of food – you wouldn't be able to turn round for legs of lamb and chickens and sides of bacon.

As soon as I stepped over the threshold, I was accosted by a bridesmaid who led me into the kitchen where the table was laden with sandwiches and sponge cake. I filled a plate with beef and ham sandwiches. On my way to a corner seat by the door I was met by Keith's mum, who poured me a mug of tea and told me to come on into the living room. 'Keith's been looking for you everywhere, bless him. I think he thought you'd got swallowed up by the family. He's over there by the window. Here, I'll give you some tea for him.'

I barely made it across the room, what with all the tea and sandwiches, and when I got there Keith was scowling.

'Where were you?' he snapped.

I was startled – part of me was still scampering through the furze with Cathy Earnshaw. 'I went for a walk,' I said. 'You disappeared the minute we got here. What's the problem?'

'It's time to be heading.'

'Well, I'll just eat this and we'll go,' I said, handing him his tea.

'Never mind that, we can eat later. Let's go now.'

'Keith, I'm starving – it'll only take a minute. And I really need a cup of tea. Those kind of roads always give me a headache. You chat to your family.'

'I already have.'

He was talking in that kind of furious whisper where every word is almost spat out, over-enunciated to make up for the lack of volume. I didn't know what his problem was.

'I'll just go over there,' I said, 'say hello to your dad and finish my sandwich. Then we'll go. There's no hurry. The bride still doesn't have her makeup on.' I was smiling at him and tugging at his shirt with my only available finger.

'OK,' he said, softening, 'but be quick. We have the rest of the day to spend with these people.'

I slithered off across the room and had a nice chat with his dad. Keith looked on while he talked to one of his great-aunts about the demise of butter churns.

It was while we were on the road to the hotel that we

had the silly argument about bridesmaids and best men. I made a casual remark that the ritual was rather silly, that it was demeaning for a girl's sisters or friends to have to be got up in an inferior dress and pretend to fuss over the bride. 'As for the best man,' I said, 'it's just an excuse for him to play the big man with all his speeches, and parade around like he's running the show.'

Keith wasn't sure whether or not to respond. Maybe I was having him on, or being flippant, or maybe I had no appreciation of the rites and rituals of marriage. He decided it was the latter and launched into a lecture on the importance of the bride and groom's lackeys. I don't know why – I had merely made an idle comment, I didn't care one way or the other – but I continued to argue, so much so that by the time we arrived at the hotel, his blood was boiling and I was fed up. We checked in in silence, and when we got upstairs Keith went into the bathroom and locked the door. I had thought that was my prerogative, but as he had taken it, I decided to change and reapply my makeup. Then I went down to the bar.

I knew things weren't going well but I was past caring. If he insisted on being a pain in the ass, there was nothing I could do except wait for him to cool off. I hadn't had a drink in ages, nearly a week, so I felt I deserved the large gin and tonic poured by the friendly barman in the poky little bar at the charming country hotel. I stayed there in the hope that soon Keith would come looking for me to apologize. I even thought it might be the perfect excuse to make it up under the covers. We hadn't had sex in ages either.

But none of that happened.

When Keith did appear in the bar he looked hassled; another scowl had formed across his face, his tie was crooked and even his suit jacket seemed not to sit right on his shoulders.

'OK,' he said, with absolutely no humour. 'Are we going to this wedding or what?'

'Of course we are,' I said, not at all sure how to take him.

'Right, then. Let's go.'

'I want to finish my drink first. Why don't you have one too?'

'Look! We either go now, or I'm driving back to Limerick.'

'All right, all right, we'll go.'

'Fine.'

'Keith, I'm sorry about the whole bridesmaid thing. I didn't mean anything by it. Of course they're important.'

'Kate, it doesn't matter.'

We got into the car and drove the rest of the way in silence.

So, it was under the cloud of this inane disagreement that we watched his cousin marry her boyfriend of several years. It was a lovely ceremony but I couldn't enjoy it. Not only because I was worrying that there was more going on between us than contrariness, but also because I believed that at this stage of my life I was pathologically unable to enjoy any wedding. I had simply seen too many. And they were all the same, no matter what flowers or folderols people used to make themselves stand out. The whole thing was mind-numbingly conventional, to be appreciated only by the couple involved and their immediate family. Why anybody thought it was a great day out was beyond me. Bring it all on at the reception, by all means, but making people sit through this pantomime of love and religion was too much.

I wished I wasn't so cynical. I wished I could appreciate it, that I could be carried away by the emotion. I wished I was fourteen again, watching Jean and Mike make their vows. I hoped it would be different when it was my turn. I kept my eyes fixed on the couple as they said they would love and honour each other for the rest of their lives. But I was experiencing more of that feeling I'd had in the bridal shop, that I was a fake. No matter how hard I tried, I couldn't visualize myself at the altar of our local church where I had been christened, where I had made my first Holy Communion, where I had been confirmed, and hear myself say those words. Perhaps that was because I wanted to get married on a Caribbean beach . . . or perhaps it was something else. I reached for Keith's hand and held it tightly. He didn't resist. For the first time in years, I closed my eyes and said a prayer: Please, God, let it be OK.

At least we were of one mind when we got out of the church. We needed a drink. The hotel bar was busy but the only alternative was a pub that liked to flaunt the smoking ban in broad daylight and didn't welcome visitors. We settled into a corner and into two big drinks. I hoped Keith had the same idea as me: if there was something we needed to talk about we didn't need to talk about it here in front of his family. We could get politely drunk, enjoy the day as much as possible, then deal with whatever it was when we got home tomorrow. I was already exhausted.

So, we had our drinks, we sat through the meal, we chatted to his parents. We made a good show of being a happy couple. There was enough noise to fill the gaps. But I began to wonder when things had changed. When had Keith's job taken over his life? When had I ceased to be the centre of his universe? I wasn't cut out for answering the hard questions.

His mother was in great form and seemed to view the wedding as a kind of dress rehearsal for ours. She examined every detail and decided what was to be kept and what should be changed. 'I wouldn't dream of interfering, Kate, but I can't help noticing these things,' she said. 'They've spent far too much on the things that don't matter. The flowers, for example, there were far too many. Nobody needs that many flowers in a church and then you have to leave them behind you afterwards. It was far too extravagant. And all these bits of nonsense on the table.' She leaned over to show me the ribboned boxes that contained more ribboned boxes. 'This sort of thing is really unnecessary. I don't mean to be telling you what to do, Kate, I know you have great taste – anyone can see that. Your outfit is only gorgeous. And that hat – but sure only you could wear it. I hate to see young people spending money where they don't need to. You have enough expenses.'

I assured her that I was into neither excessive flowers nor bits of nonsense for the table.

'And did you see all the bridesmaids she had? Those dresses must have cost a fortune and they'll never be worn again. Never. In my day, if you were lucky enough to be a bridesmaid, you'd get a simple dress you could wear to dances for years. We even wore our wedding dresses to dances. Now they pay out thousands and nothing is ever worn again.'

I didn't want to get into any kind of discussion on bridesmaids, so I just agreed.

'But it's a lovely wedding,' she said. 'Are you enjoying yourself?'

I assured her that I was.

Keith and I had never danced together, we had never had the opportunity, and I had thought we might step out at this wedding. 'I don't dance,' he said flatly. 'You know I don't.'

So I danced with his father, his uncles and one of his cousins. There's something monstrously unsexy about trundling round a crowded dance-floor with men you don't know and who don't know how to hold you. I was happy to dance with his dad, but by the third uncle it was getting harder and harder to fake a waltz. It was almost a relief when they decided to wheel out the Walls of Limerick and the Siege of Ennis. Again, I would have liked to enjoy it, to throw myself into it like the other girls, but I wasn't programmed for the West Clare Fling. I had thought this was exactly the sort of thing to get Keith going, but he remained seated. Nothing, it seemed, would rouse him tonight.

Finding him at the bar later, I tried a little old-fashioned flirtation; after all, there had been a time when he'd found me irresistible. I sidled up to him and casually suggested we take a walk outside. I knew he was very drunk, drunker than I'd ever seen him. He looked at me straight on, almost as if he wasn't quite sure who I was, and said he was sorry the wedding had turned out this way. He said he hadn't meant it to be like this.

'It's fine,' I said to him. 'The wedding is fine. It doesn't matter. But I wish you'd tell me what the hell is the matter with you.'

'There's nothing the matter with me,' he said. 'Nothing at all. Everything's fine.'

He seemed to sway gently between me and the bar. Then he added, 'I think I'll go to bed now. You stay and enjoy the rest of the wedding.'

It was so unlike Keith that I didn't know what to do. I had never had to take care of him before; it had always been the other way round. I was almost tempted to ask his mother for advice but that would have been wrong for several reasons. So, I took his hand and guided him up the stairs to our room. He fell in through the door and slumped across the bed. I took off his shoes and tie and loosened his belt. I squeezed myself in beside him and turned on the television. The late-late movie, *Brief Encounter*, was about to begin.

The following morning, despite his hangover, Keith was up and packing the car before I was awake. I wasn't sure whether or not I had a hangover, but I had a knot in my stomach. I decided to skip breakfast and join him. He was waiting for me.

'Are you ready to head, so,' he said, without catching my eye.

'Yeah, I'm ready. Do you want to say goodbye first?'

'I don't want to see anybody.'

'What about your parents?'

'Look, Kate, I'd really just like to get going.'

'OK.'

I got in beside him, and before I had my belt on he had backed out of his space without checking his mirror and was heading out of the car park at twice the speed limit . . . This was not like Keith. In fact, nothing would ever be like Keith again.

It wasn't until we were back in my flat that he told me. He emerged from the bedroom having carefully placed my bags by the bed; his own he had left in the car. He was ashen. I don't know why I was quite so unprepared for what came next. Surely I knew that things weren't right between us. Or maybe, as Keith suggested later, my mind had been occupied elsewhere. He walked to the couch and sat down. He put his head into his hands and, for a moment, he was crying. I sat beside him and put my arms round him. He didn't resist. He steadied himself. Then he sighed deeply and took my hands in his. 'It's not going to work,' he said.

'What do you mean?' I asked.

'We can't get married.'

'What do you mean?' I said again, thinking that perhaps he had lost his job or something, and thought we couldn't afford to get married. I was all prepared to assure him that we could work it out; we could get married without a wedding – it was all unnecessary expense anyway, as his mother had said. It even occurred to me that that was why he had been in such bad form at his cousin's wedding – he was afraid he wouldn't be able to do the same for me. I had it all worked out in my head.

But that wasn't it.

He looked straight into my eyes, just as he had when he'd asked me to marry him a few months earlier, and he said that I was the most gorgeous creature he had ever known. He said that he loved me more than anything in the world and that he probably always would, but he couldn't marry me.

I was afraid. What had he heard? Who had been saying things? What exactly did he mean?

'Why?' was all I managed.

'Because you don't love me.'

My only impulse was to deny.

'I do love you! I do love you!' I said, grabbing his shoulders and shaking him. 'I do love you,' I repeated. 'Why do you think I don't?'

He got up and walked over to the window. With the light behind him, his features were slightly blurred, which added to the sensation that this wasn't the Keith I knew, that somehow my Keith had been switched with a Keith who was breaking all the rules.

'You've never really loved me,' he said. 'I've always known that. I'm not a fool.'

'That's not true, Keith. I do love you. Stop saying that.'

'Oh, you probably think you do, and maybe you do in a way, but you don't love me enough for for ever.'

'Don't be ridiculous,' I said, speaking far too quickly. 'What's for ever anyway? Nobody knows if anything will last for ever. You just have to go with it and hope for the best. You said you love me, you have to believe I love you too.'

I stopped. There were so many things wrong with this conversation. 'Where did all this come from, anyway?' I asked.

'It's been coming for a while. You must have known it. I thought for ages that it didn't matter, that you'd eventually love me in the same way, or that it didn't matter as long as we were married. But it does matter. It matters a lot.'

I felt powerless. I couldn't deny that much of what he was saying was true, but I'd had no idea that he'd thought so too. And why now, when I was doing everything to try to make it work, was he so positive that it wouldn't?

I joined him at the window. He was leaning against the sill, his pose almost casual as if there was nothing more bothering him than what he would have for his tea. 'What's changed, Keith? Something has to make you think this way.'

For a while he didn't say anything. He seemed to be reflecting on what he was going to say next, or on exactly how he would put it.

'Look, Kate, I nearly got married before, but I didn't because I didn't believe I was in love. And I was right. But with you . . . with you, I was so caught up that I didn't even notice you weren't in love with me. And it breaks my heart to do this . . . believe me.' He kept his eyes fixed ahead of him as he spoke.

I didn't believe he was serious. He could still be persuaded. There was no need to ruin everything just because he was having a few doubts. 'Then why do it? We have as good a chance of being happy as anybody else. We're friends, we care about each other, we've been very happy together. I know I'm a bit flighty at times, but I'm settling down. You've helped me to settle down.'

'No. You're not settling down,' he said, swinging round to face me so that his mouth was only inches from mine. 'You're about to go back to college. You're going to have new experiences, meet new people. You're going to want to do crazy things . . .'

'Is that it?' I asked him. 'Is that what you're worried about? That I'll meet some twenty-year-old and want to run away with him?'

'No. Maybe. No.'

'What exactly are you saying?'

He walked away. He was practically striding. He walked across the room several times before he settled on the couch. His face was red and his temples were throbbing visibly. 'Kate, I don't know if you fully realize this, but not only are you not in love with me you are in love with somebody else.'

It was as if he had reached out and struck me across the face. How could he say that? How could he know it? But the worst of it was that he was wrong. Could it really be that that man was still ruining my life? I knelt beside him and, with my two hands, made him look at me.

'You're wrong,' I said. 'That's over. It's absolutely over. I care nothing for him. When he was creeping round here over the summer I sent him packing. I felt nothing for him. I know I should have told you everything from the beginning but I couldn't bear it. I was ashamed . . . Who told you, anyway?'

He was silent for what seemed like eternity. When he spoke it was as if he had just worked out a difficult problem in trigonometry. 'Oh, you mean Daniel O'Hanlon,' he said, smiling crookedly. 'I've known about Daniel O'Hanlon since the first night I met you. One of your work colleagues let me in on the secret. I'm not talking about *him*.'

I was mystified. He'd known about Daniel all along? Why had he never said anything? What must he think of me? But, more importantly, if he wasn't talking about Daniel, who was he talking about?

'Keith,' I said, 'you're confusing me. What are you talking about? I'm not in love with anybody else.'

He sighed, as if he really didn't want to have to spell it out for me. He was looking at me with a mixture of incredulity and annoyance. 'Your precious brother-in-law,' he spat out. 'Or I should say your ex-brother-in-law.'

'Mike?' I said. 'You think I love Mike?'

'Yes,' he said, rather sarcastically. 'I think you love Mike. And I think he fucking loves you back, so if you don't mind, I'd really rather not be in the middle of all that.'

I didn't know what to say. I didn't think anything I could say would be appropriate. But I couldn't help realizing that what he had said filled me with such excitement that I was in danger of forgetting I was in the middle of a break-up with my fiancé.

He was pacing again. My cheap beige carpet was beginning to show the wear.

'Do you deny it?' he asked, pausing at the window again.

I didn't know what to say. How could I say to Keith that he had articulated the one thing I'd been longing to hear for months? Whatever about my own feelings, whatever about the things I'd been too frightened to acknowledge to myself, if Keith could say he thought Mike loved me, then maybe, just maybe, it was true. How could I say to Keith that he was right, that, yes, I was wholly and utterly in love with my ex-brother-in-law despite the several reasons that suggested it was a bad idea? It was the truth and it was wonderful to hear it. How could I say to Keith that I agreed whole-heartedly we couldn't get married? That I *was* in love with another man and it was no basis on which to start a marriage?

'It just crept up on me,' was all I managed.

'Yeah?' He sounded bored.

'I've known him practically all my life. I never thought I was in love with him. But lately . . . yeah . . . I might have changed the way I think of him. But I was never going to do anything about it. You must believe me, Keith. I was genuine when I said I thought we could be happy. And I have no idea what he feels. I was never going to pursue it. You do believe me?'

'I don't think you've been having an affair behind my back, if that's what you're worried about.'

'I would never do that . . . I . . .' I didn't want to continue that line of thought but there was one thing I had to find out. 'Keith, how did you know?'

'I've seen the way he looks at you.'

'But I – I've never –'

He stood up in front of me and waved his arms about. 'Look, Kate, I don't want to become your therapist. I'm gutted enough that it's not me who keeps you awake nights without having to analyse how you fell in love with your architect friend. I don't know what it was. Maybe that you never stop talking about him. Or that your face lights up the minute his name is mentioned. Or that you go running to him when you want advice on changing your career, or cooking your dinner parties. I don't know, Kate . . . I just know it isn't me.'

I was silent. I had been told that my fiancé had observed me falling in love with the recently deserted husband of my eldest sister. I had a lot to think about. Perhaps I hadn't behaved very well. If you allow impossible thoughts to fester they can only do damage. Whatever about me, I would survive, but Keith wasn't in a good position. And it was my fault. I was a horrible person.

He went into the kitchenette and, in a few minutes, I could hear the kettle boiling. 'You're out of milk,' he said. 'I'll go and get some.'

'OK,' I said.

It was a bizarre situation. As break-ups go, it would have to rank as one of the most amicable. Apart from raising his voice the odd time, there was little other indication that Keith was mad at me. And the oddest thing was that at this minute I felt a huge affection for him. He had delivered me from my agony. He had done what I hadn't had the guts to do and I was grateful to him. He knew I would have married him, he knew I would have tried, but he also knew, better than I did, that it couldn't have worked. No matter how hard you try, you can't pretend you're not in love with someone, even if that love is inappropriate. Keith was stronger and braver than I could ever be. I admired him, I was full of affection for him, but I was not in love with him. I never had been. I think I was in love with the idea of myself with him – balanced, relaxed, together – but you can't rely on someone else to turn you into something you're not. Even if I was to remain a mess for the rest of my life, at least now I wouldn't bring him down with me.

I heard the door open and he was in the kitchenette again, making tea. I followed him in.

'I'm really sorry, you know.'

'I know.'

'I didn't plan it or even really know it was happening, I . . . I'm sorry.'

'It's OK. It's one of those things.'

'You're an amazing person, you know, you deserve so much better than me, and you –'

'Let me stop you there, Kate, before you tell me there's somebody equally wonderful out there for me. It's OK. I'll get over it.'

Despite the steely sarcasm of his tone, I knew he was right: he didn't need me to tell him anything. He handed me a mug of tea. 'I'm going to pack my things and then I'll go.'

'There's no hurry.'

He slid past without touching me.

Two minutes later he was standing in the middle of the living room, a carry-all bag in either hand. I walked towards him. I handed him back his ring. He wasn't going to take it, but I insisted. He dropped the bags and wrapped his arms round me. Our cheeks touched and our tears mingled.

'Look after yourself,' he said.

'You too.'

And then he was gone.

15

So, as I sat in my empty apartment, I had a lot to think about. To say I was in a depression was to put it far too strongly. I don't think my nature is capable of truly sustained melancholy, but life was nowhere near normal. I knew I didn't deserve sympathy, that a good horsewhipping was probably in order. Yet I missed Keith. Not in the sense that I wished we hadn't broken up, but I missed his company, I missed the solidity he lent to my life. There was a space he used to occupy and now it was empty. But something was dawning on me. I had finally realized that I couldn't keep throwing myself from one man to another without giving any thought to suitability or consequences. I was nearly thirty, for God's sake. Most people my age were in stable relationships or, at least, they weren't doing everything they could to sabotage their chances of one. Colette was the same age as me and she had two children. Nobody I knew was as determined to be a mess as I was.

The sadness I felt at losing Keith was deepening and the excitement I had felt at the possibility of something happening with Mike had subsided. It was crazy even to think it. Jean might be easy-going and liberal about their break-up, and about his seeing other women, but she wasn't going to be *that* liberal. As Marion said, she doesn't like sharing. And I had no reason to believe that Mike thought of me as anything other than his ex-wife's rather silly sister. Sure, Keith had said he thought there was something there, but I could hardly press him for details. And, yes, there had been that fantastic afternoon in my apartment. But I wonder now if I'd imagined it all; I'd lodged myself in a warp bubble where Mike was mine. Yet he had seemed happy to be there. And then there was the way he'd kissed me goodbye. In all the years that Mike and I have been giving each other friendly kisses and comradely hugs, there had never been the kind of electricity that had pervaded our semi-kiss that afternoon. And it hadn't only come from me. I knew he'd always liked me, always looked out for me, but I also knew that that was a million miles away from the kind of thing I'd been contemplating. There was nothing for it. I'd just have to get dressed, go out, buy food and face the rest of my life as it was.

I hadn't said anything to anybody else. I wasn't ready to explain, especially when I didn't have a good story ready. Everybody knew Keith was too good for it to have been his fault so it had to have been mine, and I wasn't up to being the bad guy again. I needed to be alone for a while to straighten out my head.

It was just as well that everybody was preoccupied with their own lives. Lucy and Iris were busy babying up; they had seen the obstetrician and been to the first ante-natal class. They were shopping for minuscule vests and painting a nursery; they were busy being in love. Jean's time was taken up with her new flat, and Marion and Ruth had been co-opted by Mum to help organize everything for Anna's visit. I didn't have the energy for a big family thing, in particular a hullabaloo for a sister I hardly ever see and don't know all that well anyway.

I think my reluctance to come out of hibernation might have been due partly to fear of bumping into Mike. I didn't know what might happen and since I had decided that nothing should happen it was better that I didn't see him. There was no reason for us ever to see each other any more.

We had nothing to do with each other now. Sure, he would be at the big party, but it would be a big party and I might not bump into him all evening. And even if I did we would not be alone. And if I could get over one or two meetings like that, I could work out a way to meet him occasionally and not make a fool of myself. We had agreed that we would remain friends despite everything, but he'd probably rather move on, get a new girlfriend with a new silly sister in tow. He would forget. He probably had a new girlfriend already. She was probably gorgeous and intelligent and totally together. He was probably falling in love with her this very minute –

No. I wouldn't torture myself any longer.

I'd get dressed this minute and go down to Dunnes to do a big shop. I'd buy fruit and veg, eggs and yoghurt, red meat, fish, wholemeal brown bread and maybe just one bottle of wine or maybe just two, a red and a white, because I didn't know what kind of a mood I'd be in later. Tomorrow I'd do something about my hair and I'd buy a new lipstick and eye-shadow: I needed a new look. Then I would buy something to wear at the party, something to empower me and make me feel like I hadn't just been dumped by my fiancé and that I wasn't hopelessly in love with a man I could never have.

Yes, tomorrow I'd do that.

As the day of the party approached I was feeling a bit more together. I had called Colette and asked her to come over. I needed to talk to somebody and for the moment I had to keep my troubles outside the family. She arrived with a bottle of Australian Chardonnay and a tub of Pringles – the best the petrol station had to offer. It didn't matter: she had other charms.

I told her everything. I started with the break-up and

worked backwards to my emerging feelings for Mike. I tried to pinpoint when I'd started to think about him differently but it had happened so slowly I couldn't be sure. I've always felt territorial about him – he might have been married to Jean but I was his best friend. I could say anything I liked to him, and while he might scold me and pretend to be horrified, he'd never let me down. Colette reminded me that I'd had a crush on him when he'd first started going out with Jean and suggested that maybe those feelings had never gone away, just been suppressed.

'While he was still married to Jean you didn't mind because you believed he preferred you anyway,' she mused, 'but once there arose the possibility of him being with another woman those subconscious feelings resurfaced. Jean was never a threat but if Mike went outside the family he really was lost to you.'

I didn't like her pop-psychology take on it but I still wanted her to use her skills to determine whether or not Mike felt the same way. She was no help.

'There's no way to tell,' she said. 'There's nothing to suggest he's anything other than brotherly from past behaviour, and I'm sorry to say that your testimony of recent behaviour is unreliable.'

'Who died and made you a lawyer?' I asked her, rather crossly.

'Oh, come on,' she said, 'what do you want me to say? "Yes, I think he's been in love with you all these years and he was only waiting for his wife, *your sister*, to leave, so that he could make his move?"'

'All right, all right.'

'Look, Kate, you've got to stop this. It's not doing you any good. And . . . well, none of it matters because it can't go anywhere.'

'I know.'

'I feel sorry for you,' she said, putting her arms round me, 'now it seems you have two men to get over.' She sighed. 'It's such a pity you couldn't have fallen in love with Keith. He would have been so good for you.'

'Well, I didn't,' I said, a little annoyed. 'I tried but it didn't happen.'

'It's a bit ironic. You can't fall in love with Keith because you can't help being in love with Mike. Keith breaks up with you because you're in love with Mike, but even if you are in love with Mike it doesn't matter because you don't know if he's in love with you, and even if he is nothing can happen.'

I moved away from her and crunched on a fistful of Pringles. 'You're right,' I said. 'Nothing can happen.'

'Yes, I am,' she said, whipping the crisps out of my hand. 'I bloody well am right. Look, I've tried not to be too shocked but only because I thought you had the sense to know that you've got to get over this. He's still married to your sister, for God's sake.'

'It's just that –'

'It's just that what?'

'Well . . . it would be so . . . right.'

'*Right?* How can you say that? Everything about it is wrong!'

'Oh, I know that. I just mean . . . if he hadn't been married to Jean, he would have been the guy I fell in love with.'

'You don't know that. Different circumstances . . . Anyway, it doesn't matter. He *was* married to Jean. He *is* married to Jean.'

'Yeah.'

She pulled me round by the shoulders and looked me straight in the eyes. 'You do see it, don't you? You cannot do this. You cannot do it to Jean, you cannot do it to your parents, you cannot do it to Mike, for God's sake. He's already in a bad enough state. He doesn't need you to come crying to him that you might have a bit of a thing for him.'

'I just wanted to make sure.'

'Well, now you're sure.'

As I saw Colette into a taxi I knew she was right. That was what I'd been telling myself all along. Yet so much of me ached to see him again, to allow his musky smell into my nostrils, to feel his cheek, his lips against mine. Just once – and then I really would surrender him.

By the day of the party I was more confused than ever. Anna and the family had arrived in the small hours of the morning the day before, and after a long sleep and a spot of breakfast she was demanding to see the family. I figured it was time I faced everybody, so I tarted myself up and headed over to Sycamore Lodge.

It was really strange, but from the moment I walked through the door and one of Anna's kids said, 'Hiya,' quite casually, I suddenly felt I'd really missed her and her gangly family. Then when she appeared behind her child, eight-year-old Ronan, I ran to give her a hug and felt I'd been very remiss in not making more of an effort to keep in touch. She was my sister, after all. She looked great, but distinctly different. Her hair was shorter, which made her face seen longer, more serious somehow. Anna has always combined a practical outlook with a fine appreciation of the absurd and I hoped, as I wrapped my arms round her, that she was as fond of the absurd as ever. Because I knew I was going to confess everything to her. She was family, but far enough removed for her judgement to be unclouded by that fact. She would be a good arbiter.

The perfect opportunity arose late in the afternoon. It had been raining most of the day, and as soon as it stopped Anna scouted for someone to accompany her on a walk round the area. I was first to volunteer and got us out of the house before anyone else could realize they needed exercise.

'You've got something on your mind,' she said, almost straight away.

'Have I?' I was surprised by her intuition.

'Yes. You've been hopping on one leg since you got here. Spit it out. Have you done something more sensational than leave your husband or become a lesbian?'

'I'm in love with my sister's husband,' I said.

'Which one? Not mine, I presume.'

'Jean's.'

'Ah, the lovely and talented Mike.'

'Yes. Is it terrible?'

'Well,' she said, looking up and down the road thoroughly before we crossed, 'it depends. How long has it been going on? Is that why Jean left?'

'No, no, no,' I stopped her. 'God, no! Nothing's happened. He doesn't even know. I've only just realized I'm crazy about him.'

'Wait a minute,' she said, stopping dead on the footpath. 'Aren't you about to get married to some Keith guy? I sent you an engagement present.'

'He broke it off because he thought I was in love with Mike. Nobody knows yet. I can't bring myself to tell them.'

'I see.' She thought for a while, then resumed walking. 'Well, then, no, so far it isn't terrible. It's just an awkward fact. What are you going to do about it?'

'Well,' I said slowly, 'I feel I should do nothing. It would only cause unpleasantness for the whole family, especially

Jean. I couldn't do that to her. And, besides, Mike would probably run a mile.'

'That's true – I mean that it might be unpleasant. But if you believe that this could be the real thing and not some silly crush, then maybe you'd better find out how Mike feels.'

'Really? You think I should go for it?'

'You only have one life, that you know of. It's hard enough to find someone you can be happy with, and the older you get, the more complicated it's going to be.' She paused. 'Most of the family doesn't know this, but Tom was married when I met him.'

'*What?*'

'Yeah. We've always kept it quiet. At the time there was no divorce in Ireland and, apart from that, there was the shame.' She giggled.

'Is that why you went to New Zealand?'

'Partly. His marriage was eventually annulled, but it was easier to sit it out on the other side of the world. New Zealand's been brilliant. We've had opportunities there we could never have had here. And it's a great place to bring up kids.'

'Wow! I had no idea. Do Mum and Dad know?'

'They do, but they like to forget.'

'So . . . did you break up his marriage?'

'It was already a mess, but I should probably have run a mile – he was older and he was married. But I didn't. And not a day goes by when I'm not glad I turned my back on everything the nuns taught us. So, you see, if you think this might be the real thing . . .'

I couldn't believe what I'd heard. I'd thought theirs was the most conventional of marriages. You just never know. And was she actually encouraging me to tell Mike I loved him, when I'd decided to give up hope? I couldn't decide whether I was excited about seeing him the following day, or so petrified that I mightn't even turn up myself.

Of course I turned up. I arrived on time in a new dress with a plausible excuse for Keith's absence. A relation had died. He'd had to go to the funeral. When Mum quizzed me on the details – whose side was the death on, was it an aunt or uncle, how old were they, what name would she put on the Mass card? – I realized I should have taken the time to create a back story. I mumbled some stuff about it being a shock and prayed I wouldn't be struck down for playing fast and loose with his family. I'd already done enough.

'Well, that's so disappointing,' Mum had concluded. 'I mean, it's terrible for poor Keith but Anna and Tom were really looking forward to meeting him. Maybe we'll see him tomorrow.'

'Maybe,' I said, as I backed away in the direction of the drinks table.

Mum had pulled out all the stops. From the entrance gate to the under-the-stairs loo to the compost heap in the back garden, she had painted, polished, lit up, dusted with glitter, reupholstered, revarnished – you name it, she'd done it. The length of the avenue was lit with tiny white bulbs that, in the failing light of the late-August evening, suggested a gateway to an alternative reality. I had the feeling, as I wobbled up the drive in heels I knew were too high (but too fantastic to leave behind in the sale) that I might never be the same again. The lights continued round the hall door, which was wide open to give up the eerie sounds of an Air CD being played slightly too loudly in the sitting room. My sense of disorientation continued as I walked through the hall: nobody seemed to be at home. I was just beginning to talk sternly to myself when Lucy tumbled down the stairs.

'Hi, Kate. Didn't expect you for ages. Where's Keith? Like your dress. I can't believe I'm already getting fat. Wait a minute and I'll find Mum. She wants to organize a photograph or something.'

She continued her tumble down the stairs and disappeared in the direction of the kitchen. She didn't look fat; she looked radiant. At that moment I envied Lucy. She was in love and she had her life sorted out. How had she managed it all of a sudden?

I threaded my way into the sitting room with the intention of turning down the stereo. I really liked the album and I knew who had brought it, but it was freaking me out. If I was going to survive this evening I needed to lose the feeling that I was floating in some zero-gravity universe where I'd allow myself to drift into whatever the night presented. I needed to get a grip.

Then I remembered why I always arrived late for these events. Nothing ever started on time and I hated to be on the periphery of something that hadn't yet found its rhythm. For a moment I contemplated retreating upstairs to my room for a lie-down but laughter from the patio drew me towards the garden. Beneath the syrupy giggles I could make out the warm, resonant notes of Mike's voice. If he was there, I wanted to be where he was.

He was up a ladder fixing the last of the lights to the maple tree that was the centrepiece to Mum's barbecue. I wondered why she was still asking Mike to do everything when her other sons-in-law weren't estranged from one of her daughters. I supposed old habits died hard: he was always the one called on when there was something to be hammered together or ripped apart. Maybe they thought if Jean saw enough of him she'd want him back. Then

I wondered what they might be willing to put up with to keep him as a son-in-law . . .

So Mike was up the ladder relating the story of some Christmas-lights fiasco of several years ago and Ruth was at its foot giggling as if Jesus Christ himself was doing standup. I rarely hear her laugh at something that hasn't been generated by herself, her husband or one of her children. Usually Mike's wit is way too subtle for her, yet here she was, like a groupie, twisting a length of fairy-lights between her hands and nodding as if she were his biggest fan. As soon as I stepped on to the patio, they both turned round.

Ruth continued talking, but Mike remained silent. Our eyes met, and for the first time in our lives, his look didn't carry the familiar, warm welcome: there was something else, something that didn't allow him to smile and greet me in the usual way. Like me, I don't think he knew where to look or what to say. I knew why I felt so awkward: all I could see was him sitting on my couch with his feet propped up as if he belonged in the middle of my world; and all I could feel was the faint sweep of his lips against mine. I could only speculate as to why he felt awkward.

I didn't have long to wonder, however, as Lucy breezed back, this time wanting me to come with her so she could give me my present. In my agitation, I had forgotten it was my birthday.

Before we'd got far, we were waylaid by Mum, who had parked herself in the hall to round up her daughters. Jean and Marion had already been enlisted and were trying to convince the rest of us that the sooner we got this damn photograph out of the way the sooner we could get on with enjoying ourselves. I decided to adopt the path of least resistance and planted myself beside them on the stairs. I hadn't the strength to run or to argue. Lucy and Anna joined us without any fuss; Ruth capitulated only after being reassured that she had lost weight. The picture was taken. Yet another family portrait to mark a minor milestone in our lives. At least there was no mention of including partners. I don't know how many family portraits I've sat for in the middle of everybody else's husbands, boyfriends and children. I've always been the odd one out – even Lucy has regularly scared up a short-term boyfriend worthy of the family Canon 329. But I've been consistent: no steady boyfriend, no husband, no children and, mostly, not caring.

Afterwards, I followed Dad into the living room where he was attempting to hide with the newspaper and a glass of port. He looked tired. 'Happy birthday, sweetheart,' he said, and embraced me warmly. 'I hope you like your present. I had nothing to do with it.'

'Thanks, Dad, I'm too old for all this fuss. The party's really for Anna. It's lovely having her home for a while.'

'It is that. It's nice to have everyone around.' He took a sip of his port. 'You're quiet tonight.'

'Oh, you know,' I said jokily. 'I'm turning thirty. It's time to shut up for a while.'

He laughed. 'Your mother tells me Keith isn't with you. He had a funeral?'

'Yeah.' I had to get out of there soon or I'd start blubbering in front of him. He would be so disappointed when he found out I'd messed up again. 'Hey, Dad, what about some booze? Surely you have something a bit special for tonight?'

'Actually,' he said, getting up and leading me out to the kitchen, 'I have a couple of cases of a very nice prosecco. It's superior to a lot of the champagne that's knocking around and excellent value. Come on, we'll open the first few bottles.'

The light sparkling wine would probably settle my stomach, I thought.

Back on the patio the party was beginning to happen. The barbecue had been fired up and Ruth's husband was now in charge of it. He's the type to believe that donning a gimmick apron and burning a load of red meat in front of a drunken audience makes him look manly. Mike, I noticed, had been commandeered by the kids and was helping them assemble a climbing frame Mum had bought. I was tempted to walk over and casually offer my assistance, but I was less likely to be able to stand near him without quivering than I was to attach one coloured pole to another. So I watched as they pushed him over and climbed on top of him, as he scolded and chased after them with the instructions. Once, I would have joined in without thinking twice. Now, I would never again have that kind of freedom with him.

After a while Jean and Marion joined me, wondering why I was so glum.

'Thirty isn't that bad, you know,' said Jean, heaving her legs on to the chair in front of her and crossing one over the other. 'My next birthday, I'll be forty. Now there's something to get gloomy about!'

'I don't care about being thirty,' I said, a little crossly, because I didn't: I've wanted to be older all my life.

'Will Keith be able to pop in later?' asked Marion. She probably thought I was missing him or even that I was cross with him for missing my birthday.

'What did he get you?' asked Jean. 'The consolation has to be good jewellery. I got a fabulous bracelet from Mike when I turned thirty. Oh, I was a fool to dump him before my fortieth!' She laughed.

I didn't answer.

'We've all clubbed together to get you something — oh,

except Lucy. She wanted to do her own thing. It was Mum's idea. I think it's a bit boring but she's thrilled with it. Do you want me to tell you what it is?'

'Oh, for God's sake, Jean, will you shut up?' interjected Marion. 'How old are you?'

'Relax, I won't say anything.'

I wished she'd shut up about presents. I nearly cried when Lucy gave me a beautiful antique pendant. Suddenly I wondered if I should return my engagement presents. I couldn't even remember what they were. Oh, God, I really shouldn't have come.

Soon the party was in full flight: Anna was at the centre of everything, buoyant in red cropped trousers and a red strapless top that showed off her lovely shoulders. I was still thinking about what she'd told me the day before. She had been bold enough to defy the conventions of the time to be with the man she loved, and who, really, had got hurt? His wife, it seems, had had problems anyway and was better off out of the marriage. Mum and Dad had clearly got over it. Why wouldn't they? Their daughter was happy: what more could they want?

So, who would I hurt if I pursued my insane desire for this man? Myself, if he laughed in my face and told me not to be so silly. But, of course, he'd never do that. He'd find some way to let me down gently, tell me he loved me as a sister but it could never be more than that. I believed I was willing to risk a degree of embarrassment.

Mum and Dad, of course. Mum would have a conniption for at least a week, worrying about what her sisters would think. She'd convince herself she could never go out in public again and would probably do her best to illustrate graphically how, rightly, I would rot in hell. After that, though, she might come round. I didn't know what Dad would say. Some part of me thought he'd be pleased, but another thought he'd give up on me for good.

And then there was Jean. What would she make of it? Since she'd left Mike she hadn't stopped surprising me. She had moved her life on; she was happy enough to be happy for him, there was no doubt about it. But could she be happy for me?

I continued to play with these thoughts as I pushed a sausage and an incinerated steak round my plate. I wondered if I should talk to Lucy or Marion. Lucy had shared the kind of relationship I'd always had with Mike; she understood us well. If I asked her straight out what she thought my chances were, she'd tell me. But she didn't need this: she was wrapped up in her world of Iris and the baby. I had to accept that Lucy and I might never be quite as close again. And that was how it should be. Family relationships should give way to the ultimate relationship with the ultimate person. Yet, I wouldn't have minded hearing her thoughts on this. If I got truly desperate, I'd talk to her.

Marion would listen, of course, but I didn't think she'd approve. She'd say I was being childish, wanting something I couldn't have, and that I was a fool to have let it ruin things with Keith. She'd be fair-minded and clear-sighted. She'd be everything I didn't want at the moment.

Meanwhile, I was keeping Mike within my radar. He seemed to embody everything I'd ever desired in a man. As well as loving him for reasons that were pure and noble, I craved him physically in a way I'd never experienced before. I couldn't recall a time when I'd been so engulfed by lust. It made me a little nervous that maybe my feelings weren't genuine, that I was experiencing an adolescent crush, but deep down I knew that wasn't so. Deep down I knew this was the real thing.

I watched him have a lengthy conversation with Jean while I pretended to listen to Ruth as she explained how her eldest was about to go to playschool for the first time. He was standing in front of the maple tree with a pint in his hand when she joined him; she had her back to me and I had a full view of him. They really had managed to keep everything civil between them. As far as I knew they hadn't had a single fight over anything. The house was sold and the proceeds split down the middle; Mike had said she could have the contents, but in the end she didn't want much of it. They let most of the furniture go in the sale, apart from a few things Mike had brought with him. I had no idea what they might be talking about now: Jean seemed very animated while Mike nodded every so often and said something that started her off again. I convinced myself that when he looked up he was gazing at me, and each time my heart and stomach flipped. But he was probably just staring into the distance.

I knew I was starting to obsess when I began to memorize the clothes he was wearing – a turquoise shirt open at the neck (affording a tantalizing glimpse of chest hair) with faded denims . . . and the way the last of the sun picked up the different colours in his hair – the mid-brown that had hardly faded and the strands of grey that added depth – and the contours of his face, the high cheekbones and firm jaw, the intense blue-green of his eyes . . . It was time to tune back into Ruth and her motherly anxieties, but I had clearly been out for far too long because now she was done with playschool and was trying to involve me in a plot to set Mike up with some old schoolfriend of hers. I was horrified. How dare she talk of him in that way? And the girl she was planning for him was a horrible old cow whose husband had walked out on her a year ago. I remember her at school – she was a whiny, slimy bag of misery. Just because she was separated, Ruth thought she was perfect for Mike. I had to get up and walk away.

I wandered back into the house to find more of the delightful prosecco. Some of the older kids had migrated inside to watch television. I sat with them for a while and had a fragmented conversation with Marion's Lisa about the unreality of the characters in *Home and Away*. She had a lot of opinions she was happy to share with me, but after a while it was clear that I was interrupting her enjoyment of the programme.

I wandered into the sitting room and once more considered just slipping out of the front door and going home. But I didn't. However awkward, I'd stay as long as he did. So, after examining my appearance in the hall mirror (my dress was definitely a success – the vibrant purple and orange pinstripe was nicely balanced by the ephemeral nature of the chiffon), I wandered back into the garden.

The night was beautiful. There was still a lot of heat in the air but also an autumnal note. I always love the change of season: anticipation mingles with memories of other years. I had no desire to talk to anyone; and it was as well that most people had forgotten it was my birthday. I had warned Mum that I didn't want a cake or toasts but I knew she wouldn't take any notice, so I slipped down the garden path towards the little copse. There are only about twenty trees in it, but they're large and close together so it's possible to be completely hidden from view, despite Mum's artfully placed spotlights.

As I stumbled among the beeches and elms I had no idea that I wasn't alone. It was several seconds before I registered that Mike was standing there with his back against one of the trees, and several more before I grasped that he was walking towards me with the intention of taking me in his arms and kissing me. I froze and saw him hesitate, but when he placed his arms round me and his mouth on mine there was no hesitation.

For a moment there was nothing, as my consciousness slipped off the edge of known space. When I surfaced I was only aware that the soft, tender lips touching mine were his lips; that the tongue gently probing mine was his tongue; that the hands touching my cheek, my hair, my neck and trailing down my back were his beautiful hands. Mike was kissing me truly, passionately; he was kissing me as though he loved me truly, passionately. I would have stayed inside that kiss for ever only I wanted to hear him say it. I wanted to look at his face and see it written there. When we did part he kept his hand on my cheek; he was breathing deeply and he seemed about to say something. But suddenly there was noise coming from the other side of the trees: someone was calling my name. It was Lucy, sent to find me for the cutting of the cake. I panicked. I looked deep into his eyes and then I ran.

'There you are,' said Lucy. 'Have you seen Mike anywhere?'

'No,' I said. 'No, I haven't.'

16

The following morning I got out of bed as soon as I woke. I'd been tossing and turning most of the night, and my head was still spinning. Nothing would ever be the same again – but I didn't know how things were. When Lucy had called me my first impulse had been to run, and now I wondered what would have happened next if instead I had grabbed Mike's hand and run with him out of the garden gate on to the lower road, over the bridge and, eventually, to my place or his. For that had been the last I saw of Mike that night.

I followed Lucy up to the house where everyone had gathered to sing 'Happy Birthday' and kept expecting to see him slide in at the back of the group, but he must have slipped out of the garden gate on his own. I waited and waited, and then it struck me that he might be waiting for me at home. I left as soon as I could, and ran back to Hartstonge Street. He wasn't there.

I considered going round to his place but decided against it. The next morning when I woke after a few hours' sleep, I realized that of course he wouldn't have been waiting for me. As far as he knew I still had a fiancé. As far as Mike was concerned, our kiss should never have happened. He would be feeling guilty and ashamed. I had to set his mind at rest. Then I would talk to Jean.

But I wasn't quite ready to turn up on Mike's doorstep. I knew that when I talked to him things would get complicated. So, for now, I'd indulge myself in the memory of that kiss. I had a shower, put on a pair of old jeans with a new top and set off for the Furze Bush. It would be calm there and no one would bother me.

Autumn had turned back into summer: it was warm and the sun beat down from a clear sky. The weather didn't suit my mood: I needed the gravitas of rain and a chill in the air. For me, summer was over. I wanted to hasten in the autumn and the changes it would bring. I had turned thirty. Perhaps my extended girlhood was finally at an end and it was time to grow up. I smiled to myself as I walked over the cracked pavements; I had spent the summer talking sternly to myself, and look where it had got me. I was in a bigger mess now than when I had started.

The Furze Bush had its usual breakfast crowd but my favourite table in the corner by the window was empty. I gave my order and sat down. I love to sit there and watch the bustle on the street – it's very soothing. But that morning I was interrupted even before my coffee had arrived by a grating voice. It was Angela, a former colleague at O'Sullivan and Woulfe.

'Hello there!' she said loudly. 'How are you since you left us? I must say you look great – the lazy life suits you. What have you been up to? Of course – you have your wedding to plan. You must be so busy.'

I had several options for handling this: I could get up and walk away; I could tell her a pack of lies, which she would disseminate gleefully round the office; I could tell her the shocking truth, which she could add to and then disseminate gleefully round the office; or I could just say very little, in the knowledge that she couldn't shut up for five minutes anyway.

'Oh, you know,' I said. 'Nothing, really.'

'And how's Keith?' she asked. 'I'm seeing someone my-self at the moment. Yes, I've been waiting for my Mr Right all this time and then one day he walks straight into the office. He's the guy they hired to replace you, actually. Of course, he's a little younger than me, but sure what does that matter? He's very mature.'

I was relieved to hear they had needed someone to replace me. I'd been convinced that as soon as I left, and there was no discernible difference in the workload, they'd wonder why they'd been paying me all these years.

'Oh, that's nice,' I said.

'Yes, and he's good-looking too. He has the whole package!'

'Great! Well, best of luck with it all.'

'OK, then,' she said. 'I'll leave you to your coffee. I suppose Keith will be joining you soon and I wouldn't want to impose. Alan will be here in a minute. I'll introduce you 'cos in a way I have you to thank for him.'

'Great,' I said again. 'I look forward to it.'

Angela had always got up my nose: she was one of those girls who have been obsessed all their lives with having a boyfriend, and you know that the main reason they don't have one is because of their desperation. They reek of it. I wished her the best with whatever greenhorn she'd got her teeth into, but I didn't think I could hang around to watch them moon over their croissants. So, when she wasn't looking, I got up and left.

I was on the move again. I thought about ringing Colette but I wasn't up to arguing with her and I knew she wouldn't approve. As I was passing the Augustinian church, I stopped and, for a moment, considered going in. They always used to have confession on a Saturday afternoon. When my sisters and I got older and felt our sins were getting a bit close to the bone, we'd come in here on a Saturday rather than confess to the priests who knew us at our parish church. I hadn't been in years, but I'd never fallen out with the concept of confession. I remember the physical sensation of a weight being lifted after I had unburdened myself of my juvenile crimes. Now, however, it wasn't a priest's absolution I needed (even if he would give it): it was Jean's. I kept on walking.

I rummaged for my mobile and called her. 'Jean! What are you up to?'

'Recovering. I overdid it last night. What about you? You disappeared early. Get a booty call, did you?'

'Ahm, not exactly. You up for a chat?'

'Sure. Do you want to call over?'

'Would you mind meeting me in town?' I felt it was best to stick to neutral territory.

'Fine. I could do with stretching my legs. Where?'

'What about the café bar on Glentworth Street?'

I wanted somewhere she could have a coffee and I could have a drink, and then, if she needed it, she could have a drink too.

'See you there in twenty minutes.'

'Great.'

'Hey,' she said then, 'is everything OK?'

'Sort of. I'll tell you everything.'

'OK. See you in a bit.'

I turned and retraced my steps back up town. I had no idea how I was going to tell her, even less how she might react. At one time Jean had been queen of the hissy fit – maybe I'd come to regret doing this in public.

I found a seat near the back of the café and ordered a glass of white wine. There weren't many other customers and nobody who looked like they'd be bothered to eavesdrop or get upset by a raised voice. In fact, it was unlikely that the place would remain in business for much longer –

the majority of its customers were students who brought a book or a newspaper and made one drink last hours. The moneyed working types preferred a *bona fide* public house to do their drinking.

The wine was cold and alcoholic. I could feel it shuttle through the centre of my body and radiate into every cell. I hadn't overdone it last night; I had been inebriated on something entirely different, but now I needed a crutch. I'd planned to stop at one glass but when Jean arrived she ordered one for herself and another for me. 'Hair of the dog. Next week I'm detoxing,' she said.

She settled herself on the chair beside me. 'So,' she said, with an air of open expectation, 'what's the story?'

'First,' I said, possibly in a ploy to gain sympathy, 'Keith broke up with me.'

'What? When?' She was stunned.

I'd got so used to it that I'd forgotten the impact my news would have. 'Ahm, a while ago now. Just after that wedding we went to.'

'What on earth happened?'

'He reckoned I wasn't in love with him.'

'He *what*?'

'I'd sort of been having doubts all along. I just hadn't realized he knew about them.'

'But you were happy about it, weren't you? I thought you'd decided it was worth having a shot.'

'Well, I had, but he'd obviously decided otherwise.'

'I can't believe it.' She was shaking her head and swirling her wine.

'I was a little shocked at first. I'd thought if anyone was going to do the breaking up, it would be me. But I'm OK with it now. He was right, it wouldn't have worked. I'd have been restless in no time.'

'But it's tough all the same. You had no idea, had you?'

'No, I hadn't. I hadn't been paying that much attention.'

All of a sudden she put her arms round me. 'Oh, you poor thing. I'm so sorry.' She was even crying a little bit.

'I'm OK, Jean, honestly. It's fine.' I was beginning to feel guilty.

'But you've been keeping it to yourself. Why didn't you tell anyone?'

''There was all the excitement of Anna being home and the party and everything, and I just wasn't up to all the explanations.'

She said nothing for a while, then, 'Don't kill me now, but was there something else?'

I knew what she was hinting at. 'No. Well, not exactly.'

'Kate?' Her tone was only moderately accusatory.

'I didn't cheat on him.' I paused. I didn't know how to put it. 'But there's something else I need to tell you, which you might not be that keen to hear.'

'Yes?'

'Well, at the party last night, something happened.'

'What happened?'

'I kissed Mike. Actually, he kissed me and I kissed him back.' If I talked quickly it wouldn't sound as bad, I thought.

She said nothing.

'Jean, I think I'm in love with him and maybe he is too, only I don't know because I haven't talked to him. I wanted to talk to you first.'

She still said nothing.

'I know it's weird, but I really am crazy about him. But if you say so, I'll never even look at him again.' I certainly hadn't planned on saying that, but suddenly it seemed right.

Eventually she spoke: 'You kissed? Last night at the party?'

'Yeah.'

'And that's all?'

'Oh, yeah, absolutely.'

'Did he say anything to you?'

'No.'

'And it was only that one time?'

'Yeah.' I couldn't read her. She seemed calm, but maybe this was the prelude to a violent eruption.

'How long do you think you've been in love with him?'

'I'm not sure. Over the summer. Since ye broke up.'

'Why?'

'Why ... what?' I didn't want to antagonize her but I wasn't sure what she was asking.

'Why him? Why did you fall in love with him? You were supposed to be in love with somebody else.'

'I know ... I've always liked him. Maybe when you didn't want him any more, I saw him differently. I don't know. Or perhaps I've always loved him.'

She finished her wine. She sighed. 'I don't believe it,' she said.

'What?'

'I don't fucking believe it.'

'I'm sorry.'

'There we all are, having birthday parties and engagement parties for you, and all the time you're eyeing up Mike. You're incredible.'

'I wasn't eyeing him up. I didn't even know I was in love with him. At least, not until Keith told me. And I was never going to do anything about it.'

'Until *Keith* told you?' She was looking at me as if I'd sprouted another head.

'He seemed more aware of it than I was.'

'So instead of giving you a bollocking, he sent you running into his arms!'

'Well, I suppose he didn't want me if I was in love with someone else.'

'But Mike! Honest to God, Kate, do you hear yourself? You're saying you're in love with the man I've been married to for the last fifteen years. This isn't just anybody you're talking about.'

'I know, I know – it sounds dreadful and, believe me, I was never going to act on it, but last night . . . I've never felt this way before . . .'

'Oh, Jesus, Kate, give me a break.'

This wasn't going well. It was only the memory of Mike's lips on mine that kept me from running out and never coming back.

She said nothing more for a while, then: 'So what about Mike? Has he been lusting after you all these years?'

'I don't know. I haven't spoken to him.'

'I need another drink.' She got up and went to the bar. My betrayal seemed to be written on her back as she stood there, unmoving, for what felt like an age. When she came back she sat opposite me. 'So, what's your plan now?'

'I don't have one.' I paused. 'But I thought I might go and talk to Mike. If that's OK with you.'

'Oh, fuck, I don't care. I mean, I left him. I don't want him any more. He can kiss and shag whoever he wants.' She gave a disgusted little laugh. 'But did it have to be you?'

'I'm sorry.'

'I always knew he had a soft spot for you, but I'd no idea it went this far.'

There was a coldness in her tone that made me feel sick.

'I might be getting all worked up over nothing. It was only a kiss. He was probably just drunk and horny.'

'Mike doesn't do drunk and horny. If he kissed you it was because he meant to.'

I said nothing.

'And does he know Keith dumped you?'

'No.'

'So he kissed you thinking you had a fiancé? Boy, he must have it bad.'

'I meant what I said earlier . . . about never seeing him again . . . if you want.'

'Oh, come off it! And have me painted as the evil sister who stands in the way of true love?'

'I'll do whatever you want.'

She sighed, and rested her chin on her fist. 'But tell me, Kate, is it true love? Or is it you just enjoying a good piece of drama?'

I had no intention of crying, but suddenly I couldn't hold back the tears. 'Oh, Jean,' I sniffled, 'if this isn't the real thing, I don't know what is.'

'Christ!' she said. 'I'd have stayed married to him if I'd known you were going to get your claws in.' She flashed me a wry smile.

'I really didn't mean for this to happen.'

'I know, but it has.'

'I just want to talk to him – he'll probably have changed his mind.'

'Oh, go and talk to him.'

'Will I tell him you're OK?'

'Tell him whatever the hell you like.'

We left the café together and I walked with her as far as the quays. I didn't want to leave her until I felt confident that she meant what she'd said. But, as she'd also said, it wasn't her job to make me feel better.

'Look,' she said, as we were about to part company, 'I'm not over the moon about this, but I'm not going to make you swear never to see him again. Mike and I are over. I'm reconciled to the idea of him being with other women. I wasn't ready for it being a woman I know, that's all. You do whatever you feel you have to.'

And with that she walked off.

Passing by the turn to Hartstonge Street I was tempted to go and lie down for a while; it was hot and sticky and I could have done with a change of clothes, but I knew that if I didn't keep going I might lose my courage and, after all, the hardest part was over. I went round the corner to the shop and bought a bottle of water, drank half and dabbed the rest on my face and neck. Then I set off up O'Connell Avenue.

By the time I got to his house I was trembling and although the sun was still shining, I felt a chill run down my spine. I opened the gate and walked up the path. The front and back gardens were the only things he had left untouched. The little old lady who had owned the house before him had had a penchant for kitsch and twee (although to her the winding path, the carefully trimmed shrubberies and the classical statuettes were probably the height of sophistication) and Mike had decided he liked the look. I rang the doorbell several times, but there was no answer, so I sat down on the little garden bench, drew my knees up under my chin and waited.

I wished I'd brought a magazine. Pictures of badly dressed celebrities or makeup tips for the new season would have helped me relax. I could have become utterly absorbed in what hem lengths, boot heights and lip lines were doing this winter. Instead I began to imagine what Mike would look like as he bent over one of the miniature hedges to trim a stray leaf, or how the balance of weight on the bench would shift were he to sit down beside me. I resisted getting up and looking in the window at what must now be a completed refurbishment. I knew it would be beautiful, a simple, unadorned, functional living space. I knew that even the most innocuous objects could become erotically charged. Even his neighbours, as they walked past, seemed imbued with a certain charm. Did they realize how lucky they were to be living so close to him? If he didn't come home soon I was in danger of working myself into a state of sublime panic. Luckily, he came through the gate at that very moment. He had been out for a run and was taking off his shirt. As yet he hadn't seen me.

He was breathing heavily as he stood, hunched over, one arm resting on the low pillar. The movement of his ribcage seemed forced and uncomfortable. I was about to say something when he turned. He was visibly shocked. 'Jesus!' he said, as he put his shirt back on.

'I was waiting for you,' I said nonsensically.

'I was about to ring you,' he said, his voice low and unsteady. 'I should have called sooner.'

'That's OK.'

'Look, Kate, I'm really sorry. I wanted to apologize for last night. I don't know what came over me. I – I behaved very badly.'

'No, you didn't.'

'Yes, Kate, but it's entirely my fault. I should have known better.' His voice was gathering momentum but it was still weak and dry.

'It's OK. That's what I wanted to tell you. Keith and I are broken up.'

'What?' He was truly horrified: the colour drained from his face.

'It's OK. We've been broken up for a couple of weeks. So . . . last night was OK.'

He was breathing heavily again.

'Can we go inside?' I asked.

He seemed disoriented, but then he produced a key from a tiny pocket in his shorts.

The interior of the house was beautiful. To the frenzy in my mind it seemed a haven of calm and comfort. It was becoming obvious, though, that whatever turmoil I was going through, his was worse.

'I'll make some coffee,' he said, but he went to the fridge and poured a glass of water, which he drank in one gulp. Then he poured one for me. I had sat on the edge of the couch. He remained standing. He seemed to have forgotten the coffee. 'You and Keith broke up?'

'A couple of weeks ago. He said I wasn't in love with him.'

'Weren't you?'

'No.'

'You – you hadn't said anything.'

'I didn't know what to say. It all seemed a bit ridiculous.'

'So . . . you . . .' He kept rubbing his face and running his fingers through his hair.

'So I'm not going to marry him and – and I'm free to kiss whoever I want.'

'No, Kate. You're not free, I'm not free. It's not like that.'

'Why isn't it? Mike, last night was amazing. It was –'

'It was wrong.'

'Why?'

'You know why.'

His voice had become paper thin despite the strength of his words.

'Because of Jean? She'll get over it.'

'No, Kate . . .'

'I just talked to her. She could get used to the idea.'

'No.'

'Yes.'

'No, Kate. No.'

'Why? Are you going to tell me you didn't mean to kiss me? Because I know you did. And there's no way you could kiss like that unless . . . unless you felt something.'

'Kate, it was wrong.'

'It wasn't wrong. We're both single.'

'It's not as simple as that and you know it.'

'I don't know anything any more except that I love you.'

'Don't say that.'

'It's true.'

'I shouldn't have kissed you.'

'It was the most amazing kiss of my life.'

'Don't *say* that.'

'Do you love me?'

'Don't do this, Kate.'

'Do you love me?' I was surprised at my forwardness. But as soon as I saw him again and his physical presence collided with the intense memory of his skin against mine, I knew I was going to fight for this man, even if the battle was with him.

'Do you love me?' I asked again.

He sat down on the chair opposite.

'You have to tell me,' I said. 'You have to tell me if you do.'

He kept shaking his head and staring at the floor.

'Do you love me?' I asked again.

Finally, he looked up. 'Yes,' he said, very slowly, his voice quivering. 'I've loved you for years. But like any sensible man who finds himself in love with his wife's sister, I've suppressed it. Up to now, I've done a fairly good job.'

He looked up at me. He sighed. He took a deep breath. 'I know she left me. I know we're not really married any more but . . .'

I couldn't imagine what his reasons might be.

'. . . it's not that simple. You're her sister. This would kill her.'

'Do you still love her?'

'I still care what happens to her.'

There seemed to be no answer to that. 'So, is this it, then?'

'It has to be.'

'It doesn't.'

How could he tell me he loved me, then send me away?

'I'm so sorry I started this.'

'You didn't start it. That's why Keith broke up with me. He knew I was in love with you.'

'He broke up with you because of me?'

'No. Because of me. I was in love with you all the time but I wouldn't let myself see it.'

'Oh, Kate . . . if I've ruined your chance of happiness . . .'

'I'd never have been happy with Keith. I fell in love with you because you're you. I've always loved you.'

My words were filling the cool space of his house. He could hear them, but he wouldn't pick them off and realize they were his.

'Kate, I think you should go,' he said.

'I'm not a child any more,' I snapped. 'You don't have to protect me from myself.'

'Please, Kate.'

It was no use.

I got up and walked through the front door, down the winding path and closed the gate behind me. I didn't know if he watched me go. I didn't know if he truly wanted me to leave. But that was it. I was gone.

He was gone.

17

September was a strange month. I felt like I used to as a schoolgirl when the holidays were over. No matter how good or bad the summer had been, something in the air announced that it was time to go back to school and, actually, it was a relief. Now, having been at a loose end for so long, I needed something to occupy me but my Human Resources course didn't begin until the middle of the month. It was time to stop daydreaming and find a job. It was surprisingly easy to present myself at cafés and supermarkets along with the teenagers and the non nationals and persuade them that, yes, I'd probably be able to work the till even though I had no experience. I got a job at the café bar where I'd met Jean that day. The money was awful but the hours were flexible and the work was easy.

I knew there was no way I could pay my mortgage on part-time wages so I advertised for a flatmate. I'd lived with Jean so I could probably put up with anyone. There was quite a bit of interest, but in the end I chose a shy girl who had moved in from Newcastlewest. She gave me the impression that she wanted to be left alone, which suited me fine. I didn't have the energy to make a new friend. Apart from an occasional encounter in the kitchen, I hardly saw her. She spent a lot of time in her room and I spent a lot of time out of the house.

I was throwing myself into as many different things as possible. When college opened I intended to join as many societies as there were nights in the week. I would debate,

I would act, I would watch foreign films, I would learn to play the guitar, I would embark on Dungeons and Dragons; the only society I wouldn't join was the Law Society. When I was an undergrad I had spent far too much time in the pub or crashing on other people's floors. This time I would give myself a truly liberal education.

In the meantime, though, I was scouring the post-grad noticeboards for anything that would fill my evenings when I couldn't stand the café bar any longer. I was delighted to find an array of cultural activities on offer.

One of the first things I went to was a play written by a student and performed by a mixture of other students and professional actors struggling to get a break. The theatre was a converted basement on The Crescent. I hadn't known it was there though I must have passed it hundreds of times. It was a glorious feeling to sit on my own in the dark while the seats around me filled with the kind of people I hadn't seen in Limerick since my early forays to the Belltable as a teenager: people who liked to see something new and experimental. They might enjoy it, but there was always a chance it would change their lives.

The play was called *The Enigma*, a well-chosen title. It was all voices speaking out of the dark with occasional bursts of dance or gymnastics. The actors looked like they should have been getting up for school in the morning but their commitment and enthusiasm were plain to see. After an hour I had no idea what the play had been about; the only thing I could say for sure was that I'd enjoyed being baffled. It was years since I had been to any play, not to mind one that was weird and low-budget and attended by people who clearly understood all the things that I didn't.

It was the opening night and the playwright's debut so there was a reception afterwards. I hung around because I hoped I might get into conversation with a few of the interesting people there. The men wore loose shirts and had inventive facial hair while the women had on big jewellery and very little makeup. Soon someone observed to me that the writing had been mature and daring. I wanted to ask him what the play had been about but he had dissolved back into the crowd before I could open my mouth. Then a boy told me that a gang was going round the corner for a pint. I thought, What the hell? and followed him.

As soon as I was out in the air, the only place I wanted to be was home. I didn't have the energy to talk to people I didn't know about a play I hadn't understood, especially as those people were ten years younger than I was. Perhaps they weren't as interesting as I'd thought they might be.

Mike would have put it all in context. He would have known whether or not the play was about anything. He would have made me laugh and feel good about the experience. He would have made everything clear.

Another night I went to a gig in the Green Room. The band was called The Fewer, The Better, a group of hot young musicians from Limerick. I had forgotten how easy it is to be at a gig alone: the music's too loud for talk, and if the band's good enough, all anybody wants to do is listen and watch, or maybe dance. Even I knew that this band was good but it was charming to watch so many young men make their way to the front to just stand with their arms folded and stare at what the lead guitarist was doing. You could see the awe and admiration in their faces. Afterwards I bought two CDs; one I listened to over and over until I could nearly make out all the words and could say definitively that tracks two, seven and ten were my favourites. The other I would give to Mike . . . if I ever saw him again.

Other nights I went for walks along the city streets.

I have always felt empowered by the sight of wide pavements stretching ahead of me, slightly distorted in the amber glow of sodium lamps. The city feels safe in all its Georgian concreteness; only good and exciting things could happen here. And here I felt most at ease in my limbo world – a world that contained a man who loved me but would not have me. At times it was enough to know that he loved me – had loved me for years – and at others it was the greatest injustice in the universe that we could not be together. I replayed every moment of that afternoon: his unease, his discomfort, his admission, his rejection. I immersed myself again and again in his kiss. I walked everywhere, sometimes even far enough up O'Connell Avenue to pass the turn to his house. I dreaded meeting him, yet longed to. I had so much to say to him, yet it amounted to nothing.

Then, Marion called early one morning. Dad had been taken into hospital. He had woken up in the middle of the night with pains across his chest and Mum had rung for an ambulance.

By the time I got there Dad was in his room, pale and small in his carefully ironed pyjamas; his hair, normally so tidy, was ruffled and seemed greyer than usual. Mum looked little better. She had evidently rushed out of the house without following her usual grooming routine and the clothes she was wearing were clearly yesterday's. All of a sudden my parents were frail – tragic, even.

Marion was trying to find a doctor who would tell her something about Dad's condition. All she had been told so far was that he had had some tests and it would be a while before the results were known.

'I don't think it could have been a heart-attack,' she said, 'or they wouldn't be so calm and Dad wouldn't look so well.'

'I don't think he looks well,' I said.

'Believe me,' she said, 'if he'd had a heart-attack he'd look a lot worse. He looks bad to you because you've never seen him without a shave and a collar.'

'Mum looks exhausted.'

'She needs sleep. If I could talk to a doctor I'd persuade her to go home.'

'Marion, is he going to be OK?' I couldn't conceive of anything happening to either of my parents, especially not Dad.

'I'm not an expert, but I don't think it's too bad. He's as strong as an ox.' She went out again to try to nab a doctor and I sat down beside Mum. They had given Dad something to make him sleep and he'd gone off. I didn't know what else to do so I took Mum's hand and kissed it.

'You're a good girl,' she said.

I wanted to contradict her but now wasn't the time. 'He'll be fine, Mum,' I said.

'Oh, I hope so. I'd be lost without your father.'

I could feel tears welling, so I got up to open a window. The air was cool and clear. 'Have you a comb in your bag, Mum? I'll do your hair.' It was best to stick to the things I'm good at.

'I think so, dear. I might have a lipstick too. I didn't even brush my teeth before I came out.'

'Come here. I'll do you up and then we might go home. Dad's going to sleep for a while, so you might as well get some rest.'

'I wouldn't want him to wake up to strangers.'

I could see her point, so I combed her hair and went out to find a travel toothbrush.

I've never had much to do with hospitals. Apart from the odd visit to Casualty in the small hours of the morning, I've never been 'in hospital'. The only visiting we've ever done has been for new babies and the odd minor procedure, like tonsils. Of course, Ruth was never out of hospital when she was a child, but that was years ago. I've never entertained the idea that either Mum or Dad might end up in one. They always seemed so strong.

For the rest of that first day nothing happened. Dad slept for ages and when he woke up Mum told him that everything would be fine. A doctor eventually confirmed that he hadn't had a heart-attack but they wouldn't rule out the possibility that he might have one. They weren't sure what had caused the chest pains and wouldn't speculate.

As the day went on, the rest of the family drifted in; Ruth was so fraught she had to be taken aside by a nurse and given a cup of sweet tea. Lucy and Jean arrived together, calm but insistent that Mum should go home. She only agreed when I assured her that I would stay in the house with her. So Ruth dropped us back and after I'd seen Mum to bed I found myself in my old room. I seemed destined not to progress very far.

Before I could get too maudlin, Jean and Lucy called on their way home. I hadn't spoken to Jean since that day, just texted her to say that nothing more was going to happen between Mike and me. I hadn't consciously kept it from Lucy, I just hadn't seen her, but as soon as she was standing in front of me I wished she knew: she soon detected an atmosphere between Jean and me.

When I explained, she was incredulous. 'I cannot believe it,' she said. 'How many men are there in the world and you have to go after your brother-in-law? Mike!'

I was a little hurt by her reaction. I'd been much more understanding when she'd announced that her love life wasn't exactly textbook. I felt she should understand that you couldn't choose who you fell in love with.

'Poor Jean,' she said then. 'How could you do it to her?'

'It's OK,' said Jean. 'Kate and I talked. I've come to terms with the idea.'

'There's nothing to come to terms with,' I told her. 'Mike doesn't want anything to do with me.'

'What happened?' she asked.

'Oh, he said it had been a mistake. He was drunk and a bit lonely. I happened to be there. He apologized. He's been a bit of an idiot and I've been a bit of an idiot. It's all over now.' I wasn't up to telling her that her husband had been in love with me for years but that he still cared about her enough not to let anything happen between us.

'Sorry,' she said.

'It's OK. Time to move on. I'll bag me a student before the month is out.'

She smiled wryly.

Lucy was still standing in the middle of the room with her hands resting on her spreading hips. 'I'd never have thought it of Mike.'

'Lucy, it's over. Whatever madness it was, it's over.'

'And what about Keith?'

'That's over too. And don't go pretending that Keith was the man for me because you always thought it was a bad idea.'

'I'm not. I'm just sorry things haven't worked out for you.' There was an unmistakable note of tenderness in her voice.

'Look, lads,' I said, 'I'm exhausted. I'll talk to you tomorrow.'

We kissed each other and they left.

I wanted to go to bed and sleep but I was beyond tired: I could lie on my old bed all I liked but there was little chance that I would even close my eyes. I curled up on the couch in the living room and turned on the TV.

Everything I did reminded me of Mike. There had been nights during the Christmas holidays when all of the family had gone to bed and I'd creep downstairs for a glass of water to find Mike on the floor in front of the television, his head propped against the end of the couch, watching an old western or a dodgy 1970s thriller. I'd join him on the floor, pulling a rug across the two of us and we would talk about the movie, and go to bed only when the channel closed down.

The truth was that everything had changed since Mike told me he loved me. It was as if every moment I had spent in his company had been rewritten in a different dialect. When he had kissed me on the night of the party he had meant it. When he had sat in my living room sipping wine and I had fantasized that he belonged to me, perhaps he had fantasized the same thing. And why now, when he was free to love me, did he refuse to?

Not long into my cruise of the television channels I became aware of Mum shuffling about in the kitchen. She was making hot milk and toast. Suddenly I was hungry. 'Can I get in on that, Mum?'

'Certainly, dear. You never eat enough.'

'I eat plenty, Mom, I haven't fallen away yet.'

She took the butter out of the fridge and spread it thickly across the toast. I'd forgotten the taste of real butter.

'Keith will be missing you,' she said, after a couple of bites.

I couldn't tell her more lies. Besides, it would probably bother her less now that she had other things to think about. 'Keith and I broke up.'

'No!'

'Yeah. A while ago. But it's OK. It's for the best.'

'That's an awful shame. I was very fond of him.'

'I was too. But I wasn't in love with him, not like it should be.'

'I don't know what it is with your generation. You all think it has to be like the films. You just get on with it, dear. And Keith is one of the good ones.' She sighed as she sipped her milk.

'I'm sorry, Mum.'

'Oh, don't be. You'll always do what you want. And just when I thought I'd the lot of you off my hands.'

'Yeah,' I agreed, but then I remembered Lucy. 'Lucy isn't married yet,' I added jokingly. 'I'm not the only one who –'

'Oh, I know perfectly well that that Iris girl is her . . . partner, or whatever you call it. I'm not a total fool. She's as good as married.'

I was astounded. 'Mum?'

'Yes?'

'You don't mind?'

'Why would I? I've never seen her happier.'

I couldn't believe it. 'But what about your sisters? Won't they be shocked?'

'Let them.'

'Wow, Mum, I'm so impressed.'

'Wait till you have children of your own.'

For the first time in my life I wondered if that would ever happen. And, for the first time, it bothered me.

'It's a pity about Keith. Sure you might get back with him yet.'

'Sure I might.' It seemed the kindest thing to say.

The next couple of days at the hospital were much the same. Dad seemed to be in good form, but weak. The doctors were still vague and noncommittal; the nurses were cheerful and positive. Mum had settled into a groove of getting up early in the morning to do a little housework (with her jobs done she was free for the rest of the day), then going into the hospital after lunch, usually with either Ruth or me. She would spend the afternoon tidying Dad's locker, giving him a proper shave or reading interesting bits out of the newspaper to him. Then she would have dinner with one of us, and Jean or Marion or whoever hadn't been around in the afternoon would be with Dad for the evening. It was an odd time: Dad wasn't in any danger so it felt as if we were rehearsing for something that might happen in the future. And we were all doing marvellously. I think it was that, rather than Dad being in hospital, that made me so uncomfortable.

On the third day I visited Dad in the morning. It was to be my first day at college, involving registration, orientation and an informal get-together in the evening, so I knew I wouldn't be able to see him later. There was no need to visit, but I wanted to, and I think he liked seeing me. The staff don't like you interrupting their routines in the morning but they'll allow you in if you're quick. So I was surprised to find that I wasn't the only one visiting Dad at that hour. When I arrived Mike was there.

I saw him through the glass in the door before I opened it. He was sitting on the bed and Dad was looking more animated than I'd seen him in ages. He seemed to be describing something in great detail and Mike was listening intently, his arms folded across his chest. He was wearing a jacket: he must be seeing clients later. My heart skipped a beat.

Just then a nurse jostled me as she went into the room and before I knew it I had tumbled through the door. He turned and saw me. I could swear that his first instinct, before his brain had time to take over, was to smile. He was pleased to see me. But he checked himself and the nearly-smile turned into a hesitant greeting that quickly became a farewell.

'There's no need to go,' I said. 'I'm on my way to the shop. I'm going to get Dad his paper.'

'No, no,' he said. 'I have to get back.'

Then the nurse spoke, pushing past me: 'I'm sorry now, but both of you will have to leave. Mr Delahunty and I have a little bit of business, isn't that right?' she said, smiling at Dad. She held the door and waited for us to leave.

Outside in the corridor we were unsure what to say, what to do with our hands, where to look. I wanted him so badly.

'I didn't think anybody would be here,' he said.

'Usually there wouldn't.'

'He's looking well.'

'Yeah. It wasn't a heart-attack or anything. He should be going home in a few days.'

'You must be starting college soon?' As he spoke a slight tremor was evident in his clean-shaven jaw.

'Today.'

'Oh! Good luck.'

'Thanks.'

There was nothing more to say. I let my head droop and felt sadness ooze out of every pore.

'Kate . . .'

'Yes?'

'Kate . . . I . . .'

Just then the nurse barged out of Dad's room and announced that we could go back in. Mike said no more. I watched him walk down the hallway, swerving to avoid an old man with a walking frame. I went back to Dad and burst into tears.

It wasn't my intention to erupt like that but there was no avoiding it. The tears came fast and hard. I hadn't cried like that since I was a child, hadn't felt anything so intensely since I was too young to know what it meant.

Dad, needless to say, was quite alarmed and I was all too aware that he was in hospital to avoid upsets. A hysterical daughter crying all over his sheets was not on the list of recommended activities. But he did what he has always done: he put his arms round me and held me until my body stopped heaving.

'It's all right, love,' he was saying. 'It'll be all right.'

'I know, Dad. I'm being silly. I'm fine now.'

'What is it? Is it Keith? Your mother told me.'

It hadn't dawned on me that Mum would tell him, but I was glad she had. I could never have found the words to explain to him that I'd ruined things yet again. 'Oh, Dad,' I said, 'I've made an awful mess of everything.'

'It's all right, love. If you say it wasn't right, it wasn't right.'

'Thanks, Dad.'

'It'll all work out in time.'

'I'm sorry. I didn't mean to give you a shock.'

'Oh, I'm fine. There's little fear of me.'

In fact, he did look much like his old self: his colour was back and the brightness restored to his eyes.

'So, what were you and Mike talking about?' I asked.

'Oh, I was telling him some stories from the old days. He appreciates a good story. He was good to come in.'

'He knew you'd like to see him.'

'I'm glad he hasn't let this nonsense with Jean get in the way.'

I realized I wasn't up to talking about him. 'So,' I said, 'I'd better head off to college.'

'That's great, love. You have a good time. Remember, you can do anything you want to do.'

'Thanks, Dad.'

Suddenly I wanted to go home and bury myself under the covers. It was getting harder every day. I contemplated rushing over to Mike's office and throwing myself at his feet. Surely he'd give in. I imagined parking myself outside his front door and refusing to leave until he agreed to have me. And I replayed, over and over, his kiss, torturing myself. How could he kiss me like that and then throw me away?

Instead I plugged in my new laptop (my family's present to me for my thirtieth birthday – Mum had heard a piece on the radio about modern students having to have one; it was her way of showing support for what I was doing) and set up a new email account for myself. Then I gathered up my documentation and took the bus to college.

The day passed in a blur. I signed forms, listened to talks, drank coffee and met loads of new people, most of whom seemed quite nice, but I remained on the edge of things. I followed a group outside for a smoke but I didn't even light up. I'd lost my taste for cigarettes – even the smell made me feel sick. But I wanted to make college work because, deep down, I knew that it was the only thing that would keep me sane in the months ahead.

I was tempted to go home early and skip the get-together but in the end it was easier to allow myself to be dragged along. I was in the middle of a group trading academic histories when a familiar face appeared on the other side of the room. It smiled and made its way over to me.

'Hello,' Keith said.

'Hello.'

'It's good to see you.'

'You too.'

'You're looking well.'

He was lying. I knew I looked wretched. 'Thank you. You too.'

He explained that his company sponsored the party every year because they sent a lot of their employees on the course. It hadn't occurred to me that it might be odd that he was there.

'The course is very good,' he said. 'You should enjoy it.'

'I'm looking forward to it.'

'Kate . . . are you . . . ?'

'What?'

'Are you . . . did you . . . ahm . . . ?'

'I'm not with Mike, if that's what you're asking.'

'Oh.'

'It's too complicated.'

'I'm sorry.'

'Thanks.'

'You know . . . if you ever need anything . . .'

'Oh, Keith, you've always been far too good to me. And I've been nothing but trouble for you.'

'Maybe,' he said, 'but it's been a pleasure.'

He kissed my cheek and left. His appearance had been like a mirage – our whole relationship had been like a mirage. I was beginning to fear that the rest of my life would be no more substantial.

18

I had been sitting in my flat one evening towards the end of September, watching rain fall on the street below, light but persistent; the halo round the street-lamp was dense with tiny, almost invisible droplets. I had been doing my best to fill my days with college and my evenings with work. Everything was an effort, and I was tired. I was training myself not to think about Mike but I wasn't succeeding. He was everywhere. I had been avoiding the family mainly because word was out about Keith but also because I didn't want to risk hearing anything about Mike, even by accident. I didn't know how I was going to get over him.

The buzzer sounded. For a moment it didn't register with me. It was ages since someone had called to the flat.

It was his voice. He said, 'Is it OK if I come up?'

I didn't answer, just buzzed him in.

I opened the door and stood there, waiting. Then I closed it, but immediately opened it again, and he was on the threshold, rain-spattered and out of breath.

He said nothing. I said nothing. He smiled. His gorgeous familiar smile. I smiled back. All the tension and sadness of the preceding weeks disappeared. Then he kissed me. As his lips moved over my face, down my neck, as his hands travelled across my breasts and down my back he said, 'I love you, I love you.' He buried his face in my neck. 'Tell me to go away,' he said. 'Tell me to go and I will. But tell me soon, because I won't be able to stop.'

I didn't tell him to go away. I nudged the door closed

with my foot and guided him in. Then he picked me up and carried me to the bedroom. That first time was almost painfully intense; I felt like a virgin again, which was a miracle, given how far from that state I had travelled.

But the second was slow and tender and divinely passionate. He touched me so gently, all the time saying my name and kissing me.

Later we fell asleep, but when we woke I was full of questions. I wanted to know when he'd first realized he was attracted to me and how he'd managed to hide it so well. I still couldn't believe it – all those years of amiable affection, and all the time he'd wanted to do what he had just done tonight.

'You have to let me get my breath back,' he said. 'I'm not as young as I used to be.'

'Rubbish,' I said. 'You're the best I've had in years!'

He turned on to his side. 'I've never felt like that before.'

'Well, good,' I said.

He laughed.

'You have totally blown my mind. I don't think I'll ever be the same again.'

'Oh – I hope I haven't broken you! I was hoping to have another go.'

He wrapped his arms round me and swept me off the bed on to the floor. 'Seriously,' he said, emerging momentarily for air. 'It's not just about sex – you do know that, don't you?'

'Of course,' I said smiling broadly, 'I love you like I never believed it was possible. I adore every inch of you, and it's the purest feeling I have ever had.'

I wanted to know how, with his scruples, he had managed to kiss me so ardently that night in the garden.

'I think I'd totally lost my reason by then. For so long I'd resisted you, but when Jean left and basically told me to go out and bang any woman I wanted, it was clearer than ever that there was only one I had any interest in, and she was as unattainable as ever. That night in the garden, it was a case of kiss you or throw myself in the river. I thought you'd slap my face and tell me to get a grip, but I knew as soon as I had you in my arms . . . For a moment I glimpsed what it could be like. But then I remembered Keith . . . and I got caught up in what Jean would think and how, maybe, I'd pushed her away, and I owed her something. I couldn't believe what I felt with you might be right.'

I snuggled against him, my head resting on his shoulder. He wrapped his arms tighter round me.

'All I could think of,' I said, 'was that day in my flat when you helped me prepare that meal for Lucy and the others.'

'I remember . . .'

'When you were going away you sort of kissed me – you probably didn't mean to . . .'

'I wanted to do an awful lot more . . . I was crazy for you.'

'Really?'

'Oh, yeah. That afternoon was heavenly, but it was torture, too. We had such a good time just pottering about in the kitchen. I could see a life together for us, simple, ordinary, just the two of us, as if that was how it had always been.'

'Wow! I was thinking the same thing!'

He laughed again.

'Actually, I don't know what I intended when I was leaving. I just knew I couldn't walk away from you with just a peck on the cheek.'

I couldn't believe it had been the same for him.

'Then, of course, I instantly regretted it. I mean, nothing

had changed, and here I was trying to kiss you. So by the night of the party I was a wreck. I spent the night hiding from you. That's what I was doing down there in the trees. But when you appeared, out of nowhere, I couldn't stand it any longer.'

'So you kissed me.'

'So I kissed you.'

And then he kissed me again. 'I'm so sorry for the way I treated you the day you came to the house,' he said. 'I hadn't slept all night and all I wanted was to hold you again but I was convinced it was wrong. I really felt I'd done a terrible thing. I never imagined we could be together . . .'

So I pulled him back down on top of me, and treated him to a few more of the things I learned during my years in the wilderness . . .

Epilogue: A Year Later

We were gathered at Sycamore Lodge for a small party in honour of Rosa's christening. The whole family was there; even Anna made an appearance, thanks to the wonders of broadband and video-conferencing. We had all brought something to eat so Mum wouldn't have to do too much; she refused to use caterers. 'Why on earth would I want strangers making the food for my own grandchild? I always did the food for your christenings and back then I had no one to help me.'

None of us bothered to remind her that the stories she used to tell about our christenings had more to do with fear of Limbo and painful stitches than with goat's-cheese soufflé or sun-dried tomato tartlets. Mum was in such good form that it seemed a shame to recall a time when she wasn't. Dad's retirement had made a huge difference to their lives. They had taken up bridge, they went on regular weekend breaks and had nearly finalized a trip to New Zealand. They were looking years younger, and Dad had been given a clean bill of health at his last check-up.

They were thrilled with Rosa, while Lucy and Iris were delighted with their offer to babysit from time to time. Lucy had adapted to motherhood with ease and Iris was the proudest mother on the planet. Luke, Rosa's father, never did go to Australia: he got a job in a bookshop and set up a studio space that he, Lucy and one other artist share with a view to exhibiting together. He is a regular visitor at Lucy and Iris's, and they're happy to leave him with Rosa and a bottle of expressed milk while they nip out for a walk or a quiet drink.

Iris has become a comfortable member of the family. There was no big announcement, no coming-out party; it was just accepted that Lucy had a wife, not a husband. And while I felt I'd never again have the closeness with Lucy I'd once enjoyed, she had never been happier. Looking at them now, with their baby, they're an advertisement for family life.

After Dad came out of hospital, a lot changed. The only conclusion the doctors could reach was that he was stressed and had suffered an anxiety-attack. The only cure, they said, was a lifestyle change. He had to retire. That idea stressed him all the more until Marion announced that she would like to take over the business. She'd always been interested in the company, she said, she knew its workings inside out and now that the kids were older she was keen to go back to work full-time. She'd been thinking about it for ages and was sorry she hadn't suggested it to Dad before his illness. Initially he was slow to take to the idea, but it built on him gradually. Mum was full of encouragement: she had always felt the business demanded too much of him, and she wanted them to enjoy the retirement he had worked so hard for. Shortly after Christmas, the papers were officially drawn up and Marion became managing director of Delahunty Inc. Dad and Mum went off to Killarney for the weekend to celebrate his retirement.

Jean has become very involved with her job. The travel agency decided to transfer its business to the Internet and Jean was put in charge of the operation. While the work is mainly office based it also involves travel. She bought a flat in the building where she'd been living and is perfectly happy on her own. There have been dates on and off but nobody she was particularly interested in. Weeks go by and I don't see her, which was how it used to be, but we keep in touch with phone calls and the gang of us still get together for a few drinks or a meal somewhere.

And it's thanks to Jean that Mike and I got together in the end.

She didn't believe me when I told her it had been a foolish mistake; after all, she's known Mike for a very long time. And the more she saw of me at that time, the more convinced she became that I wasn't messing around either.

'I'd never seen you so unlike yourself,' she said. 'I thought you'd have a lost weekend or two, sleep with some guy from your class and get over it. But you weren't even smoking.' She'd decided to confront Mike and, after a very honest exchange, she told him that if his feelings were real he should go for it. 'So . . . I suppose you have my blessing,' she said to him, 'if that's what you want to call it. Just . . . don't rub my face in it, that's all.'

Mike and I have agreed to keep a low profile: we have maintained a policy of no physical contact in front of family members although, in truth, we feel perfectly comfortable with Mum and Dad. Funnily enough, they didn't have any problem with Mike swapping one daughter for another. I think Mum has got to the point where nothing surprises her (she's stopped bothering about her sisters' opinions) and Dad was just glad to have Mike back in the fold. I know they're dying to ask about divorces and remarriages, but they're being tactful. It's one of the things that worries Mike: that he can't marry me.

'But I don't want to get married,' I told him, 'and I definitely don't want to get engaged.'

The events of the previous six months had soured the idea of marriage for me, and it's liberating enough to be with Mike without a label on it. He's still old-fashioned about these things, though, and has made me promise to marry him as soon as his divorce comes through.

'I'm not just being old-fashioned,' he said. 'I want to have children with you and it's better to be married when children are involved.'

I didn't argue any more. The truth was that I was excited at the prospect of having children with him. Now that my course is finished and my new job – managing a café/gallery/performance space in the middle of the city – which I love, is under way, and now that I have lived with Mike for a whole year and still have to pinch myself every so often to make sure it's real, and now that I'm thirty-one and Mike is forty-three, and now that I see how happy Lucy and Iris are with Rosa, and now that . . . and now that . . . it all seems so right . . . perhaps, perhaps, perhaps . . .

I moved into his house almost straight away. All the work was completed, including the new attic space. A spiral staircase led up to it and the room itself was almost completely white – white walls, white carpet, white wrought-iron bedstead, white duvet, white dressing-table, white wardrobe. Everything about it was soft and airy and full of light. It was a girl's room.

'I did it for you,' he said. 'I knew it was insane. I was halfway through when I realized what I was doing, but the minute you said it should be a bedroom, I could think of nothing else but you, here, in this room. I hope you like it.'

I loved it.

I love it so much I even manage to keep it tidy. It has become the perfect space in our house; it is a centre of calm where I often lie during the day to reflect on how lucky we've been. It is where Mike often finds me when he comes home from work and we lie there together for hours, just talking. It was where I asked Mike when he first fell in love with me.

'I'm not sure,' he said, 'but I remember an Easter weekend you were home from college – I'd say you were in Third Year because you were doing your nut about exams –'

'Third year?' I interrupted. 'That long ago?'

'That long ago.'

'Wow! And you never got tired of me in all that time?'

'No. I never got tired of you . . .'

'Anyway, I was in Third Year . . .'

'Yes, and you brought this pimply weed of a boyfriend home with you, and all weekend I couldn't work out what my problem was with the guy. He was utterly harmless, yet I found myself mentally plotting his slow and painful death . . .'

'I remember him – Conor Moloney. I dumped him after exams. I was only using him for his notes.'

'I'm sure he's never got over it.'

'Anyway, you were plotting his death . . .'

'Yes, and I couldn't work out what my problem was with this poor geuck and then I realized it was because he went round the place with his arms splayed across your chest and he kissed you openly in front of everyone. I couldn't believe I was jealous and I presumed it would go away. I didn't really think I was capable of falling in love with my wife's baby sister . . . But it never did go away . . .'

Even Ruth's less annoying these days. There was a period a few months ago when she reached a peak: in the middle of her kitchen extension she suddenly had an epiphany that it wasn't a new kitchen she needed but a whole new house. So while her builders continued the demolition of her existing home, she got into her car and visited every show home and for-sale sign in the city. She even had plans drawn up, with Mike's firm, for a dormer bungalow on its own site. It was while she was in the throes of negotiating a price on a site fifteen miles outside Limerick that my mother told her not to be so daft. 'Exactly why do you want to be stuck miles out in the country, with no one to talk to and no shop for miles?' Ruth thought again and decided that a new kitchen and a holiday were probably all she needed.

Things were quiet for a while and then she announced she was pregnant. So far the pregnancy has been problematic: she's had back pain, constipation, diarrhoea, intermittent vomiting, swelling of the limbs and high blood pressure, yet she seems to be in her element. Right now she's carrying on a fairly normal conversation with Iris about the benefits of breastfeeding.

When I told Colette my news she was stunned. She thought the whole thing was outrageous but typically me. 'You're the absolute limit,' she said. 'Only you could run off with your sister's husband and make it sound reasonable. And what about poor Keith? He must be devastated.'

It turns out that Keith has managed to survive. I ran into him recently and he made a point of wishing me and Mike well. (He had heard from somebody.) He said he'd never forget me but he was still glad he'd done what he did. He told me he was seeing a girl he'd known years ago in college who had recently started work at the plant in Shannon. He said it was going well and he was happy. He looked happy. I know I should have been more honest with him from the beginning, but at the time I don't think I was capable of it. I'll always owe him such a lot.

As for that other guy, I bumped into him too. It was Christmas and he was queuing with three of his kids outside Santa's grotto on O'Connell Street. I saw him from the other side of the road. The kids were hopping round him, singing, dancing, excited at the prospect of seeing Santa. And when he turned to rescue one child from walking under a cyclist, he looked happy too. He looked, if I remember correctly, as he had when I first knew him, when I didn't think he was the master of all evil. It was a nice image to take with me.

But nothing is as nice as the image before me now: my family gathered round the big mahogany table in the dining room, each perfectly content in their own way. And the best part of all is him, of course, sitting opposite me, in the middle of a mock-argument with Dad about the merits of some rugby-player, while my mother butts in every so often to repeat her mantra that rugby is a very dangerous game. Meanwhile, I pick at my honey-glazed quail and sip my champagne, confident, at last, that I have got it right.

Acknowledgements

Many people have helped me so much with their encouragement, excitement and belief, in particular: Vivienne McKechnie, Jo Slade, Maeve Kelly, Roisín Meaney, Claire Culligan, Damhnait O Riordán, David Burns, Gerry Greaney, Paul Grimes, Joan McGarry-Moore, Niall Moore, Joan McKernan, Pat Burke, Vivienne Graham, Noelle O'Kelly, Enda Grimes, Sheila McCarthy, Fiona Regan, Norma O'Brien, Mary Conlon, Lisa Kiely, Paddy Dalton, Sinéad Donnelly, Pauline Goggin, Marie O'Driscoll, Siobhán Nash-Johnson, Gordon and Úna Cosgrave, Patrick and Linda Cosgrave, Geoff and Mary Griffin, Anne and Jim Cosgrave.

A huge thank you to Áine McCarthy and Ita O'Driscoll at Font for so much support, guidance and patience! Also a huge thank you to Patricia Deevy, Michael McLoughlin, Cliona Lewis, Patricia McVeigh, Alison Walsh, Hazel Orme and Ann Cooke at Penguin who have done so much to make this happen.

And of course to James, Dharma and Maya for not being there one hour each night, and for being there the rest of the time . . .